THE SPOILT KILL

THE SPOILT KILL

MARY KELLY

With an Introduction
by Martin Edwards

Published by Poisoned Pen Press, an imprint of Sourcebooks,
in association with the British Library
P.O. Box 4410, Naperville, Illinois 60567-4410
(630) 961-3900
sourcebooks.com

Originally published in 1961 in London, England, by Michael Joseph.

Library of Congress Cataloging-in-Publication Data

Names: Kelly, Mary, author.
Title: The spoilt kill / Mary Kelly ; with an introduction by Martin Edwards.
Description: Naperville, Illinois : Poisoned Pen Press, 2020.
Identifiers: LCCN 2020020883 (print)
Classification: LCC PZ4.K299 Sp4 PR6061.E495 (print) | DDC 823/.914--dc23
LC record available at https://lccn.loc.gov/2020020883

Printed and bound in the United States of America.
SB 10 9 8 7 6 5 4 3 2 1

INTRODUCTION

Fourteen years after its original publication in 1961, *The Spoilt Kill* was reissued in a new edition and hailed on the dust jacket as 'one of the most distinguished novels of crime ever published.' The book was only the fourth published by Mary Kelly, but it had earned her a Gold Dagger award from the Crime Writers' Association for the best novel of the year, and it remains one of the finest British stories about a private investigator. Yet by the time that encomium was written, her career as a writer was already at an end; she lived for a further forty years, but never published another book.

The Spoilt Kill marked a departure for Kelly. She'd previously published three novels about Inspector Brett Nightingale which she later described as 'sins of my youth.' This apprenticeship yielded *The Christmas Egg*, recently republished by the British Library and Poisoned Pen Press. *The Spoilt Kill* is written in the first person, the narrator being an inquiry agent called Nicholson. Yet there is a curious link with the early books: While driving towards Sheffield, Nicholson passes the scene of a car crash. The car in question is the same type that Brett Nightingale used to drive; he isn't mentioned by name, and we can't even be sure that he was killed in the accident, although he never reappeared in Kelly's work. This was her way of moving on from one protagonist to another, a characteristically cryptic updating of Sherlock Holmes's apparent demise at the Reichenbach Falls.

This is a private eye novel of a very different kind from the books about such legendary Californian gumshoes as Sam Spade and Lew Archer. The mean streets that Nicholson walks are in the heart of Staffordshire's potteries. He has been hired by an old-established pottery business, Shentall's, to look into a case of industrial espionage; a cheap foreign manufacturer is pirating their earthenware and undercutting Shentall's on price. Luke Shentall, the young head of the firm, is convinced that Shentall designs are being passed on by someone inside the business, and he wants Nicholson to track down the culprit. There is a nicely assorted bunch of suspects—prime among them is Corinna Wakefield, the chief designer. Corinna has a mysterious past and a tendency to drink too much, and Nicholson's task is complicated by his growing attraction to her.

The book's short first section ('What Happened') opens with the discovery of a body by Corinna and Nicholson, while she is conducting a visitor tour of the pottery. The corpse is found in the ark, a cylindrical brick-lined vault used to store liquid clay, known in the jargon as 'slip.' Nicholson recognizes the dead person 'in spite of its slimy mask,' without revealing his or her identity, before giving us, in a lengthy flashback ('What Happened Before'), a detailed picture of the events leading up to this shocking find.

In other words, this book is a 'whowasdunin,' a story in

which part of the puzzle, and part of the pleasure for readers, concerns the mystery of the identity of the deceased. An early example of this kind of detective novel was Anthony Berkeley's *Murder in the Basement* (1932), and it's a type of story which has attracted a variety of gifted crime novelists, ranging from the American Patricia McGerr to Britain's Julian Symons, and among current practitioners, the cultural commentator Mark Lawson, whose *The Deaths* (2013) is an excellent example of an undervalued branch of the genre, and Lucy Foley, author of *The Hunting Party* (2019).

The third section of the book ('What Happened After') recounts the investigation of the two central puzzles, the industrial espionage and the killing. The characterization, as always with Mary Kelly, is crisp yet sophisticated, and an impressive feature of the story is the way in which crime appears to be a natural consequence of particular personalities and patterns of behaviour. There is no sense of contrivance, of stock figures being manipulated to suit the plot. When one considers the whole body of her work, it is fair to say that plot was not Mary Kelly's strongest suit; this was a complaint made even by that gentle critic, H. R. F. Keating, who admired her writing. But in *The Spoilt Kill*, the marriage of people and plot works splendidly.

Another great strength of the novel is its backdrop. Workplace settings have been employed to good effect since at least the days of Dorothy L. Sayers and her advertising agency mystery, *Murder Must Advertise* (1933). Kelly broke fresh ground by choosing a deeply unfashionable location, a factory in Stoke-on-Trent. She vindicated this daring choice by making superb use of the background, both within Shentall's and outside, evoking the rugged industrial landscape with a striking lyricism.

A gap of three years separates the publication dates of *The Christmas Egg* and *The Spoilt Kill*, and during that time Kelly wrote *Take Her up Tenderly*, a novel which has yet to be published. It was turned down by Secker, publishers of the Nightingale books, and so, astonishingly, was this book. Rejection prompted Kelly's move to Michael Joseph, who were rewarded at once when *The Spoilt Kill* pipped John Le Carre's *Call for the Dead* and Allan Prior's *One Away* to the Gold Dagger; the trophy was presented to her by Sir Compton Mackenzie. Her delighted publishers hailed her as 'the new Dorothy L. Sayers,' but although Kelly admired Sayers, the two women had little in common as crime novelists, apart from a shared ambition to write fiction of high caliber.

At this stage of her career, Kelly was one of the most promising British women crime writers of the post-war era. Agatha Christie, Margery Allingham, and Gladys Mitchell were still highly popular, but the future, it seemed, belonged to the likes of Kelly, Margot Bennett, Shelley Smith, and Celia Fremlin. Yet Bennett and Smith gave up the crime genre all too soon, and so did Kelly.

Nicholson returned in *Due to a Death* (1962; aka *The Dead of Summer*), a book so bleak as to make *The Spoilt Kill* seem almost cozy by comparison. That story is narrated by a female character, rather than by Nicholson, and the setting is Gunfleet, a fictionalized version of Greenhithe in Kent. Kelly and her husband, Denis, both keen amateur botanists, went hunting there for rare orchids in the pre-regeneration era when, as Denis says, 'it was a backwater off the A2 with a ship's chandler, an inn and a jetty, a tiny remnant of the nineteenth-century Thames-side Kent that Dickens knew.'

A restless writer who cared little about commercial

success, Kelly then abandoned Nicholson in favour of writing stand-alone novels. Five appeared between 1964 and 1974, but the rest was silence, so far as the reading public were concerned. Fellow novelists such as Keating and the Canadian Eric Wright urged her to keep going, but she preferred to concentrate on other interests. Towards the end of her life, she decided to write another book, drawing inspiration from the nursery rhyme 'Ding dong bell.' The story was to concern a drowning in a well in Surrey, and was meant to be slyly comic. However, she did not finish it before illness intervened. She died in 2017, more than forty years after her career as a published novelist ended. Writing had been only one facet of a long and fulfilling life, and at that time her books had long been out of print. Her books aren't always easy reads and they are not to everyone's taste. But such a gifted and interesting novelist deserves to be remembered, and it is a pleasure to welcome back into print this book, her masterpiece.

Martin Edwards
www.martinedwardsbooks.com

I
WHAT HAPPENED

I had been spying on Corinna for over two weeks; spying on her for pay. So when at half-past two she came out of the art room, naturally I saw her from my carefully chosen position, through the door of the library, which I always kept open, and naturally I got up and followed her; with the difference that after the events of the morning I no longer bothered to conceal that I was doing so.

She walked as far as the cloakroom used by women staff, and half turned on the threshold.

'Why don't you come in?' she asked, trying a sarcastic inflection that didn't quite come off.

Why not? I thought, and followed her. After all the place was only a cloakroom, literally, with a wash-basin and a rail for the women to hang their coats. No one was likely to come in at such a time, and if they did, Corinna wasn't the one who had to worry about explaining her presence.

The narrow window disclosed a section of the city of Stoke-on-Trent; a row of bottle kilns blocking the gap between blackened brick buildings, and beyond them a factory chimney and the peak of a slag heap, wraiths even in the middle distance. There was no far distance, only a grey blankness of cleaned smoke mixed with the drizzle that seeped from low-lying clouds.

Corinna was letting soft tepid water from the drinking tap trickle into a mug. An earthenware mug, of course. There aren't many plastic mugs in Stoke, at least in public places; not even plastic cruets in canteens; always pottery.

She took a small tube from her handbag and shook out a couple of tablets.

'What's that?' I asked, too quickly. It was stupid of me. My mind, set on edge by the crackling tensions of the morning's work, had taken a melodramatic leap. All the same, I wanted to be sure.

Without a change of expression she held out the tube, a commercial aspirin-codeine compound.

'Headache?' I asked.

She looked at me sullenly. 'My insides enjoying their revenge, that's all. Something you never have to take into account.'

There's no answer to that, their ultimate weapon for beating you down as a lout. 'Revenge?' I said. 'On what?'

'Barrenness. They make you pay for the waste, whether it's your fault or not.'

She put the tablets in her mouth and swallowed them with a gulp of water. I hoped for her sake that they would work quickly. Showing visitors round the works was a long, tiring business; and it was hard on her, one way and another that she should have to do it today. But there, it was her turn, and she accepted without question that she would go on as usual, in spite of everything.

She straightened the collar of her blouse. 'Be useful, since you're here,' she said. 'Is my back tidy?'

There was one loose hair on her shoulders. It was long and shining—she didn't pay the hairdresser a small fortune for nothing; might have been fair or grey, an ambiguity which presumably accounts for the description ash-blonde; and hung limply from my fingers; the spring of youth had left it. I looked at the white face reflected in the mirror, at the lines which today were so marked. She was lucky, at thirty-five, that they were still individually distinguishable. But then, she'd had no children, she'd known only the second-best pain.

In the mirror our eyes met, and turned quickly away. She pressed her hands against the front of her skirt.

'I must have a drink,' she muttered. 'Just a swig, not enough to kick against the tablets. Otherwise I can't face the afternoon. Visitors!' She shot a sour look out of the window at the kilns and the leaden sky. 'You'd think the place was a spa, the way they come.'

She went to the coat rail, shoved back the hangers and put her hand in the pockets of her suède jacket, for her flask; then in the other pocket.

'Left it at home?' I asked.

She stood still for a moment, with her back to me; then turned round and without answering went out of the door. I followed. She said nothing, merely glancing at her watch as we walked along the corridor to the showroom.

The visitors were there already, stepping nervously on the polished wooden floor, making unnaturally wide turns round the corners of tables and cases, with their elbows tucked into their sides. They looked more or less the same as last week's batch; quiet, well dressed, more women than men in the group, and this time no children, for which Corinna would be thankful; their curiosity and instinct to touch must have added to the strain of showing round. Half the visitors would be strangers to Stoke who had come to the city primarily to see the other half, their relations or friends; and quite properly the first and most important part of their entertainment was to be shown round a pottery. I counted them. They were all there. Shentall's don't permit more than ten to a party; and that's quite enough to be let loose among their fragile ware.

We walked in together, through the luminous display of bone china, milky white with pastel flowers for middle-class wedding presents, crimson and gilt for city banqueting services, pink, brown and green prints for the North American market. At all of it the visitors smiled with unwinking approbation.

Miss Ashe the curator came forward. 'Oh, Mrs Wakefield, there you are.' She turned from Corinna to me. 'I wonder if you'd mind if we looked in at the library, Mr Nicholson? I wouldn't have disturbed you if you'd been working there, but perhaps you could give us just a few minutes—'

'Of course,' I said, 'as long as you like.'

She thanked me, collected the visitors, and led them through the door into the library. Corinna went with them. I hesitated; but I couldn't bring myself to inflict on her in front of Miss Ashe the humiliation of my tagging presence. I suppose I might have listened to the official commentary on the portraits and photographs that hung round the walls. Matthew Shentall, master potter, who founded the firm in 1788. His son and successor James. James's partner, Edward Hope. William Shentall. Henry Shentall. The late James John Shentall. Mr Luke Shentall, the present head of the family and firm. But I knew them by heart and I could make my own comments.

I went downstairs to wait, wondering whether the visitors had admired the hall as much as I had when I arrived, whether they'd been as charmed by their reception. The oiled oak walls hung with blue and white plates were no more than an adequate setting; the jewel was in the lighted cubicle: Judith, sweet apple dumpling Judith, the receptionist, the girl at the switchboard.

I couldn't see her. I walked across and put my head through the open window marked *Enquiries*. She wasn't there. On the desk by the switchboard lay a small white lace-trimmed handkerchief crumpled into a ball. Judith, Judith! Suppose Mr Luke had a call from Tiffany's? But it was none of my business.

After a few minutes, the visitors came down. I stood back in the angle of the stairs till they had all gone through the door, then walked after them into the yard. The air was soft and close, and the fine drizzle seemed rather to float than to fall. Clay-whitened water lay like milk between the cobbles over which the visitors picked their way, past the line of parked cars, acid bright against the smoky wall.

'Are those kilns still used?' a woman asked timidly.

She meant the two black, brick bottle-ovens partly embedded in the side of the building.

'No, those are preserved, for the time being, as souvenirs and for storage space,' Corinna explained. 'We have gas-fired tunnel kilns now; you'll see them later. There's very little coal firing left in the industry, and even that will be gone in a few years.'

One of the men in the party murmured something about the Clean Air Act. As she turned to agree with him and, perhaps, to enlarge on the subject, she caught sight of me standing on the fringe of the group. She flushed, and without discussing the Clean Air Act, walked on to the clay bank.

'This is the raw material,' she said. 'China clay, ball clay, Cornish stone—'

A chorus of exclamation cut her short. I remembered being surprised myself by those grey and mud-coloured heaps lying on the ground in wooden pens, like sheep.

'Doesn't it get dirty?' someone asked.

Corinna could barely fetch the required smile. Anyway, I thought, half-hearing her explanations, it is dirt, isn't it? Earth of a sort. Decomposed felspar. Can dirt get dirty? Or dirtier?

'But what about the rain?' said a visitor.

'Weathering is good for it,' Corinna answered shortly.

I knew why she was short. She was suffering agonies of embarrassment because I was there, watching and listening, making her feel like a schoolgirl at an oral exam. Perhaps she believed that, like an examiner, I was quite at ease, even enjoying myself. I couldn't tell her that I wasn't. There was nothing either of us could do to help the other.

She went on mechanically rolling off the usual information.

'This is the slip house,' she said, 'where the process of manufacture starts. In fact this is the earthenware slip house, but it's much the same for china. First the crushed clay is mixed with water, in specified proportions, in what's known as a blunger. The resulting liquid is called *slip*. This is passed through a fine mesh which retains any coarse impurities or grits that may have persisted so far, then over a magnetic screen which draws out minute iron particles. If these were left, they'd appear as dark brown spots on the finished ware. Next, the slip goes into a filter press to have surplus water squeezed out, then through a machine called a pug mill, where it's sliced, chopped, and pressed, in order to have removed as much air as possible. That's to reduce the shrinkage during firing to the minimum. And when it's pushed out by the pug, and sliced into conveniently sized lumps, the clay's ready for shaping.'

Inside the slip house it was cool and wet, and quiet except for the soft throb of the machinery and the whistling of two men shifting the great dripping concertina of the filter press. There was a smell of damp earth, such as you get in a deep cellar or a dungeon.

Corinna stepped forward to point out the machines she'd mentioned: the blungers, which were shown only from a distance, the screens, the press. The pug, with its thick extruding pipe of clay, claimed, as usual, most attention. Analysts, the whole pack. Corinna left them to stare for a moment, and came across to me.

'Are you going to carry on with this farce through the entire tour of the works?' she asked in a low voice.

'I'm afraid so,' I said, 'and I think the word *farce* was ill-chosen.'

The grey eyes, so apt for tragedy, looked steadily up at me. 'You can't trust me, can you?' she said.

That wasn't strictly true; it was rather that while I was paid I *mustn't* trust her. But I said nothing; and saw at once that almost any words, however hard, would have been easier for her to discount than that silence. She held her lower lip with her teeth, and her eyes grew red and sticky. I thought with consternation of the visitors, even glanced for a moment at the idea of taking over the tour myself.

She walked away, half a dozen steps across the floor of

the slip house, as if to put a little distance between herself and the rest, to give her a breathing space. She stood with her back to the men working the press, struggling for control of her face. And then—I don't know what made her do it. Why did she do it? She bent down and lifted the trapdoor off the ark.

The ark isn't shown to visitors; not for reasons of secrecy, but because it isn't particularly interesting. It's a cylindrical brick-lined vault, about eight feet deep, in which the slip is stored till it's needed in the press. Two gently rotating paddles keep the clay particles in perfect suspension.

I glanced at the visitors, to make sure they were still engrossed by the pug, then back at Corinna.

Alarm gave my insides a wrench. Something was wrong. Her face, staring down at the ark, had the stupid owlish look of wits scattered to nothing that follows a shock. There were three steps to her side. I took hold of her elbow, and looked into the ark, which was less than half full. There was something—

A body. Christ, Saviour! there was a body sprawled over one of the paddles, a body, partly held by the junction of the paddle with the shaft. The grey-white slip had splashed and soaked its clothes, coated its hand, run over the tongue in the open mouth, over the eyeballs, the face, the hair, the whole down-dropped head. No room for doubt; it was a dead body, lying like a statue fallen and crooked, a blind, grey slimy statue slowly turning round and round. But it was a body.

Reaction came, half a minute late, my heart knocking and leaping inside me, a hard hot lump bursting to get out. Corinna's arm began to shake as if she were holding a drill. Quickly, I bent down and lowered the lid of the ark. Then

I took hold of her, one hand on her back, the other behind her head, and pressed her face against me.

'Sh! don't make a fuss,' I whispered. The silly insults one offers in moments of panic. She wasn't the screaming sort. She was going to faint; I felt her sway. With one furious second of prayer for a steady voice—I, the agnostic, old habits die hard—I called to the men at the press.

'Arthur, take the visitors next door and ask them if they'd mind waiting a minute. Mrs Wakefield's ill. They can watch the cups being jollied. Run up to Miss Ashe and ask her to carry on the tour from there. Harry, here a minute. Get the paddles of the ark stopped. Then find Mr Luke and, whatever he's doing, tell him to come down. Tell him it's urgent. There's been an accident.'

I shifted my grip on her without letting go. 'Come on, Corinna,' I said quietly, 'just as far as the wall, then you can sit down.'

She managed to walk, leaning on me, with her head bent as if she were watching our feet crossing the clayey floor. There was a box of some sort pushed against the wall. I sat her on that, keeping my hand on her shoulder. She leaned her head on the wall and closed her eyes.

One of the men came across from the pug. 'Hullo,' he said, 'what's the trouble?'

Lamely, I repeated that she felt ill; a half truth, an excuse, to keep things calm for as long as possible, like the word accident. Accident? Not a hope, not a chance. The man from the pug had the only word for what was happening, what was about to happen. Trouble. Trouble, linked with Corinna from the start. The paint shop, the library, the slip house, the art room, Etruria, Dovedale, Endon, the party; this was the culmination of their half-grasped tensions.

Death. A body, which, in spite of its slimy mask, I'd had time to recognize.

Trouble. A sea of troubles, in which, in my shock, I felt I was drowning. And like a drowning man, with some things clear, some gone, all at a fevered distance, I remembered.

II
WHAT HAPPENED BEFORE

The first words Corinna spoke to me alone, standing outside Mr Luke's office, looking perplexed that she, and not another man, had been asked to take charge of me; spoken not with the local accent, not with any special accent, just accepted Standard English in a low-pitched voice that could have come from anywhere between Tyne and Avon.

'I want to comb my hair. Perhaps you'd wait in the hall.'

I didn't mind. It gave me a chance to take a good look at the reception desk, or rather at the girl, who had already impressed me. She sat by the switchboard seriously adding up a column of figures. Her head was bent over the paper, she bit the end of a pencil—perhaps she found the arithmetic difficult—and the light in her cubicle shone down on the neat bun of fair hair and the pale yellow cardigan. A nice girl. Pretty in a quiet way, plump rather than slim, with downy skin and a winning smile that went well with the soft Staffordshire speech with which she welcomed you. The quintessence of good, simple, amiable, well-brought-up girl.

I heard Corinna coming down the stairs, and had time to

turn my eyes to one of the plates hung on the walls; a blue and white landscape of trees and ruins.

'Is this Shentall's?'

'We wouldn't hang up another firm's ware. That's old stuff, about 1850. They were trying to nick Spode's market. Do you like it?'

'Not much, in itself, but it looks well against the wood.'

'Oh yes,' she said, glancing at the Enquiries desk with a half smile, 'it finishes the picture. If you're ready we'll go over to the canteen before the crowd comes.'

We sat down at our table as the one o'clock hooter sounded for lunch; and through the open tops of the windows the signals of other factories, other potteries, blew their different notes in the next thirty seconds, according to the sharpness of their clocks; a noise like a ragged woodwind chord that breaks four times daily from industrial cities.

Then they came, of course, as Corinna had said they would, pouring through the doors, mashing the silence with their talk and the clack of plates and the miniature thunderclaps of metal trays. The table filled. Mr Anthem, the elderly doyen of the designers; Mitchell, Johns, and Olive, Corinna's colleagues from the art room. To all of them she introduced me in the only way she knew; a writer who was going to revise and bring up to date the short history of the firm and illustrated brochure. This information was received with calm cordiality and no surprise. They spoke to me occasionally, from politeness, but they had too much to say to each other not to fly off into a strange technical vocabulary that was beyond me. Glost, frit, reduce, biscuit, resist. And kill. Again and again, kill, kill, kill. Till someone said 'Hullo, Fred!'

A hand set down a bowl of tomato soup on the Formica. I looked up, and saw Freddy.

Freddy! Years ago, early in my teens, I read with avidity a book by Rider Haggard, of which I remember only the beautiful queen of a fantastic country who keeps herself young and immortal by regular dips in a sort of fiery fountain of life. She takes this bath stark naked, of course, no wonder I was impressed, stands in the middle of it, irradiated with essence of life. And that is how Freddy appeared, though clothed, and male.

He was about twenty-six or twenty-seven, with a compact, muscular body. Perhaps it was the power latent in those muscles that gave him his air of vitality, helped by bright blue eyes and the black hair that sprang back so thickly from his forehead. But on the whole I think it was simply that enthusiasm for life sometimes found in a certain sort of spoilt person. Oh, they're not wanton, these people, not brutally wilful, destructive, piggish. They're open-handed, they retain an easy optimism that can exasperate cynics and other less amiable souls. But they are spoilt all the same, spoilt by life which has never thwarted them with any of its miseries and misfortunes and which in gratitude they therefore adore. A sort of mutual back-scratching. And there was one of these spoilt optimists, breaking a slice of bread into his soup and stirring it round, gazing at me with curiosity which changed, when Corinna introduced us, to a gleam of amusement. Thus he acknowledged the word writer; he, Freddy Lumberdine, electrical engineer.

He had a *Daily Telegraph* folded down so that the crossword lay facing him, and he frowned at it as he spooned up his soup.

'Slack morning, Fred?' asked Mitchell.

'Fair. Got through it all but one. Fifteen down. Angling for winged messenger and lady diarist? Blank O blank E blank blank blank E.'

He broke off to whistle softly at a girl passing the end of the table; an automatic response, with nothing personal to it, let alone lecherous. But his attention was diverted. He began a conversation with Johns and Mitchell—quick energetic speech clipped by the north midland accent—and the unfinished crossword was forgotten.

I kept thinking about it, for want of something better, but without seeing the pattern it was rather difficult to envisage solutions, and none came to me till we were all at the tea-drinking stage; tea from white glazed pots, not an urn.

'Dovedale,' I said to Freddy. 'Fifteen down.'

He looked at me with surprise, took a pencil from his pocket and filled in the squares. 'The literary mind,' he said, grinning. 'There. Dovedale. On the doorstep and I couldn't get it. And you're a stranger. Want to come sightseeing? I'm just running into Hanley.'

Should I stay with Corinna? No. That would be too much, after only an hour's acquaintance. I thanked him.

'Laying in for tomorrow, Fred?' asked Mitchell.

'More on the plate than that. I want to post my coupon.'

There was an outburst of laughter.

'You can't do it twice, Fred lad,' cried Mitchell.

'I can try, can't I? Anyone else want into Hanley?'

'Please,' said Corinna. 'I want to see the hairdresser for tomorrow.'

'Ah, tomorrow!' said Freddy with relish. 'Come on then, girl, hurry up, finish your tea.'

—

His car was a new Consul, of the same colour as the tomato soup he'd had for lunch. He opened the door.

'Squeeze in front,' he said, 'there's room.'

He backed the car out of the line and swung it across the yard. He glanced at us with bright eyes, as if to say *Neat that, wasn't it?* and switched on the radio. Music came tinkling out, light, easy-going strings. Freddy sighed, stretched, settled back in the seat, and turned out of the works gate up the cobbled slope of Rush Street.

'Do you do much writing?' he asked. 'Mostly reports, I dare say?'

Reports. That made me jump, though I realized almost at once that he meant firms' reports, speeches, brochures, et cetera. He saw me as an embodied ghost of the personal column, I suppose. 'Yes,' I said, with my ready casuistry, 'mostly reports.'

'You're staying in Stoke the weekend?' asked Freddy. 'Anything to do tomorrow evening?'

'No. Why?'

'Like to come round to my place? We're having a few people, mostly from the works, some of those you've met. Corinna here, of course.'

I thanked him. His friendliness played into my hands. 'What is it?' I asked. 'A birthday?'

'Just a celebration.'

'He had a win on the pools and it's burning him,' said Corinna.

'Shrouds don't need pockets, love,' he said with a grin. 'Get off!'

The last was half shouted, half snarled, at a lorry which had moved rather sharply in front of him, a lorry stacked with large straw-coloured barrels. I wondered what could be stored in unseasoned casks. I should have guessed, in Stoke. Pottery, always pottery.

'Nice day, isn't it?' said Freddy.

I looked with astonishment at the grey clouds covering the sky.

'He means nice for here,' said Corinna, 'not actually raining.'

Freddy laughed. 'Our Town!' he said to me.

Our Town! That grey haphazard sprawl, that welter of shallow hills and twisting roads netted with little streets; six towns that had spilt outwards and run into each other as their native industry swelled. Burslem, Tunstall, Longton, Fenton, Hanley, Stoke. Later I could see differences between their centres, at least, assign characteristics. On that day I saw only the confused legacy of past opportunism and nineteenth-century industrial expansion. Houses, factories, chapels, laundries, shops, and potteries, built as needed, sprouting along the roads that linked the six, till they touched; no plan, no architectural consistency, only on all sides the unity of dark red brick blackened with soot, more or less, according to its age. Black, throwing into acid relief the lemons and oranges and sharp green apples in a small fruit shop, making them look artificial, indecently bright; black, on the newer buildings a mere rubbing—the newest of all glittered with glass and colour, their raw edges cutting the poor old neighbouring crumbs; black, ugly, but not repulsive, not hostile, not boring like other industrial towns; *like* no other town. There was something different, something to attract, to interest, to compel respect; purpose, self-containedness; and, after London, a strange sense of people being alive and conscious of where they were living. So that when Freddy turned his bright eyes on me and said 'Well?' I could truthfully answer, 'I like it.'

'Get off! Ugliest town in Britain,' he said, with a smile of satisfied pride.

'Une belle laide.'

That went down very well; at least with him.

We called at the post-office, a tobacconist's from which Freddy emerged carrying about three hundred cigarettes, and a hairdresser's.

'Your hair's fine, love,' said Freddy as Corinna came back to the car. 'What do you want to go having it done for?'

'To keep it fine. Thanks all the same.'

Freddy emitted a fearful snarl as the red bulk of a bus pulled slowly and inoffensively out of the kerb in front of him. 'Where the hell are *you* going?' he shouted. 'Buxton via Leek, not up my radiator!'

'Is it far to Buxton?' I asked.

'About twenty-five. You don't know these parts at all, then? We'll have to show you the sights.'

'Chatsworth,' said Corinna.

'Get off,' he said, grinning. 'We had a day's out to Chatsworth last summer, a few of us. Pouring rain all day, on and off, and she had to run the length of the terrace in a cloudburst. She's never forgot it. Dovedale, now—ever seen it? We'll have to go.'

His eyes gleamed. Already he was planning the next party, without for a minute losing consciousness of his pleasure in handling the car, in sitting back relaxed, whistling to the music that ceaselessly tinkled from the radio.

The kilns, the bottle ovens. Everywhere and anywhere they appeared, singly or in clusters, strung across a grey distance as in the three square inches of smudgy photograph I remembered from a school textbook, or piercing a slate roof behind a clutch of little shops at a street corner. From one of them thick black smoke was billowing across the road at a height of not more than twenty-five feet.

'Someone firing,' observed Freddy for my benefit.

'Still?'

'They'll be a small firm, one family. Not in the Shentall sense, really one family. Dad, uncle, sonny and co. They'll still be on the bottle.'

'His facetiousness for using a bottle oven,' Corinna explained. 'And if you mean why still the smoke, I suppose they haven't got round to cleaning it yet. They'll have to hurry up.'

'Ah, it must have been ripe in the wicked old days of coal,' said Freddy, cheerfully. 'Multiply that by six hundred. Think of it! Our incomparable city, wrapped—no, plunged—no, shrouded that's it, shrouded in Stygian gloom. Or Cimmerian gloom, if you like.' He shot a look at me, the crossword arbiter, the literary mind. 'You wouldn't have been able to keep your hair so pretty in those days, Corinna!'

Yes, it was easy for Freddy, brimming with life and contentment. Compliments didn't have to be wrung from him; they were the overspill, the surplus, the assistance to underprivileged areas.

We were turning into Rush Street when it began to rain, and by the time he had rather showily slid the car back to its place in Shentall's yard the fall was quite heavy. Corinna and I ran across the cobbles to the entrance hall, through the swing door, wiped our shoes on the rough mat that lay inside to prevent desecration of the polished wooden floor. Freddy followed a minute later, shooting through the door with such force that it was still settling back to place in a series of diminishing shocks while he was halfway up the stairs, which he took three at a time, leaving behind a trail of grey-white footprints, the right fainter than the left, where the foot had briefly touched the mat as a springboard.

'That slightly mars the picture,' said Corinna.

The picture. In the reception desk the light still shone on the neat bun of fair hair. The girl was leaning forward, looking up the stairs after Freddy.

'Doesn't she have any lunch?' I asked.

'Oh yes. She comes back on time, that's all. We're late, you know. Hence Freddy's haste.'

We went upstairs, and turned towards the library. Down in the hall the girl had come out of the cubicle and was squatting by the trail of footmarks, rubbing them out with a yellow duster.

I turned to Corinna. She shrugged.

'There'll always be someone to clear up after Freddy,' she said.

'What's her name?'

She looked away from me. 'Judith.'

—

The grand tour of the works followed that afternoon. Then I learned for the first time the all-important distinction. China. English, uniquely English, bone china—china clay, Cornish stone and bone ash, the calcined bones of oxen. Earthenware—all clay, china clay, flint and Cornish stone. It's a question of a different body. Different degrees of plasticity, different drying times, firing times, firing temperatures; and finally a different product; one vitrified and translucent, the other porous and opaque.

A different body!

And on that afternoon I heard for the first time the slap of a pancake of wet clay being flung on a plate mould—

Must I remember that? Why? Why above all the other first sights and sounds?

The casting, for example, uncannily still and silent, long trestles of porous plaster moulds, dishes and jugs and pots all whitely coated inside with what looked like uncooked batter. The rough grey of raw teacups, nearly breakfast size before drying and firing shrinks them by an eighth. The turning—ware partly dried, leather hard, trimmed on an electric lathe, where the turner touches the clay with the bright knife, and grey parings fly off to land in a pile on the bench like the snips round a cobbler's last, carefully to be swept up and used again. Ware finally dried, white-hard, powdery, the texture of children's bubble pipes before the days of wire loops; ready for its first, biscuit, fire.

The firing. A gas-fired tunnel kiln two hundred and fifty feet long, firing zone temperature twelve hundred degrees centigrade; nothing but words, until you walk the length of the silent grey block and, staring through the tiny peephole at the side of the doors, see the long darkness barred in the middle by orange flames, flaring and trembling, as if the fringe of the sun were boxed up in the walls of the oven. Yet it's quiet, all quiet. When you tour a factory you expect to be half deafened by pounding machinery; but one doesn't pound a bone china plate. There was plenty of mechanization at Shentall's, but all gentle, nothing violent, nothing loud. In her explanations, Corinna didn't once raise her voice. The one noisy process I didn't reach, on that first day. The loudest sound was the music relayed through the works between quarter to four and half past.

By that time we were in the paint shop, breathing in the

smell of oils and turpentine. The workers were all women and girls. They sat in their overalls, singing with the music, some of them, filling in patterns already outlined on the ware, working in delicate small strokes with fine brushes. Each had her own collection of pots and rags and colours with esoteric ceramic names—Tinslow's Orange, Cottimore's Blue—clustered round a half-empty cup of tea. The teapots, white glazed earthenware, undecorated, stood at the end of each row against the upright that divided the benches; an upright thick with pictures cut from magazines—film stars, babies, kittens, royalty, all curling at the corners, all alike. The attempt to individualize each workplace had recreated a community.

There was a slight little girl, with masses of auburn hair piled loosely on top of her head, burnishing a gold pattern, which leaves the kiln after firing as a matt brown surface. Her small sharp face was bent over her work as she rubbed at the plate with cloth and sand. She didn't look up once. After a minute I followed Corinna, who had walked away with what seemed to me foolhardy carelessness and speed among the stacks of finished ware that surrounded us on all sides, some on trolleys, some even on the floor, where they were covered with grey dust. She'd stopped to examine, for some reason, a rose-patterned saucer and I waited for her, staring rather vacantly at a wicker basket.

A young boy in grey overalls was approaching, carrying a pile of tea plates in his hands. Very young, he looked; his large ears stuck out from his head. Following him was a man, a tall man in a suit, coming up silently; and, about to overtake him, he brought up his hands behind the boy's ear and clapped hard.

The boy jumped, swerved, his leg struck the wicker

basket, the plates shot out of his hand in a downward arch and landed with a brittle ringing clash.

'The smashing of fine bone china has an utterly distinctive sound,' observed Corinna calmly. 'You've just heard it.'

The boy was standing still; only his lips moved, and that rather savagely, so far as I could read the first letter they were forming. Already an elderly man in overalls had appeared, holding a dustpan and brush with which he silently set about sweeping up the fragments. A woman hurried out of the paint shop.

'How many?' she asked the boy, in a resigned voice.

'Three. No, four,' he muttered, scowling.

'What was it?'

'Burnet Rose.'

'You'll get it! That's the new one.'

'I know, I *know*,' said the boy, sickened and angry. 'It wasn't my fault.'

'Oh yes, it was.' The man in the suit came forward. 'If you'd been holding them properly they wouldn't have flown out like that. And look at your shoes. You know you're always slipping. Why don't you have the sense to wear rubber soles? Anyway, there's a lace undone.'

The boy put his foot on the basket and started to tie the lace. His face and ears were scarlet.

The man turned to us. 'One of your guide turns, Corinna?' he asked. A cold voice, used to chiding, with the obsessively pure vowels and clipped consonants that can be heard in any of the prestige areas of London.

Tersely, without enthusiasm, Corinna made introductions. His look passed over me, appraising, disparaging, dismissing: a hack writer, clean but shabby. That was right, that was what I had to be; inconspicuous and safe.

Meanwhile I took note of his suit, dark, discreet and expensive. He showed it to advantage. He was tall and well built, very handsome in the straight-cut marble-jaw manner; a pale face without humour, set off by a thick sweep of black hair trimmed correctly short at the back. He must have been about thirty. He was an accountant. Dudley Bullace.

I'd seen the name before, scrawled in chalk on the wall near where I'd parked the car. *Theyt a bugger Bullace.*

Anyway he'd gone; he had no time to spare for us. The boy went too, in another direction, and we came in for some of his scowl, innocent as we were. It was enough that we'd talked to Bullace.

'Poor Albert,' said Corinna. 'He's a calamitous boy. If he'd lived in a Greek myth he'd have stopped all the thunderbolts.'

'Why did Bullace clap? He must have known what was certain to happen.'

'Bullace has a mania for efficiency just for its own sake. He's for ever showing everyone else how to do the job—which doesn't make him popular, especially as he's so often right. Albert, for instance, was carrying carelessly and his shoelace was dangerous. There could be ways of pointing it out to him pleasantly. But Bullace has to be offensive. Or defensive.'

I stored that remark in the back of my mind, reflecting that Bullace had no doubt tried to instruct her in the principles of ceramic design.

'He's not a local man, is he?'

'Oh yes. From Burslem. That accent's laid on—vocal stockbroker's Tudor. He's got his elbows out, and he thinks that'll help him.' She paused. 'He's Freddy's cousin.'

'Good heavens. Well, they have the same sort of hair.'

'Yes, they have,' she said, surprised. 'You're quite observant, aren't you?'

I was observant enough to see that she seemed tired.

'Let's stop at this for today,' I said.

'But you haven't seen ground-laying or the enamel kilns or lithographic transfer printing—'

'Tomorrow. No, that's Saturday. Some other time. Otherwise you'll miss your tea.'

She smiled. 'I suppose you mean *you* want some. All right then, we'll stop. I'll send a girl along to the library with yours. Any preferences?'

'The red-haired one who was polishing the gold.'

'I meant preferences as to tea.'

'Thank you. No sugar.'

She sent the red-haired girl, all the same. Janice. She was quite happy to sit on the table and talk while I drank tea from a bone china cup.

'You're a writer, aren't you?' she said, in her soft Stoke voice. 'What d'you write? Stories?'

'No, the truth.'

'But what'll you do here?' she asked, puzzled.

'Rewrite the firm's booklet.'

'Oh that!' Her eyes brightened. 'Will there be new photographs?'

'I expect so.'

'You ought to ask Mr Bullace. He's got a lovely camera, a German one. You should see the ones he took of the works dance, with a proper flash and everything. Oh I hope there's new photographs—the others are all old-fashioned, all the women have their hair in buns.'

'You've got your own hair in a bun.'

'Not like that!' she said indignantly. 'They're old ladies—old-fashioned buns.'

'Earphones,' I suggested.

She went into peal on peal of giggles; a sound which was regularly to accompany my cups of tea, twice daily, for the next fortnight.

When she'd gone I sat down to work. Work! The first of those hours I was to spend at the desk, scribbling innocuous notes for the benefit of anyone who might put their nose into my headquarters; and when I'd sufficiently blackened the page to give colour to my ostensible business, I'd sit thinking about the truth. Through sheer vacant staring the image of the library sank into my brain, as the coloured metal oxides sink into the glaze in the silent fires of the kiln. The grey walls with their dark pictures and shelves of stiff books, the worn black leather top of the desk, the green rectangle of blotting paper; the rococo inkstand in white porcelain, encrusted with gilt scrolls and painted with sprays of flowers, which, as I learned later from Corinna, had been turned out by Shentall's in the early nineteenth century in imitation of a French model.

I took paper from one of the brass-handled drawers, the one that didn't lock, and began to write. It wasn't difficult. The walls were lined with technical treatises, old catalogues from as far back as 1798, histories of pottery, of the Potteries, of Staffordshire, even the previous history of the firm, the one my efforts were supposed to replace.

Supposed. What would he produce to account for my supposed work? A book of his own composition? Or wouldn't he bother? Do nothing, leave them to draw their own conclusions, to guess, after I'd gone, my true occupation.

I thought you might pose as a writer. That was his

suggestion, thrown out rather diffidently towards the end of the first interview; which was already embedded in the past, though only a few hours distant, overlaid with the day's impressions.

Luke Shentall. He was younger than I'd expected, young to be at the head of the firm, younger than me; tall, with the spread look of an athlete out of practice, broad face, sifted with Demerara freckles, creased forehead, receding toffee-brown hair, no trace of Staffordshire speech sounding through the muffle of public school and Oxford and directors' standard English.

How he scrutinized me, during that polite preliminary skirmishing, judging whether I was what he wanted, whether I was safe to be let into the secrets of Shentall's; and suddenly without warning, coming to the point, when, I suppose, I'd passed his fitness test.

From the side of his desk he lifted two cups and put them on the edge near me.

'Look at these,' he said, 'and tell me what difference you see between them. No, don't pick them up. Just look from where you are.'

Two cream-coloured teacups, trimmed with a band of stylized periwinkles and leaves that circled the waist, if you could say that a cup has a waist. To me they appeared identical and I said so.

He handed them down. 'Now turn them about, see what you think.'

I picked them up and in my amateur way looked first at the foot of each. On one the word Shentall was impressed, together with a sign like a nought between parallels. The other was bare. The foot rim of the named cup was plain, the other indented with three notches. The colours of the pattern on the unnamed one were darker, on close inspection, and on the stem between the last periwinkle and the handle was cramped an extra leaf that threw the whole design out of balance.

I pointed to these differences and set the cups down. 'Beware of unlawful imitation?'

'Except that it isn't, exactly. The named one is ours, Vinca on Clarendon, Vinca being the name of the pattern, Clarendon the name of the shape. The other was made abroad. It's obviously a direct imitation, intended to deceive, but if we were to challenge the maker he could point to the three notches and say that on their account the shape was not Clarendon and that the design, on account of the extra leaf, was not Vinca. So it wouldn't be unlawful imitation. He'd be technically right and there'd be nothing we could do about it.'

'Surely you have some legal protection or redress? Aren't your designs registered? What about copyright?'

'We have a couple of hundred in current production. We don't register them all. You have to pay, you know—and *why*, when there's this loophole of an extra flower? Even supposing someone didn't bother with the loophole, brought out a full replica. Would you embark on costly long-distance litigation of uncertain outcome? Copyright cases are always tricky. On balance it's cheaper to grin and bear it. All you can do is to caution the public every so often, tell them to insist on the genuine mark, buy from reputable dealers, and so on.'

'But the copies damage your prestige?'

'Not exactly. This, though not a patch on ours, is not complete trash. All the same no one who knows Shentall ware would pick it up and say "That's their pattern, it must be theirs, my God, they've fallen off!" They'd say "It isn't Shentall. It's the pattern but not the quality." And if they wanted Shentall they'd make sure they got it. But imagine the people who put quality second to appearance or, more likely, don't appreciate any difference in quality between the two cups—it's not so easy for anyone outside the trade, especially when the imitation's as clever as this. Those people will be buying simply because their eye is taken with a particular pattern. The name Shentall isn't going to weigh two beans with them, they won't even know it, so how can it lose prestige? What they see when they go marketing from shop to shop are two apparently identical tea services one of which is a good deal cheaper than the other. They wouldn't be human if they didn't leave the Shentall on its shelf. That's where it hits us, in sales. And no sales mean, eventually, unemployment, a point some people forget when they talk as if sales were just too sordid to be considered. That again is where these people are clever. They rarely try their competition in china, which is limited in sale by its high price. This is our tableware they're copying—fine earthenware, in other words, for which there's a much bigger demand. However, that's merely a technical point, aside from the real issue.'

'That you can't trace the foreign producer?'

Shentall looked at me as one might look with ironic pity at a child, amused by its naïve remark but sad to think that in time its innocence will have shrivelled like your own. 'We know that,' he said gently, 'from long and bitter experience. If you're a potter you have to live with the idea of imitation, you get used to it. What I'm concerned about is something much more disturbing. You'll have realized that there are two aspects to a pot, the shape and the decoration. When we introduce a new shape it involves installing new moulds, new profile tools and so on. And as that's a considerable expense it doesn't happen as often as patterns are designed to suit existing shapes. That was the case with the tea service from which this is the cup. The shape we've been making for some years. Vinca, the periwinkle pattern, is new. So new that it's not yet on the market.'

'Then how did they make this copy?'

'Exactly.'

'I see, begin to see, rather. How long does it take you to bring out a new design?'

'At least twelve months. In fact Vinca's been in preparation that long already. It's a complicated process, getting a simple band of flowers on a teacup. In this case the designer made a drawing, on paper as it happened, that caught the eye of Cardamine, our art director. He showed me, I liked it, our American market representative happened to be present, he said *that's it, I can sell it.* Cardamine got Mitchell, in the art room, to copy the design on a cup—just in water colour, to demonstrate it in the round, make sure it was practicable. That was all right. The other directors saw it, we formally decided to go ahead. Right. What next? The pattern in the round has to go back to paper, *from* the pot, so that the lithographer can engrave it for the transfers to be made. That's done by covering the cup with tissue paper, outside, of course, waxing it so that it fits taut without a wrinkle, trimming it, then cutting it open, which gives you the shape of the cup flattened out. Trace round the tissue on paper, and into the outline you can dispose the pattern in such a way that when it's made into a transfer it fits on the model as originally conceived.'

'Who does that? The designer?'

'Good heavens, no! It's a specialized job, a technique, highly skilled. Then of course it has to be reduced. That's to say arranged to suit the other pieces of the service. Obviously you're going to need more pattern on a plate and a teapot than on a cup and saucer, and in a different disposition, though of course it's easier with a running pattern than with a central figure, for example.'

'Wait a minute—doesn't the designer do a whole service, show you exactly what he wants on every piece?'

'No. Well, he could if he took a fancy to, but it wouldn't make any difference, it would be reduced in the usual way, working off the teacup and saucer for tea sets and the plate for dinner services. Why?'

'It seems to have got a long way from the designer, that's all.'

'We won't discuss aesthetics,' he said briskly. 'The lithographer then makes engravings, we work out what ceramic colours will give the effect of the original design, transfers are made, trial pieces fired and if necessary modifications are made. Then of course you have sample batches for showing to buyers and key retailers, advertisement to prepare—well, you have the idea, I hope. Seventy-five per cent of what we make is for export, and I've told you Vinca was aimed primarily at the American market. Until, last month, one of our representatives happened to walk past a display of ware in a New York store. I needn't tell you the rest. Or rather, I have told you.' He paused. 'Of course, these people undercut us with their cheap unlimited un-unioned labour, and of course they can produce quicker than we can—they haven't our standards, nor our working hours. But even so, to have the information, put it into operation, and market the ware before we're off, that means one thing only. They had the design to work from at a very early stage, almost as soon as we did. So early, therefore, that it must have been passed to them from someone inside. Someone from here.'

'Don't you allow visitors on the premises?'

'Yes, often, in the afternoons. But they never go in the art room. The guide keeps an eye on them, they'd be missed pretty quickly if they slipped away. Not to mention the almost impossible chance of the art room being empty at that time.'

'Could a visitor see it on the works?'

'Seeing wouldn't be enough for such accurate copying. Anyway by the time it's recognizable on the works it's nearly ready for dispatch. That's the time element. If they didn't have the design till we'd got to the stage even of transfers hanging up in the works I very much doubt if they could have caught us up, let alone passed us. As they have.'

'All right. Someone from inside sent out—what? A prototype or a drawing, I suppose. What about the cup on which the design was first demonstrated in the round? Would it be kept?'

'Yes.'

'Where?'

'Oh—just about. Back in the art room till it got cleared out.'

'You mean just lying about?'

'I suppose that sounds unbelievably careless. It has no value, though, once it's seen by the people who need to get an idea of it. It's the drawing we work from.'

'So someone may have stolen this prototype—'

'No. As a matter of fact, by a bit of discreet grouting in the cupboards of the art room, I've found it, the cup and saucer.'

'Drawings, then. What about the original design?'

'That gets passed from hand to hand in the course of the processes I described. In fact at the end it was handed back to the designer, who wanted to keep it. That's accounted for.'

'Isn't it duplicated, or filed for reference?'

'Oh, there's a pattern book, of course. We have all the designs, past and present, over the last fifty years, and most of them for the fifty before that, as well as a great many from the earliest years of the firm. But the drawings for the files are made from the finished product, though for historical interest we do hold on to a lot of originals, when the artist has agreed to part with them.'

'All right. Who would know that a new design was going into production, apart from the people immediately responsible?'

'Difficult to say. It isn't kept dead secret, that would be impossible, and really unnecessary. There's no locking away of work—sketches, transfers, anything of that kind. We just keep it pretty quiet, especially in the case of a new shape. Of course a new body would be hushed up as much as possible. Less so a pattern. People are free to talk shop in the canteen and wherever they like. But they're used to being discreet with outsiders. Just a sort of secretive tradition, if you like, dating from the days when a potter would back his fortune on information from a couple of workmen who'd run away from another factory.'

'So in theory anyone at all could know.'

'In theory. In fact I think you can exonerate the works and concentrate on the staff. That's not inverted snobbery, it's a question of knowledge and access. The first the works sees of a new design is the transfers rolling off the machines for them to apply to the ware. And as you've heard, that would be too late for anyone to do what we're investigating. In its early stages the drawing and the prototype and everything to do with it are at the art room end of the building near the offices. And although there's a great deal of come and go, it's on the part of the staff, especially the art people. The factory's on piece work, and in that case you don't get up and stroll over from the slip house to pass the time of day with your friend at the glost oven.'

'So outside the art room, staff are most likely to be in the know, by proximity. Also by proximity, it's easier for them to steal.'

He flinched slightly, said nothing.

'But even to slip a piece of paper in a pocket is to take a great risk when people are about,' I went on. 'That suggests lunch hour, which isn't dead safe, or night. Is there a night shift?'

'No. Only a couple of men always here to draw the cars from the kilns as they're ready and push the next load in at the other end. There's the lodge-keeper who works the middle shift from two till ten, then the night watchman. And neither he nor the men at the kilns would think anything of seeing staff working late.'

'Overtime on the works?'

'No. Production's geared to the amount that can be put through the kilns, there's no point in piling up more.'

'Cleaners?'

'They come in every evening, straight away, as soon as work's over. I don't think it sounds much like a cleaner's job.'

'Someone might be using one of them. You have to consider everything. But I was chiefly thinking of them as a hindrance to whoever wanted to get at the art room after hours. Now let's have a roll call of suspects. First the designer.

Then the fellow who put the design on the cup. Then the American representative and the board of directors—'

'What!'

'Why not? They knew from the start, didn't they? Before the reducer or whatever you call him and the lithographer and all the rest got to work. Everything is possible. Anyone can do anything at any time.'

He looked at me hard. 'Do you really believe that?'

'Experience had forced me to.'

'I'm sorry,' he said. 'Such determined pessimism must make your life very miserable.'

'It's the optimist who comes a cropper,' I said. 'If you expect the worst you can't be hurt when it comes.'

He shook his head and smiled slightly. 'All the same I'm afraid you'll have to count the board out, and the American representative, if only for the reason that they all know what's happened, though no one else does. The board also knows about you. One can't take a step like that without consultation.'

I thought he could have taken it very well and with every reason. But if he was willing to pay me for working half strung from the start, that was his affair.

'Another thing,' he said. 'On the other foreign pieces—the plate, the jug, et cetera, the pattern's been reduced in a form slightly different from ours. It's still recognizably the same design—after all, these people are potters themselves, they have the technique of reducing, they'll already have had our shape Clarendon to build on and long experience of imitating our colours—but there is just that difference which proves that they had only the cup and saucer to work up from. As we did. In other words it was passed out before being reduced, let alone engraved.'

'So you want me to scrub out the people responsible for both those processes.'

'Well, strictly speaking, no. They're all so close together, the art side. But you see, these men, Johns, who reduced the design, Mitchell who painted it on the cup, Whaley who engraved it—they've been with the firm years, their fathers and their grandfathers were with the firm—I know, I know, it means nothing. Anyone can do anything at any time, as you'd say. But *why* should they start now, after years of faithful service?'

'Pressure of some kind.'

'Yes, but there is just this point. The person for whom it would have been easiest of all, who could have passed out the design earlier than anyone else—'

'The designer.'

'Exactly. The designer, you see, is an outsider.'

'Commissioned for this one work?'

'No. I mean not a Potteries person, joined the firm only six years ago. There is just that. Not that being born in Stoke immunizes you from all fault,' he went on rather hastily, 'I simply mean that if one isn't so sure of a person's background and character—'

'That's all right,' I said. 'I see what you mean. Besides, it seems that what was made and painted and passed out was either a replica of the design itself or scale drawings of the prototype cup. Anyone who did either must be a skilled artist. Or else—'

He looked at me expectantly and said nothing.

'There's one thing that can be used by someone not knowing one end of a brush from the other,' I went on. 'Something comparatively quick and easy and inconspicuous. A camera.'

He nodded. 'I knew you'd get that far without difficulty. And I'm sorry, but we have a flourishing works camera club. Mitchell started it about five years ago. He's very keen.'

'Mitchell who painted the cup?'

'I shouldn't read too much into that.' He paused. 'They have an exhibition of members' work twice a year, down in the hall, and meet every other month in the canteen. Someone's got a cine camera and they also project transparencies and so on. I've a standing invitation, but there's always been some engagement to stop me from going. I believe everyone enjoys it.'

'You could have a camera without belonging to the club, I suppose,' I said. 'Have you a list of members?'

'I haven't. Mitchell will have. But then—'

'You don't want to ask in case the offender hears of it, takes fright, and slips off overnight with a whole fistful of designs.'

Mr Luke lowered his eyes and looked uncomfortable. 'Partly that. There comes a point, you see, when in my position I'm stuck. I don't think I'm boasting or deluded to say that the atmosphere in our works is as friendly and cooperative and democratic as any you'll find. All the same I couldn't suddenly begin to ask all manner of personal questions without attracting attention. Nor could the other directors.' He paused. 'And so we have you.'

'Yes. May I ask, why not the police?'

'Hardly their territory. It's bad for us, but is it a crime?'

'Theft, breach of contract, fraud. They have their scientific ways and means, you know, powders and stains and closed circuits and beams. They're quick and clever in their field, whatever it's the fashion to say.'

'I don't doubt it. But you'd only need someone in the

slip house to be the detective sergeant's cousin, or play billiards or watch Stoke City with him, and there'd be the end of secrecy.'

I didn't believe him. He just didn't want the name of his firm in police records—a common attitude, and understandable, though quite irrational. 'There are good private agencies,' I suggested. 'Cotton's, for example.'

He looked up at me suddenly.

'Why did you leave Cotton's?'

So he knew that. Well, why didn't I tell him? Tell him that I was sick of divorce and adultery, jewels and wards, sick of checking insurance risks and combing the past of high-powered metallurgists for debts, alcohol, the Party or a homosexual liaison, and above all, that I hated being stood over with a stop watch. *You're slow, too slow. We're paid by result. Truth, the whole truth? Forget it. Forget ifs and buts, pros and cons, forget our client's sadism, meanness, avarice, vulgarity, any one of which qualities she possesses to a degree that would provoke a canonized eunuch: is her husband committing adultery with his secretary in a flat in Half Moon Street every Wednesday from five to six thirty, or is he not? The answer, the facts, and quickly.*

I didn't tell him, though. I said I wanted a change; and it was his turn to look disbelieving. He picked up a seal with a long porcelain handle and began to twist it round and round in his fingers.

'You see,' he said, 'there's always been a Shentall at the head of the firm, from father to son in direct line, and so I hope it will go on. To me there's no distinction between business and family. And I don't want a file of our private affairs stacked in an inquiry agent's cabinets for any chit of a filing clerk to read and chatter about.'

'Suppose I chatter?'

'That's a risk I have to take. You didn't chatter about George Lanning, I gather.'

So that was who recommended me. I wondered briefly how they knew each other. 'That was much more easily settled,' I said. 'Straightforward theft. This may take some time.'

'Look, I know your terms. I agree to them. I don't expect miracles. Just see what you can do for me. Go anywhere on the works, speak to anyone, ask what questions you like. You'll find everyone most cooperative—'

'How do you propose to account for me and my questions?'

'I thought you might pose as a writer who's come to do over our illustrated booklet. Could you sustain that?'

A writer. That shouldn't be too difficult. Hadn't I been scribbling privately for years of my youth? Journals, erotic verse, long blistering unpublished letters to newspapers and magazines, even, once, a few chapters of a metaphysical novel. The memory of them made me smile slightly as Mr Luke elaborated his ideas.

'Of course you just use that as a cover,' he said, 'don't let it distract you. Concentrate on what's relevant.'

'Everything's relevant. Every word, every silence. How can you know at the start what's important and what isn't? You have to receive before you can select.'

'Well, you work in your own way. But I think we'd better acquaint you with the designer first. I'd be sorry to lose a good worker. However—'

He touched a switch and spoke into his desk. 'Miss Chapman, ask Mrs Wakefield to come over, would you?'

'A woman?' I said.

'Yes. A widow. She's been with us six years now, came from a textile firm in Manchester. I'll get her file sent up on some pretext, you can see her references, they might be of interest.'

'Can a textile designer turn over to pottery like that?'

'The chief thing is that they should be good designers, good artists. Then we can train them, teach them what's practicable. Besides, we want her ideas, not her skill. We have that. She provides the drawing. The technicians, if you like, translate it into terms of a pot. As it happens Mrs Wakefield's very hard working, very conscientious. Since coming here she's taught herself a lot, or let other people teach her. Now she can try out her ideas on the ware as well as anyone.'

A knock. The door opened. He smiled.

Mrs Wakefield. Already she was Corinna, already faintly predictable; and of course it seemed as if I'd seen for months on end the long, back-swept grey-blonde hair, the severe nose, the curving mouth so often compressed, the remarkable eyes, so clear and so beautifully shaped under rather thick greyish eyebrows; eyes that seemed ready to suffer. Fanciful notion. The effect of heartbreak was probably due to the disposition of the lids, or it was something I imputed in advance, knowing that already she was cast as victim; the persecutors being myself and Luke Shentall.

Towards the end of the afternoon I thought I'd better go to see him, if he was still to be seen at half past five on Friday. He was. His secretary showed me in, and I told him how I'd passed the day.

'When I've met more of your staff,' I said, 'I'd like to go through the salary sheets.'

He looked rather blue at that, as I'd known he would.

They're all the same. They engage someone privately because they imagine they won't have to show them anything, that it will all be done by chat and intuition.

'Very well,' he said, resigning himself. 'Let me know when you want them and I'll give you a clear hour in here.'

He wasn't going to let me out with them. Well, I could hardly blame him.

He handed me a few sheets of paper from his desk. 'Mrs Wakefield's references. All there was in her file, apart from her cards. You might say she's completely negative.'

Negative, with those eyes!

'What I mean is that she doesn't do anything except be there and get on with her work,' he explained, seeing my look. 'She's never off sick, not once. She never comes in here to complain, even when Anthem's tamed one of her designs out of all recognition. She's really too avant-garde. An idealist, not concerned with what will sell, only with what she thinks is good—what she knows, what I know, is good. We'll sell her ideas in twenty years' time perhaps. In the meantime, they won't do. What disturbs me, what I find unnatural, is that she never protests when you tell her so, just goes off without comment and turns out the semi traditional design you want. Only better than most.'

'Yet you can say she's negative when you're so impressed with her work.'

'Ah, but *personally* we know nothing of her. She doesn't mix. She's not standoffish, she just doesn't appear to go out or be visited. One gets to know these things. And she doesn't say much. You see?'

I saw. What he meant was not negative but reticent. I put the thin sheaf of testimonials into my wallet. 'I'll keep them safe,' I said.

'Well, of course they're only copies, but confidential,' he said. 'Are you staying in Stoke for the weekend?'

'I'm invited to a party.'

'Freddy,' he said, and added as an afterthought 'Lumberdine.' He smiled, naturally. The thought of Freddy would have raised a smile in any but the sourest. 'By the way,' he said inconsequently, 'here's an example of her work.'

He held out a white china tea plate, decorated with yellow wild roses set against sprigs of their own blue-green leaflets; a light spiky design in pale colours.

'The first batch through,' he said. 'All that's left of it.'

'Burnet Rose.'

He looked at me with surprise. 'Have you heard?'

'I was there when they were smashed.'

'Albert!' he said with a sigh. 'What I call a quiet week is one that passes without his name being cursed in the works. If he isn't having a glorious smash-up he's putting sugar in Miss Ashe's tea or giving lip to the glost manager.'

I could have told him that for once Albert was not entirely at fault; but there was no need to add informer to my name as well as spy.

'He'll be all right in time,' he went on. 'His father was just the same at that age. We started together—though I was twenty-one and he was sixteen. Oh yes, I had to do it the old-fashioned way. Three months at this, three months at that, right through the works, before I was even allowed to see the inside of the offices. Mind, I was an under-manager of whatever section I happened to have reached, and John Roach was only the fetch and carry, like Albert, at that time. He's a section manager himself now.' He smiled. 'Well, I hope you enjoy the Lumberdine party. You should, if I know Freddy.'

Yes, I'd enjoy it as much as I could enjoy anything I was putting to a double use. I thanked him, said good night, and left.

Mr Luke—it was impossible not to call him that when you heard the name on all sides. He puzzled me; or rather his position did. If I'd been called on to command I should have preferred to step to it fully fledged, not to have been watched by the ranks through my slow training, progressing by trial and error. Since it was essential for him to learn at first hand what was involved in the manufacture of pottery, why couldn't he have worked for another firm, as the sons of medieval barons were sent as pages to neighbours' castles to learn courtliness? Later, when I understood something of the conservatism, the intense almost narcissistic family feeling, and the fanatical suspicion of other potteries that characterized Shentall's, I remembered that question, and saw its answer. But I wondered at the time, thinking of Mr Luke. His chemistry degree put him right with the crystal structure of clays and silicas; and his working-through must have laid the foundation of his Christian-name familiarity with the workers and their generations, in which he persisted with apparently unaffected ease, looking on himself, not without justification, as combined paterfamilias and blood brother to everyone in the works.

That's why it hurt him, I suppose; for he couldn't hide that it did. It must seem to him a personal injury from someone nourishing an incomprehensible grudge against himself, the firm, the family. To me it seemed too complicated for spite, which daubs, spoils, and smashes. The stealth, the pains taken, the risks to livelihood that were involved all added up to one word; *money*. For all Luke's information about staff and access and cameras, it was money that I had chiefly to look for; money needed or money spent; someone poor, desperately, habitually, or suddenly; or someone merely greedy; or extravagant. That was why I wanted to see the salary sheets. As for wages—time enough to think about them when I'd fruitlessly exhausted the staff. The great thing was to remember that nothing was impossible; nothing, and no one.

I went across the corridor to the art room. The door stood open. The drawing boards were bare, the papers, paints, models, and angled lamps had been pushed back to leave the tables clear for the weekend and the cleaners. There was no way of telling which was Corinna's place. I'd find out in due time.

I took the testimonials from my pocket and read them where I stood. They told me little I hadn't known; her maiden name, where she had lived her youth, the barest chronology of her adult life. Conscripted for the last throes of the war, three years at the art school, then at twenty-three to work in the London office of an industrial design consultant. At some time in the next two years, marriage. At twenty-five the move to the Manchester textile firm. Four years later the move to Stoke. There was no mention of when the husband had died; though it seemed unlikely to concern me I should have to find out. And did she have children? I needed to know everything about her.

Mrs Wakefield. That was what Mr Luke called her. John, Albert, Freddy—but not Corinna. She was different; a valuable asset, but a reticent outsider. Not a Potteries person. Could she help having been born in Alton, Hants, instead of Burslem, Staffs? But I had to admit that it wasn't prejudice that made her number one suspect. Anyone would have thought the same.

I was sorry. I liked her.

—

The museum in Hanley; clean, bright, and razor-sharp, a new building with big windows and yellow bricks which under the new dispensation stand a fair chance of keeping some of their colour; to one side a big space glittering with parked cars; doors approached by a smooth pavement flanked by grass and flowerbeds, in which lines of primulas, daffodils and hyacinths struggled stiff-headed under the grey sky.

There I was to meet Corinna at one o'clock—oh, I'd arranged that without difficulty, somewhere between the ovens and the paint shop on the previous afternoon. Poor Corinna. She couldn't refuse to take pity on a fellow outsider alone in the strange city. In fact I met her two hours early, as she was taking a short cut through the car park, carrying a cobweb shopping bag distorted with parcels.

'Are you going to or coming from the hairdresser's?' I asked.

'I'm going in a quarter of an hour. Meanwhile having coffee with the Darts—oh, you didn't meet him yesterday at lunch. He works in the accounts.'

'With Bullace, then.'

'Yes, with Bullace,' she sighed.

'Don't you want to go?'

'I couldn't get out of it. I met them along the road, and they asked me.'

'Husband and wife?'

'The wife invited, but the husband will join us.'

'Are you alone? Want some moral support?'

She smiled. 'If you can bear it.'

'As bad as that, is he?'

'Poor Colin! No, it's Gillian.'

Gillian! She was an icicle, a narrow brittle icicle wrapped in a tightly belted scarlet raincoat that exactly matched her lipstick and flattered her crisp black hair and blue eyes. She was in her middle twenties, good looking in an orthodox way, though you wouldn't have turned to look twice at her; a shell on the beach, one of thousands.

'Is Colin coming?' Corinna asked, having presented me in my false colours.

'He should be here. I've been waiting ages. I can't think what he's doing.'

The three sentences were uttered each at the same level of languid complaint; the voice of the suburbs of London. As we sat down her look went from Corinna to me with a faint surmise; but the flicker of interest expired after a couple of seconds. She seemed to assess us as just two more figures in a landscape of unrelieved boredom.

'Are you going to this party affair of Freddy's?' she asked Corinna, when the business of ordering coffee had passed, leaving us empty handed. 'You are? Well, what are you going to wear? I mean'—without waiting for Corinna's reply—'I don't know what sort of a do it will be.'

'I should wear whatever you like,' said Corinna. 'I can't imagine Freddy insisting on formality.'

'It's not a question of him, it's what everyone else will be doing,' she said with a fretful anxiety that approached animation. Convention is seldom so outspoken. 'Oh—there you are,' she went on, 'I thought you were never coming.'

The husband had arrived, loaded with packets and parcels, several of which he dropped on the floor in his attempts to be rid of them. All his haste was directed to freeing his hand simply in order, as it turned out, to offer it to me with gauche insistence as Corinna repeated the maddening introduction.

'Why on earth didn't you dump all that in the car?' Gillian complained. 'I can't think why we have it if you don't use it.'

'Well, time was getting on,' he apologized. 'I didn't want to go all down there. I got held up at the chemist's.'

I led off with remarks about parking space in Stoke, a subject on which Dart grew quite expansive. Gillian, however, maintained a silence that suggested both scorn for our talk and reproach for not including her against her obvious will, and after a time the zone of coldness that surrounded her affected us, numbing our conversation.

'Do you work for a pottery too?' I asked, despairing, in a deadly pause.

'No,' she said, 'I'm a secretary at Tiller's.'

'Machine tool people out at Longton,' put in Dart helpfully.

'We don't belong here,' Gillian went so far as to volunteer, with a certain emphasis. 'We're from the south.'

Yes, I could see her *south*; gables and rock gardens sickly with laburnum and mauve aubrietia. About the husband I was not so sure. There was something much stronger in his speech, some suggestion of Islington or Camberwell or Bow, which I shouldn't have noticed, or not to the point of refined diagnosis, if he hadn't taken such pains to suppress it, thus accentuating his inevitable lapses. It may have been part of a general anxiety that seemed to harass him.

He brought out cigarettes and offered them, but Corinna, with a glance at her watch, refused. So did I; not exactly thinking what I was saying, looking at what Dart had pulled out of his pocket before he could get at the cigarettes. It lay on the edge of the table, a yellow packet of film.

'Do you belong to the camera club?' I asked hopefully.

His face brightened. 'Yes, not half!' he said, carried away by enthusiasm. 'Are you interested?'

'Don't encourage him,' said Gillian languidly. 'The time and money he wastes already!'

That quenched him, naturally; and my potential information also. Yet I felt his mortification as much as my disappointment. I looked at Gillian. She swallowed some coffee, pulled a face, and added two lumps of sugar.

'Poor Gill,' said Dart, feebly attempting to rally, 'you like a powder out of a tin, don't you? This is real—real.'

Those two reals! Only a phonetician could adequately describe them; but in a crude lay approximation they were *rill* and *reeyall* respectively; the loose-tongued, back-of-the-mouth Cockney and its immediate nervous correction which was no improvement and only involved all four of us in a moment of acute embarrassment.

Luckily there was Corinna's appointment to break up the meeting; and I made an excuse of carrying her shopping.

'If you're not going to need this bag before lunch I'll put it in the car,' I said when we were outside.

'Thank you. I didn't know you had a car.'

'I should take more care to mention it, like Gillian.' I paused, rebuked by the compression of her lips. 'What sort is it, Dart's, do you know?'

'A cream Zephyr, one of the old ones.' She looked at her watch. 'I must go. Museum at one?'

'Museum at one.'

I had nothing to do. Or rather I had so much, the task was so vast and amorphous that any beginning I might make must seem a mere futile nibbling. So I followed as usual my first idle whim, walked down to the car park and looked for cream Zephyrs.

There were two. In one a child's harness and a blue rabbit lay tumbled on the back seat. Of course, Gillian Dart's insistently *nullipara* look might have been deceptive. They might have had children. But when I looked in front I saw two crammed shopping baskets next to the driver's seat. It wasn't, it couldn't be theirs. Dart had all the shopping with him. The other Zephyr was so remarkably dirty that at first I thought it was stone- or buff-coloured, not cream. The flat top of the boot had been used by children as a sketching block; with their fingers they had drawn faces, flowers, noughts, and crosses, and one wag had scrawled *Please clean me mister,* enclosing the message in a neat scrolled lozenge. I took my handkerchief and rubbed it out. Dart had enough to bear.

'Mr Dart?' said someone beside me.

I turned round. A neat dark man with a high colour and greased hair looked up into my eyes.

'I'm not Mr Dart,' I said.

He seemed taken aback. 'Oh. I thought, seeing you clean the car—is he a friend of yours, perhaps?'

'I know him.'

A pause.

'You see I've just called at his house,' he went on, 'and he's out, unfortunately. I suppose you don't happen to have seen him?'

Sometimes I dislike my habitual suspicion, which puzzles ordinary, frank people and makes life so wearing. But how did this man know Dart's car and his name, yet not his appearance? Of course there could be dozens of legitimate reasons. 'No,' I said. 'I haven't seen him. Sorry.'

He frowned, and glanced at his watch. 'Too bad. Maybe I'll knock into him anyway.' He nodded to me, and walked off, though he seemed to hesitate, as if unwilling to go.

I turned and headed with brisk purpose for the museum, but at the porch I looked round.

He was back at the car, tucking a paper in the windscreen, as if he were giving Dart a ticket. It took him about three seconds, and he was gone, really gone this time, walking down to a blue A40 which he drove away towards Stoke. I watched it disappear, then went over to the dirty Zephyr.

It wasn't a ticket in the window, of course; it was a card, tucked face to the glass, so that it presented a blank white back to the outer world. I slid it out and turned it over. A business card. J. D. Lawrence, Northern Security General Finance Company; a Manchester address; and added in pencil: *regret to have found you out when I called this morning, J.D.L. (Area Representative).*

I slipped it back in the window and stared at the car. *Please clean me mister.* Well, the inside was clean enough, clean and empty, lacking those touches of clutter that make cars so homely and dear, the wrapped loaf, the worn gloves, the child's pot. There was nothing in the facia pocket but a map and a box of sweets, the sort that is full of pink and green fondants and fudge. I glanced over the dials, the little clock, below which were the patchy remains of one of those gilt and coloured transfers sometimes stuck on by the dealer. Victor Mot—, it said,—ue St,—field.

I looked up towards the centre of Hanley. Crossing the road, standing against the maroon back of a P.M.T. bus, was a tall, thin figure laden with shopping and parcels. I retreated to the porch, to wait.—ue St. That was probably Montague, or Bellevue. But—ffield? that could be Sheffield, the obvious, or Driffield, or Nuffield, or Swaffield, just to take the first to spring to mind. There were sure to be others. Not that it mattered what had been rubbed off the transfer, or only to my curiosity, as habitual as my suspicion, which drives me always to try to fill in missing pieces, however trivial.

Dart saw it, as soon as he reached the car, of course. He didn't even wait to put away his parcels, two of which he dropped in the awkwardness of pulling out the card. He stood with his back to me, reading it, quite still. The soft wind flapped his mac against his legs and lifted his brown hair into disorder. At last he moved, screwing up the card and flinging it away. With difficulty he dug the key out of a pocket, unlocked the door and put away the shopping. He hesitated. Then he went to where the crumpled card was lying by the rear wheels of the next car, bent down, picked it up, and carried it right out to the pavement, where he dropped it in one of the city's litter bins.

He sat for some time in the driving seat before backing out; not the last word in elegant reverses. If my car had been parked next to his I should have had an anxious moment for the paint.

Changing my mind about the museum, I walked out and asked a passer-by the way to the public library.

—

Corinna seemed rather impressed, not to say surprised, to discover where I was staying.

'Not all writers live in garrets,' I said, pulling in behind the black statue of Josiah Wedgwood.

'I'm sorry. I didn't mean that.' She paused. 'I suppose some do, though. Beginners perhaps, or daemonic artists obscure in every sense.'

'I see. Once you make it pay it can't be art.'

'I didn't say that,' she said quickly, with an almost frightened look. 'There'd be failures, artistic failures, in a garret, I'm sure.'

'Ah, those poor deluded ones! There's only one thing to do when you can't get money for giving your soul an airing. Sell it.'

She turned her grey eyes on me. 'Do you believe that?'

'Sometimes,' I said, 'it depends how much I have in the bank. As for the hotel—that's Mr Luke's headache.'

She looked at me thoughtfully. 'He must want it badly, this history of the firm—I suppose to coincide with the publicity campaign they're planning for the autumn. Anyway, generosity isn't a weak point with him.'

I opened the door, hoping to distract her attention. Truth the two-edged weapon, or whatever the saying was. On just that little careless sliver of it I'd cut my fingers. I simply couldn't have her reflecting on the oddness of my position in that dangerous way; but it had been my own fault, a stupid indiscretion, one of the slips that bedevil the person who makes even the slightest compromise with truth.

Still, to walk into the hotel with her made up for it. Against the convention she hadn't changed her wedding ring from left hand to right; and it certainly didn't displease me to have her taken for my wife.

She looked round the dining-room; apprehensively, it seemed to me.

'I wondered if we might meet Bullace,' she explained, seeing that I had seen her. 'He has lunch here every day in the week, but perhaps not Saturday.'

That must take a neat bite out of his salary, I thought crudely. 'Why not the canteen?'

'Not good enough.'

'I thought lunch yesterday was very good.'

'I didn't mean the food,' she said. 'After all, even Mr Luke has the same, though it's sent into the directors' dining-room. Perhaps that's what gave Bullace the idea that to lunch in the canteen is socially damaging—gives you the working class cachet. I told you he's set on pushing up. He's leaving in September, going to the great metropolis, goal of a provincial's dream.'

'Leaving pottery, then?'

'Yes, going to be junior accountant for a steel firm. Quite a step up, you see. As far as brain's concerned, he deserves it. He's very good, quite outstanding. That's the trouble. He can't make allowances for lesser mortals. You're bound to see a lot of him as he runs round prying into everyone's work, making sure it's properly done. Besides, he knows it's the sort of thing you see asked for in the high-powered situations vacant—wide experience of production, sales, and administration method.'

'Who's he going to?'

'Brace Lanning,' she said.

I sat still for a moment. It didn't matter. It could do no harm. He wasn't there yet, he could know nothing of what had happened. They wouldn't have told him at his interview that the junior accountant he was to replace had been dismissed over a couple of false entries and three forged cheques. There'd been no public disgrace, no prosecution, the amount was too small, to them, to justify the unpleasantness. But of course it's impossible to prevent speculation and gossip. The office would have guessed something, if not exactly all. Bullace would learn. But that would be September, and by then I should be finished with Shentall's, and he too would have left. Besides, had they, at Lanning's, connected me with that dismissal? Yes, probably. I should have used another name, then, or now, or both times, or always. But I hate that, the last degradation, the denial of identity. In any case, I didn't see how it could cause trouble.

Our meal was not clouded by the appearance of Bullace. I questioned her closely about her work, with what she must have taken for a touching interest. I *was* interested, in fact; not just professionally. Certainly she answered everything frankly, and about her latest design, just finished, she was quite excited. Apparently it was a formal pattern, cobalt blue on white, suggested by Persian decoration.

'Will they have it?' I asked.

'Oh yes,' she said, with calm certainty. 'The Almighty himself has said he's pleased.'

'Mr Luke? Don't you like him?'

'He's all right.'

I looked at her. Perhaps Mr Luke was right to distrust her compliance. Open rows are better than rankling injuries. But I couldn't see Corinna in the role of smiler with the knife. Her comment sounded to me more weary and indifferent than anything; as if to say, why should you expect me to *like* anyone?

'I want to call it Isfahan,' she said suddenly, 'the design, I mean. But of course that won't get through.'

'Speaking commercially, I don't think I can blame them.'

She smiled, unexpectedly, a lovely one; and all was well.

'What are you doing this afternoon?' I asked.

'Nothing,' she said, surprised.

'Would you like to come into Sheffield? The weather's improving. It might be quite a pleasant drive.'

'Aren't you forgetting Freddy's party?'

'I didn't mean to stop there. It won't take long at all. You'll be back in plenty of time.'

Her eyes began to sparkle. 'I'd love it.' She paused and looked at me with some embarrassment. 'It's years since I was driven—apart from being squashed like a shrimp in one of Freddy's outings.'

Well, that was something, I suppose, to own a car and be able to drive it. As long as it gave her pleasure, that was something.

The sun was shining, through a fine grey film, bringing out tints of powdery brown in the long black wall of the railway that flanked the road.

'There's just one thing,' she said. 'Would you mind going through Endon? That's where I live, about four miles out. I've some steak in my shopping bag and it won't enjoy the drive to Sheffield so much as I shall. We could go on through Leek, Buxton, and Chapel. That's over the Pennines, of course, but I don't suppose they'll trouble a car that calls itself Alpine.'

'You know a lot about cars,' I said. 'I suppose it's the design of them that interests you.'

'Oh yes,' she said, 'the design.'

Endon, then. Where she lived. Poor Corinna, I'd known that already.

There were two little boys walking along Station Road, two stocky little things with brown legs and the dark shapeless clothes that betoken a poor family. The one on the outside was smaller than the other; and quite suddenly he sprang out in the road, in front of me.

It was all right, I wasn't going fast, I braked. But he had quite a shock, and then, immediately, another. The elder boy seized him, dragged him back to the wall and gave him two hearty whacks round the shoulder, clout, clout! His small grubby face was tense with the spasm of anxiety and fear, and in his relief he belaboured the erring one's back, railing in a dialect so thick that I couldn't get a word of it.

I looked at Corinna, we smiled, and I drove on. At the corner we had to wait for a long line of traffic to pass before we could turn; so long, that the two little boys passed us. Their arms were linked, and the elder, with bulging cheek, was in the act of offering to the younger a lumpy paper bag, into which his fingers were already digging. They were brothers. That cuff had had the quality of blood-love, the deep unconscious instinct to protect—

'Coming?' said Corinna.

The road was empty. I turned.

—

I'd looked up a map of Sheffield in Hanley Library. The name was not Montague or Bellevue but Prague Street, and it didn't take long to find; a short row of small to middling shops; grocer's, chemist's, radio dealer's, Launderette, florist's, tobacconist's, newsagent's. And Victor Motors. I had thought that it might be combined with a filling station, but no, it sold only second-hand cars of high quality; or so it claimed.

I stopped opposite the newsagent's, bought a local paper, in which I found what I wanted, and, leaving Corinna, walked over to the showroom. Credit by arrangement, easy terms. The cars all looked decent enough, small to middle range; nothing outstanding, nothing very new, nothing older than about eight years. I made sure there was no Morris Minor convertible displayed for sale, opened the door and went inside.

A young man came forward.

'Good afternoon,' I said, 'I've called about the '57 green Morris Minor convertible you advertised in the paper—if I'm not too late.'

He looked blank, poor fellow.

'Are you sure there isn't some mistake, sir?' he said. 'We've no Minor convertible at the moment.'

I looked taken aback, I hope.

'Just a minute,' he said, 'I'm really quite sure we haven't, but I'll ask—'

Obliging chap. His mind wasn't really on me and my problems, I could see, but probably with United at home, or moving forward to half past five, tea, and the evening out with his girl. Still he was affable without effort, the customer drill came easily even to a semi-absent mind. He opened a door at the back of the shop. I had a glimpse of an oily yard and pile of tyres.

'Ed!' he called. 'Mr Victor say anything about a '57 Minor convertible?'

'Not to me. Could ring the other shop and find out.'

The young man shut the door and came back to me. 'I'm sorry, there does seem to have been a mistake,' he said. 'We could probably get you one—or you might be interested in something else?'

I shook my head. 'Perhaps my eye slipped a line to the next advertisement. Did I hear that there's another branch?'

'Oh, that's not cars, sir,' he said with a smile, 'that's ladies' wear. Mr Victor owns both. But I know it's no good ringing, because he's gone away for the weekend. I'm sorry.'

I laid my hand without looking on the wing of the nearest car. 'That's not bad,' I said, 'but I must have a convertible.' I hesitated, as if I might yield to a little persuasion. 'What *are* your credit terms?'

'Well, of course that depends on the government. Anyway the bigger a deposit the customer can manage the better it is for him. We never like to take less than a fifth deposit, with two years to pay, in any case, though when things are easy it has been done for less—but that's by special arrangement with Mr Victor.'

'I see. Do you deal with the Northern Security Finance Company? A friend of mine works for them, Lawrence.'

'Yes, we do,' he said, 'but I don't know the name.'

A few more polite exchanges and I extricated myself. The episode seemed pointless. It was the sort of thing that I was always doing, that I felt I might as well do as not. I could have asked more loaded questions; but to do that too early was a mistake I prided myself on never making. That was why I was too slow for Cotton's.

'Going to get rid of your car?' said Corinna, as I returned.

'Lord, no! I'm like the Miller of Dee. I love my car, she is to me as mistress, child, and wife. But I might want something faster,' I added, just to tease her.

She didn't smile. 'You want to die like the man in the Jaguar, I suppose,' she said.

Just before Sheffield we'd crept past a dark green X K lying with its bonnet crumpled into a broken wall and its hood torn back and flapping, surrounded by the whole horrible set; blood, police, ambulance, stretcher.

'I don't think he was dead or they'd have covered his face,' I said. 'And it may not have been his fault. He was entitled to drive fast along there. Perhaps another car made him swerve.'

She said nothing. At the time, when we'd passed, she'd merely raised her eyebrows; but no one could have failed to be sickened by the sight of those red gelatinous pools and the face against the blankets, like an antique marble bust.

'Are you cold?' I asked. 'Would you like some tea?'

'No, thank you,' she said. 'No, truly not.'

I didn't press her. She knew her own mind. I drove off to find some petrol.

The town was crowded, and the traffic an appalling Saturday afternoon clot. There were queues of cars at the pumps of the filling station, and dearth of assistants. I switched off, and settled down to wait, watching the people passing on the pavement.

There was an old woman, dressed all in black, bent from the hips, creeping against the wind, barely able to raise her feet in their clumsy boots. Her shiny cloth coat reached almost to her ankles; and in spite of the coldness of the day she wore a straw hat, a black straw hat. Her face was not wrinkled, the skin was stretched too tightly over the bones; and it was difficult to tell whether her mouth was fixed in a smile or a rictus, but on the whole I think a smile; for her pale watery eyes expressed it too, a look of simple childlike pleasure and pride. Almost under her chin she carefully held a tiny bunch of flowers wrapped in white florist's paper. They must have been violets, to judge from the dark shadow at the top. Just one bunch. I watched her creep past the bus stop; and then it was my turn at the pump.

Four gallons was enough. I paid, and waited for change, and drove off. The old woman was still walking, though a straight half mile of shops lay ahead. I knew what it was. She couldn't afford both bus fare and flowers. With a pang of guilt I slowed the car as we passed her. It was an absurd gesture, of a kind with my useless regrets that the car was a two seater, so that I couldn't offer her a lift. In any case she might only have been alarmed if I had.

I glanced at Corinna, and nearly drove into an island. She was in the act of taking a swig from a fair sized hip flask.

'You *are* cold,' I reproached her.

'No, it isn't that,' she said, 'not that at all.'

She offered me the flask, but I shook my head. She looked paler than usual.

'Are you sure you're all right?' I asked, remembering the smashed X K.

'Yes,' she said, 'I'm fine.'

I didn't insist; she was not a prevaricator; and for a long time we drove in silence.

'How long have you been at Shentall's?' I asked, at last.

'Six years.'

I knew it, of course, together with her age, her salary, her excellent health record. 'Why did you come here, north?' I went on.

'You go where the work is.'

'I wondered if you had family connexions here, that's all.'

'No.' The answer came, sharp and decisive; and she felt its sharpness herself, for after a minute, as if to soften a rebuke, she added: 'I've hardly any family connexions. Just a few cousins I know by name.'

'Parents?'

'No. Dead, both.'

'Relations by marriage?' I said, trembling inwardly.

'I don't see them. I never did.' She paused. 'Nor did he.'

That was enough; more than enough. We went on in silence.

—

The party. Corinna swore that she would take herself, so I dropped her at Endon and went off to dine alone; and at about half past eight I drove out to Freddy's.

He lived on the outskirts of Stoke, in an area of semi-detached houses that followed the usual pattern of the twenties and thirties—gables and bay windows—except that instead of being faced with pink and cream pebble-dash as in the south, they were built of local red brick; less blackened with soot than the old buildings, merely touched.

Outside Freddy's was a line of cars, and the sound of music and laughter from within was only partly subdued by drawn curtains. When I rang the bell, the door was opened by Freddy himself, beaming, jubilant, holding half a glass of beer in his hand. 'Come in!' he cried. 'I was beginning to think you'd lost your way.'

He was dressed in a very dashing silver-grey suit; and I saw him shoot a glance at my feet which plainly spoke his relief that I hadn't spoilt his party by wearing my suède shoes, which taste the brush not more than once every other month. As his own shoes always shone like new-split conkers, I could imagine him dogmatizing on the necessity of polish as a leather preservative.

He led me into a room that ran from front to back of the house. Most of its furniture had been taken out, but prominent among what remained, pushed against the walls, was a long sideboard, the whole of the top of which was stacked with bottles and glasses in profusion. The cleared floor space was crammed with dancing couples, half the girls from the works, it seemed, floating their short skirts like powder-puff Christmas presents.

'Let's see,' said Freddy, 'who do you know—ah! Gillian, you've met, I hear.'

My usual party luck was in from the start; though Gillian Dart seemed more lively than she had been in the morning. God knows what agony of indecision she'd suffered before choosing her papery silk dress, dappled flame and vermilion, with huge splashes of blue and peacock green; but what with her black hair and her metallic eye shadow, she looked, in her brittle way, quite dazzling. I guessed that she was at her best at a party; in fact, like all persons of limited mental resources, she needed continuous company and entertainment; and in the café that morning she'd had only her husband and dull us. All the time I was passing these rash judgements, I was smirking for dear life and asking her to dance, which she did rather well. But her animation was only superficial; her eyes didn't lose their flinty languor. So I made conversation, listened to her answers, smiled, noted her almondy and expensive perfume; and looked for Corinna.

She wasn't dancing, she was standing against the wall. How pale she was, and severe, against Gillian, and among that flower-burst of girls. Pale hair, pale face, lipstick her only make-up as far as I could tell; and a straight black sleeveless dress. Yes, she was right to wear that; her neck and arms were beautiful. I manoeuvred for a better view. Why, *why* did she affect those loose and muffling jackets? She had such a lovely figure. At least, it appealed to me. I began to be impatient of Gillian, couldn't smile with such facility as before, so much I looked forward to dancing with Corinna.

Yet when I did, how disappointing it was, like pushing round some clumsy schoolgirl who has to concentrate on getting the steps right; the same tense, resisting body, the same monosyllabic replies. She was nervous because she danced badly, and her nervousness made her worse. That was all, it must have been. For she couldn't have sensed through the palms of my hands the suspicions which even for the space of one short dance I couldn't leave alone.

The party went on as such parties usually do, with dancing and frequent drinking and spasmodic outbreaks of noise and laughter. Freddy wandered about permanently holding the half glass of beer. I was introduced to his mother, a short, cheerful, hardy woman, and to his numerous sisters—all older than him, all married, all dark midlanders with the same smiling blue eyes. Bullace was there, obviously condescending to be nice, the management suffering for the sake of good labour relations, and Janice, my Hebe from the paint shop, with luminous lipstick and a child's slender legs under her paper bell of petticoats. I danced with her once; after Corinna, it was like holding a feather. Johns was there, from the art room, and fat freckled Mitchell, and even the luckless Albert, in a light blue suit with red tie. Dart danced with Corinna after I'd left her, and as partners they were not conspicuous for their grace. From time to time I caught glimpses of him at the sideboard.

Everyone moved around a great deal; a situation of which I took advantage to look over the other rooms; prying as usual. Like Bullace.

The house was in good repair, spotless, decorated throughout in slightly off-key colours, startling, unusual, and weak: 'contemporary' intentions, diluted by time and democracy, and even then imperfectly grasped.

I went upstairs and stood for a moment on the landing, listening to the sounds of the party rising from below into the quiet. Then I found Freddy's bedroom.

It was done out in what he must have considered manly taste, grey paper and dark wood. Against the wall stood a narrow bed, covered with a white quilt; over its head a crucifix. On the bedside table, a shabby black book—I knew what it was even before I'd picked it up. The Roman

Missal. Inside on the flyleaf, in an unformed hand, F. Lumberdine, September 12th, 1945. I flicked through the pages that fell open at key dates marked by red ribbons and holy pictures—Easter, Low Sunday, Ascension, Corpus Christi, the Assumption, All Saints, December 8th, and January 21st St Agnes, an unusual one. I sighed, and put the book down. There were photographs on the table—Mrs Lumberdine, younger, Freddy, as a child, in white shorts and blouse, looking solemn, First Communion. And there was Freddy, juxtaposed with the casualness that only a devout Catholic can achieve, riding a donkey at Blackpool Sands. It was rather a touching photograph—he was obviously going to slide off sideways at any minute, and an older boy was struggling to hold him on. So perilous was Freddy's angle that the two dark heads almost touched. I would have looked at the single shelf of books, but hearing voices at the foot of the stairs I slipped out of the room, without turning off the light, and wandered down with an appearance of ease.

—

Supper was taken in a narrow room further back in the house, and it was a crush, grab as grab can. Needless to say, there was lavish provision, and the coffee was passable enough for Gillian Dart to wince as she tasted it. Everything was humming along happily when someone, into a pause, said, 'Letting the firm down, Fred!'

Freddy made querying sounds through a ham sandwich. 'Oh, the cups,' he said, swallowing, 'they're hired, of course. How d'you think we'd get this lot the same out of one small household?'

'Strange enough, we haven't any Shentall ware, have we?' said Mrs Lumberdine. 'Bar that old plate of Dad's.'

Bullace held up his cup. 'It might just as well be Shentall's,' he said.

Immediately there was a shout of protest.

'That quality?' cried Mitchell. 'Look at it, would you? I reckon Luke would go through the roof on a blue balloon if he saw a transfer join like that—or if he *saw* a transfer join!'

'Perhaps,' said Bullace, in his chilling voice, 'but it might just as well be one of our tepid designs.'

Freddy was into the breach like a flash. 'Here,' he said, snatching a stray bottle of Cordon Bleu from the window-sill, 'have a shot of this in it and you won't care if it's got a pattern of dogs' tails and old tin cans.'

Bullace smiled. It made a world of difference to his face; I could see the change in the way some of the girls looked at him. The slight hostility was melting from the air, and all would have been well, but for Gillian.

'I know what he means,' she said, 'I don't really see how they can help being a bit out of touch. Everyone knows the lead in design comes from the Continent.'

'Well,' exploded Mitchell, 'we're not in the days of stage-coaches, are we? Here, only last week there was a delegation from Germany going round the works, all smiles and *ach!* and *wie da schön!* We have trained market research—'

'Maybe,' said Gillian. 'I still think if you're stuck up here you can't help turning out something provincial.'

'It can't be that bad,' said Johns, shortly, 'it sells.' He looked not at Gillian but at Bullace. 'And if it didn't sell there'd be no accounts to keep, so *you'd* be out of a job. Besides most people are conservative, you have to break their taste gently.'

'And anyway,' said Freddy, 'what's fashion? A fickle jade.'

He grinned at me, acknowledging my writer's right to the crossword cliché. 'You go all out on every latest vogue and in a few years you're left with a load of dated lumber. Whereas with traditional—'

Bullace made a gesture of impatience. 'Aesthetically—'

Freddy seized his lapel and tugged it. 'Well, an accountant has no business to think aesthetically.'

'In the long run—'

'In the long run,' said Dart, suddenly, 'we'll all be a cloud of atomic dust, so what does it matter? You might as well eat off roses as—'

'God, roses!' said Bullace. 'How weary I am of roses on china!'

'Can't be helped, Dud,' said Freddy. 'Flowers and pots they go together, they're naturals. Even the Chinese, the ones the art brigade ram down your neck, they were always bunging on a bit of blue bamboo. Then there's all that other stuff—Bristol, Sèvres, Chelsea—' Freddy waved all non-Staffordshire pottery to a second-class limbo.

'Exactly,' said Bullace, 'there's no originality in industrial pottery design. It's all derivative, approximations, modifications. If they'd only employ an artist potter to design for them, you might get true originality.'

'Originality my—foot,' said Freddy, provoked at last. 'What the hell can you do original with a plate? Or a cup, or a jug? If you muck 'em about, you don't get originality, you just get something odd—no, what's the word?'

'Bizarre,' I suggested, 'grotesque.'

'Thanks,' he said. 'I tell you, pottery's limited, it can't help itself. All the hand-potted boys do is copy earlier back, that's all, stuff that's not so well known—the middle ages, China, Egypt, Ur of the Chaldees. You look in the museum sometime and you'll see what I mean. Only you mustn't call that copying, that's inspiration, the *influence* of tradition. All right, I'm not saying they *do* copy outright, I'm not doubting their honesty, their—'

He turned to me.

'Integrity?'

'That's right. Well, I think once an idea's expressed it's anyone's property. What gets me is that you call theirs inspiration and you call the industrial designer's derivation.'

'Cheers up!' cried Mitchell. 'Mr Frederick Lumberdine appeared for the defence. Thanks, boy. Same for you, some time.'

'All right,' said Bullace obstinately, 'leave that. But why so anaemic, why always such washy pastels? Now Scandinavian—'

'You mean insulator porcelain with a coloured slip?' said Freddy saucily.

Bullace gave up in despair.

'Pottery!' said Dart. 'Can't we ever get away from it?'

They looked at him in surprise. Stoke people don't get sick of pottery, I suppose, any more than they get sick of the sky. And how can you get away from it in our civilized life? between bricks, cups, plates, tiles, lavatories, sinks, sewage pipes, conduits, insulators, laboratory ware, firebricks, coke ovens, and finally the super-refractories to line the combustion chambers of the rockets that will defend your civilization and wipe out the other chap's, if he doesn't get in first.

But Freddy, with a remark I didn't catch, provoked a general laugh. The hint was taken, and pottery design was smothered in a blanket of trivial conversation.

Who had taken part in that rather significant discussion?

Significant, that was to say, for my purpose. Freddy, prominently; Bullace, aggressively; Gillian, from mere stupidity; Mitchell, with an indignation that didn't go very deep; Johns, briefly; Dart, hardly, and in a very general way. Well, then, who were conspicuous by their abstention?

Corinna.

I looked round for her. She'd gone. She had been standing beside and a little behind me; I'd fetched and carried coffee and sandwiches for her, I'd half seen her, over my shoulder, when Gillian made her remark about provinciality; but absorbed in the remarks that followed I hadn't seen her go. Well, was it so suspicious that the designer of Burnet Rose should have slipped away, at the point, for example, when Bullace affirmed his weariness of roses? She couldn't bear his proximity, that was all. Crudely, he was a pig, a crass and thoughtless pig.

I looked at him, standing alone, quite close to me. I'll go and talk to him, I thought; but at that moment Freddy cut in.

'Here, Dud,' he said quietly, grinning, 'chew your disgust out on this.'

And he lifted up, right in front of Bullace's chin, a large home-pickled onion, gleaming, grey-brown and globular, stuck on the end of a fork.

Bullace didn't smile. 'Freddy,' he said, 'take that plebeian object from under my nose, would you?'

'Get off!' said Freddy. 'When you were fourteen you knocked back a whole jar with me at one sitting.'

'That was then,' said Bullace.

There was a pause. Then Freddy put the onion whole in his mouth, crushed it between his teeth, and stood there, crunching it. Neither of them moved, each stared at the other with a mutual challenge. And yet in Freddy, his blue eyes smarting with the strength of the onion, didn't that long look have more the appearance of a plea?

The sloppy bulk of Mitchell moved across my sight.

'I say,' he said, 'you know the stuff, don't you! *Bizarre, integrity, grotesque.* Fred's walking dictionary.' He grinned and shuffled away.

Bullace had moved. Freddy was already turning to Janice, threatening to pull off one of her jingling eardrops, while she dissolved in giggles. And Freddy's mother came up to me with a plate of cakes.

'You'll have one of these, won't you?' she said. 'Must sample my eldest girl's baking. Mary, that is, the one by the door—lives over at High Lane, Burslem. We belong to Burslem, really, you know, we came here at the end of the war. We ought to move again, now that the girls are married. It's a big house for just us two. Still, Freddy likes it, you know. He keeps it nice, puts a lot of his money in it. I expect when he marries he may want to take it over.'

'Will that be soon?'

She laughed. 'He's not planning it, so far as I know, and he's not close, is he? Oh, there's plenty of time.' A gleam of pride appeared in her eyes. 'And plenty to choose from.'

I wondered why she confided in me in this way; but when she'd left me, and I was looking at her from the other side of the room, I realized that we were the only two, of all those present, whose hair was grey.

—

After supper, more dancing. Corinna was not to be seen; but I couldn't miss Gillian Dart, standing at the side with a petulant expression on her face. There was nothing for it, since I was so close, but to ask her to dance again. Her liveliness was wearing off. She had exhausted the interest of the provincial party; or perhaps the discussion of pottery had made her cross. We danced in silence, and I was relieved when I could decently hand Gillian back to her husband. Not that he noticed. He was mixing himself a drink.

Freddy came up to me and gripped my elbow. He raised his half glass of beer, which looked suspiciously like the same half glass as he'd had when I arrived.

'Here's to a brave man,' he said in a low voice.

'Why? How?'

'Dancing with Corinna, and twice with Lady Dart.'

'What demands bravery in dancing with Corinna?'

He hesitated, grinned, and drew me out into the hall. 'You know Mitch, old fat Mitch? Well, two years ago at the works social, he waxed rather merry and made a gentle pass at Corinna—nothing crude, Mitch wouldn't. Just wanted to show how fond of her he was, you know. They nearly had to treat him for frostbite. No one's tried it since. Not that I mean you were trying anything,' he added hastily. 'It's just that Corinna's rather the works iceberg. Now Mrs Dart—' His eyes sparkled. 'Quite a dish!'

Blind, then, the man was blind, in that respect; dazzled by a flaming dress and a bright lipstick. I would have settled it that our tastes differed, except for what he'd said about Corinna. How could he so misjudge her eyes and voice and mouth and throat, not to go any further? But then, perhaps, unlike me, he'd refrained from looking her over, hadn't permitted himself that licence. I remembered the bedside table. Blind wasn't the word; blinkered would be better. But at that moment I hadn't time to explain myself, or ponder on Freddy's character.

'You've got a nice bunch of girls here tonight,' I said, 'but you haven't asked the sweetest of all.'

'Who's that?'

'Judith.'

He looked away quickly. 'No, she isn't here. Ah! Jack, Margaret!' He greeted, with relief, I thought, a couple who'd just come from the room into the hall, and with a nod to me he walked over to join them.

I went back to the dancers. Bullace was standing inside the door.

'Hullo,' he said. 'Did you enjoy Sheffield?'

Damn his eyes! 'I wasn't there long,' I said, controlling myself. 'I didn't see you.'

'I was waiting at the lights, by the filling station,' he said. 'I went in to see about a car, as a matter of fact.'

'What do you want, an executive's Rolls?'

He didn't exactly flinch—it was a look as if he were resisting a schoolboys' hand-squeezing contest. So he was, in a way; that was the quality of my remark, childish, outrageous, feeble, the uncontrolled reaction of a moment's stupid alarm. Bullace wouldn't have discovered the episode of Victor Motors, even if by coincidence he'd gone there himself; and that, putting the small shop and Bullace side by side in my mind, I thought most unlikely.

'No, I was after something more in your own line, in fact,' he said, taking it so well that I was even sorrier that I'd spoken. 'But I was too late, the snip had gone. Ah, here's Corinna.'

And he walked away, leaving us together.

Oh well, to hell with Bullace. They'd put on a waltz, a nice slow easy waltz. I held out my hands.

'Why?' she said.

'What a question!'

'Can't you answer it? There must be some special reason why you're willing to suffer my dancing.'

Her candour unnerved me, the directness of her clear eyes gave me a pang for my deception.

'I'm a glutton for punishment,' I said. And after that we danced together all the time.

—

It must have been about twelve when Freddy came up and squeezed my elbow.

'Sorry to interrupt your dance,' he said, looking very embarrassed. 'Could you come outside a minute? You too, please, Corinna love.'

We followed him into the hall.

'Look, could you do a good turn?' he said. 'Could you take Dart home? Gillian can't drive, you see, and he can't, the state he's in. I'd go myself, but I can hardly leave everyone. Some of them may want to be going soon, and I ought to be here—'

'Yes, that's all right,' I said. 'Will there still be buses, or shall I have to walk back?'

'No, you drive his car back here, and he can collect it when he's fit. That's why I wondered if you wouldn't mind going too, Corinna. I know it's a lot to ask, but you could be guide home, and besides it would be less mortifying for Gillian. Would you?'

She nodded. 'Where is he?'

'I've got him in the car, all ready. Gillian's waiting. He's not too bad, as far as locomotion's concerned, I'm sure you'll be able to manage.'

Yes, we'd manage, we'd have to; the older ones, the responsible ones; supposedly responsible, at any rate.

'Here, Corinna, put this on, girl,' said Freddy, snatching up a thick man's cardigan. 'You mustn't catch cold.'

We went out, down the garden path, to the cream Zephyr. Gillian was waiting for us by the door.

'I'm sorry,' she said tightly, as if words choked her.

'That's all right,' I said. 'Corinna's coming to show me there and home again.'

She nodded, and got in the back of the car beside Dart, who was slumped in the corner of the seat. He must have been solidly and steadily packing it away all the evening. It was none of my business, yet. My business was to drive the car, and that was enough; more than enough, a nerve-racking strain, to press down and get no response from the exhausted engine but a soft helpless wheeze like the laugh of someone with half a lung. I pushed slowly up the numerous hills of Stoke, sweating every time a cylinder missed; the little cough was so blatant in the silence that filled the car. Neither of the women spoke, and there was no sound from Dart.

The trouble, the difficulty, came when we had to get him out. I had him halfway to a fireman's lift, which seemed the best way of dealing with him, when Gillian pulled me back.

'No,' she said sharply, 'make him walk. He can. He did for Freddy.'

Thinking of neighbours—at that hour!—I looked round. Every window in sight was black and empty.

'Give me the key,' said Corinna. 'I'll open the door.'

Gillian came round to the other side of Dart and gave him a shove that nearly canted him over. Without regard to saving her face, I kept one of his arms round my shoulders;

and thus, swaying and scuffling and stumbling against some sort of stone beading that defined the path, we half carried, half dragged him into his home.

Ignoring Gillian's unwilling looks, I helped to take him upstairs; and I should have liked to hear Freddy's comment on the single beds, on one of which we laid Dart out.

'It's all right, I'll manage now,' said Gillian, and forced herself to add, 'thank you.'

She was flushed and her lips were tightly folded. I felt sorry for her, after all; I didn't relish witnessing such agonies of shame.

'I'll drive back to Freddy's and you'll collect the car later,' I said. 'Good night.'

'Wait!' she said urgently. 'Don't say anything—ask Corinna not to—don't say anything to the others.'

I shook my head. *The others!* The thought, the fear of them, must dominate her life.

I couldn't see more of the house than the hall: white paint, a blue carpet, and anemones in a bowl on a little mahogany table. Corinna was waiting for me, and we went out, closing the door very softly. Neither of us alluded, then or ever, to what had just happened.

'Don't go back the same way,' she said, 'I want to show you something. Just drive on. Don't hurry.'

We crept along the road between the dark houses—late Victorian, like Dart's, quite large, with hedges and full-grown trees in their gardens.

'We're in Newcastle now, you know,' she said, seeing me peer about. 'Newcastle under Lyme. Quite separate from Stoke. Historic borough, royal charters, that sort of thing. They touch, but they're separate. Stop here. That's it. Do you mind getting out?'

We stood on the brow of a steep hill which dropped away on the far side of an iron railing; below lay a black smoking pit, here and there glowing red, prickling with hundreds of lights.

'Etruria,' said Corinna.

'What?'

'That's what it's called, down there. Etruria Vale. It's where the great Josiah Wedgwood built his factory. Called it Etruria in admiration for Etruscan pottery, I suppose. Imitation of the antique was all the rage then. They're not there now, of course, Wedgwood's, I mean, they're out at Barlaston, all clean and electric, in the fields, and where they used to be, down there, is an iron and steel works.'

I stared down into the pit, at the black buildings silhouetted against the flushed sky, buildings, some of them, flickering within, as if a river of liquid gold were rolling through them. Clouds of steam and smoke drifted across the shadowy vale, rosy steam, lit from the fires below. There was a continuous hollow rushing sound, broken by clanks of shunting. An engine, raised on a bank, black against red, like a slide, moved slowly backwards and forwards. The whole pit seemed to breathe as it worked; for though it was past midnight on Saturday, and the Newcastle neighbours' windows were dark, naked lights on gantries and signals glittered all over Etruria.

Suddenly a deep orange glow spread over the sky, swallowing other reds in its brightness; a reflection of what we couldn't see but what I knew to be there: a forty-foot slab of red-hot coke, packed solid, pulsing, sliding into the night air, pushed from the coke ovens of the steel works.

'Lovely,' I said, thinking of it.

She turned and looked at me. 'Do you really think so?'

'Yes.'

'So do I,' she said. 'But I suppose we'd better go back, if only to say goodbye to Freddy.'

'Did he really have a win on the pools?' I asked her, as we turned away from the pit.

'What do you mean? That it might have been dogs or horses?'

'No. Was the money a win of any sort? Have you seen the cheque?'

'Of course not. What do you think he was going to do—put it in a frame?'

'I was wondering whether he mightn't simply have made up an excuse to throw a party.'

'Freddy wouldn't need an excuse,' she said.

'I wonder if Bullace ever wins.'

'You don't imagine he'd lower himself to fill in a football coupon? He doesn't mind taking the drink that the pools have paid for. That's different.'

'I was surprised to see him there this evening.'

'I told you, they're cousins. Freddy would never leave him out. He's not the dropping sort.'

'Well—Bullace hasn't dropped Freddy either.'

'Hasn't he? You'll never see them together at work.' She paused. 'They were brought up together, you know. Bullace's parents were separated—mother went off with a neighbour and Mrs Lumberdine took Dudley. I suppose she felt moral guilt at her sister's lapse, or something, and one more in that family couldn't make much difference. Anyway, I think the father used to send money.'

'Besides, he'd be company for Freddy, among all those girls,' I said. 'He doesn't live there now, I gather.'

'No,' she said, 'not since he left the university. He was

clever, you see, won scholarships, did well in exams and training. Now he's gaily kicking away the ladder.' She laughed shortly. 'Dudley, pushing himself up for all he's worth, lunching at the North Staffs, lodging in some refined guest house outside Newcastle, and in theory he's politically quite pink, *Guardian* and *New Statesman*. Whereas Freddy never sees anything but the *Telegraph*, loves his fellow men, sits in the canteen as a matter of course, and votes as blue as a wet weekend. You have to laugh, or you might cry. To hear them arguing about pottery! Both pigheaded, both part right, part wrong.'

'I wonder what Mrs Lumberdine feels,' I said, 'about Bullace, I mean.'

'Oh, she has Freddy.'

So what more could she want?

When we returned the party was already breaking up. Freddy almost embraced me, such was his gratitude for having one of life's difficulties swept out of his path.

I gave him the key of Dart's car and went to look for Corinna. She was standing in the hall, with her loose jacket, alas, covering the dress and all else that I so much liked.

'Ready?' I asked.

She looked embarrassed. 'I'm going with the Johns, do you mind? I came with them. I often do. They go back to Leek, you see.' Suddenly she looked up at me with that nervous placatory air that I'd seen in her before, outside the hotel when we were talking about artists in garrets. 'Don't be offended.'

'Don't be silly,' I said, astounded.

And before I could add a word of reassurance, just as I was smiling at her strangeness, she'd turned and gone, without even saying good night.

Etruria. That's where I went. Up the hills in a car that didn't cough, to look at Etruria, to stand smoking staring down at the red darkness. All those workers! And in the day, in the week, all those thousands of other workers! In the steel works, in the gas works, in the factories of Stoke, in the potteries. The hundreds in Shentall's alone—how could I dare to admit them to my list of possible pirates? when at the party alone there was Bullace who spent to the bottom of his purse, in order to look successful, in order to be successful; Freddy, who might or might not have won the pools, who liked the big house, who poured out money on maintaining it in its excellent state of repair and off-key decoration, so that he could have it when he married, Freddy who thought that an idea was anyone's property; Mitchell, fat cheerful Mitchell, instigator and expert of the works camera club, he who had painted the prototype cup and who had been, a couple of years back, so heartily snubbed by Corinna. There was even Dart, poor fellow, about whom I knew little beyond what I'd seen; and that was enough—another large well painted house, also a well painted wife, perfumed, silky, despising Stoke, dreading the neighbours, dominated by *the others*.

I put out the cigarette, started the car, and drove down the hill.

Also at the party had been Corinna.

—

Questions. No one seemed to find it surprising that I should wander about the works, asking so many. Particularly I liked to talk to Roach, Albert's grandfather, who stacked ware on the trolleys to be sent into the glost oven, china glost; that was to say, for the second firing, after the biscuit had been dipped in glaze. Roach had been working for Shentall's for forty-six years, and his greatest delight was to recount, and doubtless to embroider, tales of the old days of coal, when all ware had to be packed in fireclay boxes called saggars, to protect it from specks and fumes; when men climbed ladders inside the bottle-shaped kilns, carrying piles of saggars on their shoulders, and darted in and out of the opened still-hot ovens to clear them, for economic reasons, as quickly as possible without letting the fire drop too low; when a miscalculation of temperature could ruin a whole kiln full of ware, distorting shapes and changing colours and possibly with a small firm ending the career of the potter and the living of his workmen; and when, similarly, a fault in the body turned out pots that were twisted, shrunken and collapsed, like genetic mishaps of a nuclear disaster. I'd seen a sample in the Hanley Museum. Wasters, they called them, for that's what they were, waste, waste, fit only for the shraff heap.

Shraff! Dialect, doublet of scrap, I suppose. Until clay is fired it can be remodelled, thrown back with water and reduced again to slip; hence the careful sweeping up of snippets from the work benches. But once it's fired, it's finished. If it's wrong it can only be smashed and thrown out—time, work, money, all for nothing. And Shentall's standards were cruelly exacting. For the tiniest blemish a piece was rejected, and such was their pride that they wouldn't let out second pieces at reduced prices but, so that no one should point the finger at a Shentall fault, exposed the weaklings on the hillside. For they had their faults, even Shentall's; though thanks to scientific control they no longer suffered the major disaster of a spoilt kill.

Kill. Local pronunciation of kiln. It no longer sounded sinister to my ears, nor did the word body for the prepared clay. China body, earthenware body, feldspathic body. Sometimes when I stood in the slip house and watched it squeezing out of the pug, grey, damp, and inert, I was reminded of a true body, human and dead, a corpse. I mentioned this to Mitchell one day as he happened to be passing on some far-fetched errand, and we laughed. Laughed!

'No, it's all safe, now,' old Roach would say, regretfully. And then he would add, with brightening eyes—'Mind, it does happen sometimes, you get one of those cars come off the rail in the middle of the tunnel. Then there's a cafuffle—why, they have to cool down the oven, see, for the men to go in and clear up the smash and put things to rights. Meanwhile there's no ware coming through to be glazed, or decorated, as the case may be, and they're all twiddling their thumbs, while on the other hand the biscuit piles up waiting to go in. And they all get on to you, but there's nothing to be done but be patient. As always, in pottery.' And all the time he talked, he'd be placing plate after plate on its pins, without a glance, never missing one.

Pins, props, thimbles, bats—kiln furniture they call it; refractory fireclay supports that hold the ware in position on the trolley or separate each piece from the other by the finest of fine points. When they unpack plates and saucers at the other end scraps of the supports break off, fused with the glaze in the firing. Women chip away these crumbs with sharp chisels, removing also, inevitably, flakes of glaze, leaving three equi-distant rough patches on the bottom of finished saucers and plates. It's the one process that makes a noise; a continuous rapid chink, chink, like a hedge full of angry blackbirds. Albert's aunt worked in this department;

but the middle generation of Roach was chiefly represented by his father, who was manager of a section of the printing shop, where long narrow sheets of transfer paper were draped on lines over the benches, giving the place the air of a laundry.

Clay! They give it to cases of nervous disorder; it soothes them to pull it about. Was that why the works was so calm, because of the satisfying tractability of the raw material? But there, you have to be calm when at any minute you may be passed by a man balancing a four-foot plank of cups on one shoulder. You have to be patient, as old Roach said, with clay, as with people.

And on the whole they *were* patient. The chart of breakages was low; it would have been lower, but for Albert. Of course there were tensions and minor rows. The glost manager complained that the biscuit manager didn't keep it coming through; the biscuit blamed the slip house; and the slip house, who dealt with the clay in its most plastic and malleable state, went steadily on as usual, fortifying my belief in the affinity of clay with human nature. As a corollary I came largely to share Mr Luke's conviction that all that's good in pottery must be touched, at some stage, and in some degree, by human hand, however much assisted by mechanical devices.

I once asked Corinna about labour relations.

'Good,' she said. 'Everything done with discussion and negotiation, works dance, cricket match, outing, the lot. One big family.'

'I thought the family idea was démodé?'

She shrugged. 'People are fools enough to imagine a family must be happy. They think it can't be a unit without a welter of gush and kisses. The strongest families are the ones that never think of themselves as a family, they scratch and squabble, and then act together by instinct in a crisis.'

Corinna. She was working late almost every evening on a design she wanted to thrash out. I stayed too, under the claim of preparing the booklet, taking my notes into the art room every evening when the others had gone, pleading that I was lonely in the library. She smiled sardonically, and said nothing. At first she worked by the door, ready to run, I suppose. But as the days passed she didn't bother to leave her place in the middle of the room; convinced, no doubt, of my tameness.

Whenever she packed up, so did I. Then I drove her home to Endon; always only to the end of the road. She was still that much afraid—no, reserved. Something was there, some resistance. But she had no idea, or perhaps the wrong idea, why I was so much with her. Well, and which *was*, by that time, the wrong idea?

As she had predicted, I saw a lot of Bullace, stalking round the works, laying down the law, displaying the *Guardian* and his beautiful clothes. He was much better dressed than Hansell, Brassick, Tombey, and Cardamine, the directors, although in Mr Luke he met his match. On the second Wednesday I found him in the library looking through my notes. He made no apology, simply said 'Very interesting, all that,' gave me a cool, semi-approving nod and walked off. I didn't want to antagonize him, or anyone, so I took it quietly. There was nothing damaging, in any case, for him to see. All the same, he'd given me a shock; especially when on the following day he was absent. But as I made haste to find out, he had leave.

Apart from that incident, two weeks passed without alarms. Mr Luke continued to rule with Gilbertian benevolence—a despotism strict combined with absolute equality—Albert to break china, Janice to rub up gold and bring me cups of tea, Judith to put through calls and answer enquiries. I often regretted that it was impossible for me to ask questions over the phone, for I had few chances of hearing that soft sing-song voice. Unlike Freddy. I was always catching sight of him in some part of the works, his white shirtsleeves rolled neatly above his elbows and his blue eyes sparkling me a greeting as he chattered for minutes on end to some crony at the other end of the factory, or even outside. Mitchell, too, was inclined to be a rolling stone. His large, paint-stained figure shuffled into sight in most unlikely places; he seemed to wear permanently an easy-going grin. Dart continued pale, basically well-meaning, and quite ineffectual. One day when the considerate Bullace had parked across the back of my car, he offered me a lift into Hanley, and I discovered why the Zephyr's engine was so tired; he'd hacked it to death. Every few minutes he apologized for the jerks and crashes of his gear changing. Like Freddy he switched on the radio, but there was no relish in his gesture; it was simply something one did to a fixture in one's car. Poor Dart, poor Colin. Only once did he startle me. Suddenly, out of the blue, into a pause, he said 'I like Lumberdine.' And nothing more.

Of course he did. Freddy the fountain of life, with hair like split coal and shoes like chestnuts, frowning over the crossword, stirring bread into his soup, scowling and shouting abuse at harmless buses and lorries—how could he help liking him? There was no one who didn't.

I worked. I hadn't spent years with Cotton's for nothing. I filled whole notebooks with information in my shorthand code; salaries—even now, some wages—relationships, dependencies, commitments, habits, standards of living; the fruits of my hours of double study at the works. The patience, my God! with which I tortured conversation to take the turn I wanted. No wit, labouring to introduce after dinner his *bons mots* polished in the afternoon, ever took such trouble as mine. And, after all, for a few lines of code in the notebook.

Thus, from the middle-shift gatekeeper, to whom I suggested, unnecessarily, that my constant late departures must give him some trouble:

'No, no, no trouble at all. I like people to work late, it livens things up for me, having to open the gates. Yes, I shut them about ten to six, most of them's off by then. Bill sees to shutting up Rush Street side, over by delivery. About six, he goes off. No other gate, no—unless you count the loading bay, no one uses that but the lorries, right down other end, it is, leads out to Mile Bank. Despatch foreman sees that's closed at half five when they go off. Oh, if anyone works late and haven't a car to get out, like the cleaners, say, they walk through the side gate here. I'm always in the lodge till ten, I'm bound to see anyone, so it's left open. Pat locks up the lot when he comes on, of course, the night watchman. The office, they're here all hours sometimes, and Mr Luke too. Well, you've seen for yourself there's Mrs Wakefield, since you come out with her. She's a worker, you know! Then you get that with the artists, they get carried away. Olive, no, not so often, but it does happen. And Mr Mitchell, he has the camera club, of course, every two months. Not so much Mr Johns, a family man, he is. Mr Bullace! You can see him leaving his office unless everything were just so. People talk, but I say if a man's got a good brain and uses it he deserves to get on. What's it to do with anyone, his private life? We're all in glass houses, aren't we? Of course if you're not too fond of work it comes hard. Young Mr Dart, now, he stops because he feels obliged to when Mr Bullace is sweating at the books. Not that Mr Bullace has to sweat. I reckon it comes pretty easy to him, easier than to others. That was just my way of speaking.'

If only they all had his way of speaking! How much easier it was for me, and more rewarding, than the brevity of Judith's demure responses. For not even Judith was spared.

'Don't you get lonely in here all day, Judith?'

'Oh no. I hear people's voices.'

Yes, little clam, you must know most of what goes on.

'I've seen you working at sheets of figures. I suppose that helps to pass the time.'

'Yes. Sometimes Mr Luke sends down the easy ones when Miss Chapman's busy.'

'But what do you do when she isn't?'

'Well, I read. Mr Luke doesn't mind. He's seen me.'

'Only read?'

'Sometimes I knit, or do some sewing.'

'You'll make a good housewife, then, when you're married.'

A deep deep blush. The soft Staffordshire voice.

'I might not be asked.'

Dear God! how sweet, like a fresh baked apple dumpling, warm, soft, scented and ready to melt. Yet above all how transparently good. Sullivan, Judith Agnes, age twenty, wage seven pounds thirteen and six gross, parents living, brothers two older, sisters two younger, father's occupation welder, mother's housewife, religion Roman Catholic. I'd written that out with loving care and neatness.

And this, from Johns:

'Of course Corinna's very quiet. I don't know why she hasn't remarried though. She's quite good-looking.'

He rises in my estimation; he has judgement.

'Her husband? Never knew him, none of us did. She was a widow when she came here. Tragic, I suppose, so young, as she was then. Not that she's old now, but you know what I mean.'

A pause. I know.

'Anyway, her private life's her own affair. But still waters run deep. Of course, no one really knows her, not even Olive. You'd think a female colleague—still, perhaps not. Olive? Well, she's good, of course. We're all good artists at Shentall's, didn't you know? But no, not like Corinna. Corinna has style.'

Collecting such trivia I passed my days. In the evenings after I'd taken Corinna home I'd go for a walk, usually under the dripping railway arch to where the Trent made its way through tufty grass to the sewage works; and there, by the puddles and the gasometer and the barbed wire and railings that fenced the brown gape of the brickworks quarry, I'd shove my thoughts, if I could, into some sort of order. If not, I'd give up and drive round the towns, learning them—hilly residential suburbs cleft with vistas of grey and iron; shopping centres where stucco and paint and vitreous façades almost concealed the sooty brick; town halls, valiant parks, grim black churches, isolated and rearing, heaps of eroded slag, micaceous rocks of new colleges, factories, offices, thrusting sheer above surrounding waves of low slate roofs that dipped and sagged with age. Progress and consciousness were gradually but ineluctably sponging down the past. An improvement, of course; but it was impossible not to murmur occasionally, from the deep forgetful rosy well of sentiment, a sad farewell to the old bottle ovens and the soot.

On the Friday of the second week Bullace came back to plague us; Freddy remembered the projected excursion to Dovedale and rushed about the works making up a party for Sunday afternoon; and Corinna's 'Persian' design was passed by the board, as I learnt when Mr Luke called me in at five o'clock.

'We can't keep it dark, you realize,' he said, 'it has to go through the works.'

'Yes,' I said, 'and it might be better for your purposes if you broadcast the news rather more than usual. Don't just wait for it to filter through in the course of production.'

He looked at me unhappily. 'You think it will precipitate—'

'It might, that's all. It's a possibility worth watching.'

'But how can we watch Mrs Wakefield?'

'I'll do as much as I can,' I said coolly. 'If you tighten security here at the works and in time you discover that your dinner service is duplicated, you'll be certain that she's the one responsible—passing her drawings out from home. Unfortunately that takes time and doesn't save this particular design. It isn't the first she's done since Vinca, is it?'

'No, there was Burnet Rose, and of course she helped in some composite efforts. What may have happened to all of them God only knows. Besides, what's to prevent her copying someone else's work?'

I turned to go, then remembered. 'The new design—are you calling it Isfahan?'

'We are not,' he said, dryly. His smile faded. 'How did you know about that?'

'She told me.'

He looked at me; the familiar look that all my employers give me in the end; not knowing whether to admire or despise me.

—

While I was driving Corinna home I let her tell me, as if it were news, that her design was accepted.

'I'm going to take you out to celebrate,' I said.

'You can't this evening. I teach at the art school from seven to nine.'

'Tomorrow, then?'

'Thank you,' she said. 'What's it to be, lunch?'

'Followed by driving, since you like to be driven, then we'll have dinner, and then I'll teach you to dance.'

'No,' she said soberly, 'that's too much. You mustn't.'

On the contrary, I must. 'Why not?' I asked.

She turned her eyes on me with such candour. 'I don't want to put a strain on Mr Luke's generosity.'

'Don't worry. There's more than Mr Luke between me and indigence.'

So she accepted.

I picked her up at the bus stop that evening, only an hour or so after I'd taken her home. I drove her to the art school, I met her outside at half past nine, I drove her back to Endon, to the corner of the road, by the lamp. She'd gone very silent, giving me a subdued and thoughtful goodnight. I couldn't meet her eyes. I could no longer think of what I was doing, or I should have had to stop, even I.

There was another side road fifty yards on, where I parked the car. I walked back, stood in the shadows by a garden wall, and watched the light in her windows, which naturally I'd known long since through my spying. When it went out I still waited.

In the morning she would be shopping, which was a danger point before which I was helpless; then at the hairdresser's from eleven, then safe with me till about five, when I should have to leave her to change for dinner. Then she would be safe again all the evening, and I would watch her light go out. Sunday morning was a great unsupervised space, until, as arranged with Freddy, I should collect her after lunch on the way to Dovedale. For that dangerous time, and for Sunday evening, something might be—must be—provided in due course, thus leaving her only the early part of Saturday and Sunday mornings in which to make phone calls, or more likely, post letters. That couldn't be helped; such rifts, short of sleeping with her, I could hardly prevent.

Corinna, Corinna. Couldn't she post a letter without a black mark? No, she couldn't, she who had no husband, no family, no friends. What would she want with letters?

I waited half an hour. Her light didn't reappear. She didn't come out. She was in bed, perhaps asleep. Shivering with cold, I went back to the car and drove away.

—

But Sunday morning defeated me. I'd simply failed, in invention or determination, to find a plausible excuse to keep her in sight.

I did my best to redeem the lapse by ringing her up and spinning out conversation for half an hour; but couldn't prevail on her to lunch with me. That made me nervous; and promptly at half past one I left for Endon.

It was a fine day. Outside Stoke the sun shone brightly in patches through the loose clouds rolled and broken by the wind. When I arrived she was sitting on the broken pillar of the gate, wearing an old riding mac and a red scarf over her long, uptwisted hair.

'I saw the Darts pass the end of the road about ten minutes ago,' she said as she sat down beside me.

'Have I made you wait? I'm sorry.'

'No, I wanted to sit in the sun. It's so warm. Why are you tearing up this road? I know you can drive fast.'

'I thought we'd catch up with the Darts.'

'And pass the time of day as we drive along side by side? Anyway you'll probably overtake them without trying. Colin's very careful.'

'He hasn't much choice. There's hardly a wheeze left in that car. How long has he had it?'

'About eighteen months, more or less. Would you like a cigarette?'

She lit one for me, and put it in my mouth; then one for herself. She was looking tired, the lines in her face were marked and shadowy. I'd kept her out too late the night before, and made her dance too much. I had to.

The entrance to Dovedale was rather impressive, bald humps of limestone, scurfy with yellow grass, looming towards each other on either side of the narrowing road. Turning into the official car park, I saw that the Darts had that minute arrived. The cream Zephyr stood on the end of the line, and Dart was paying the attendant. Gillian, bored by such transactions, was waiting with her back to him. She barely managed a wave and smile as we came in. How typical of her, and of her difference from Corinna, were her clothes. Because it was Sunday Corinna wore an old raincoat that never appeared at work. Because it was Sunday, Gillian wore a smooth dark green suit and little stab-heeled shoes.

Dart shambled across to us in his usual shame-faced manner, kicking a stone as he came.

'Hallo,' he said, 'shall we wait here for the others?'

'No,' said Gillian, 'it's cold.'

In fact the wind was much stronger, and of course much fresher, than it had been in Stoke. We crunched across the car park. Gillian shivered.

'I'm freezing,' she moaned.

'You should have brought a coat,' said Dart.

'I didn't know we'd have to get out and walk,' she fretted.

Dart's face brightened. 'Here comes Freddy,' he said.

The tomato-soup Consul, looking rather low, swung in at the gate, its horn tooting in a music-hall rhythm. Freddy was grinning and mouthing inaudible greetings at the wheel; and when he had manoeuvred the car into a space we saw why it rode so close to the ground. A youth and a girl followed him from the front seat, and from the back he unpacked five giggling girls, dressed in short skirts and bright shaggy sweaters, so alike that they seemed the uniform of some advanced, expensive, and slightly fast finishing school.

He herded them across to us like a sheep dog, tightening the bunch with darting sallies and threatened slaps that provoked shrieks of feigned terror.

'Hullo,' he said, approaching us with a grin. 'My friend Mike, his sister, and a few friends.' He waved vaguely at the girls. 'Well—shall we go?'

Gillian didn't need to be asked twice. She walked off in

front, we followed, and Freddy and his flock lagged a little behind. Apart from their chattering and the quiet scuffs of our feet, the only sound was the rattling of the stream beside the path. Occasionally we had to flatten into single file to let a car creep by. A large patch of cloud had covered the sun, casting into shadow the limestone scree and thin grass of the slopes that closed round us. A solitary kestrel hovered overhead.

Dart took out his camera.

'For goodness' sake, what is there to film?' said Gillian sharply. 'I don't know what we've come all this way to see. Anyway you might wait till the sun comes out again. If it does.'

Dart put his camera away.

A little further on, the dale widened to an open space where, in spite of prohibitory notices, several cars had stopped. At this point the stream was crossed by a line of stepping stones; quite easy ones, for the water, though fast, was shallow. Dart went over first, followed by Gillian, who made for the tea stall on the far bank.

'Would you like some tea, Corinna?' I asked, when we had crossed.

'Thank you, I carry my own refreshment,' she said, tapping her pocket.

An outburst of shrieks made us look round. The last two girls were teetering in midstream, hunched together on one stone, while Freddy, grimacing and flapping ogre-like behind them, threatened to push them in.

Dart watched with a faint grin. 'Fred's a clown,' he said, admiring from a hopeless distance. Gillian turned her back, disgusted.

I looked at Corinna. She was watching Freddy rather sadly.

'Let's go on a bit,' I said.

We walked upstream along the steep-sided valley. The left slope was dark with woods that came right down to the water, which was perfectly clear, with green hair-like weeds streaming flat under its surface.

'May I ask an impertinent question?' said Corinna, suddenly.

'You may. I don't have to answer.'

'How old are you?'

'Forty-four. Why?'

She looked up at my hair. Those eyes were incapable, surely, of dishonesty.

'Oh, that,' I said. 'Anyone would think it was a snowdrift. It's only grey.'

'Silver,' she corrected.

I wasn't to argue with an artist.

'What was it?' she went on. 'Illness, or the war, or what?'

'Nothing so romantic. It just went.'

She nodded quietly, and we turned, and made our way to the stepping stones, from the direction of which shouts and laughter suggested that a certain amount of horseplay was still going on.

'Freddy's in an outrageous mood today,' I said.

She smiled indulgently. 'Freddy!'

'Have you noticed that although he threatens, he never touches these girls?' I said. 'He's with them as he is with drink—the half glass of beer at the party where everyone's swilling.'

She looked at me with such quick comprehension that I knew she'd noticed that too.

'Yes,' she said, 'Freddy makes a lot of noise, but he's really very sober and very chaste. He's a Catholic you know.'

'Does that give him proprietary rights in chastity?'

'I just mentioned it,' she said, her forehead wrinkling with the nervous anxiety that saddened me; it was the expression of someone used to having rows break over her head, rows that she'd try to avert, wearily hoping that her explanation would be allowed.

Anyway, her remark wasn't the *non sequitur* I'd implied. I remembered the crucifix, the missal. Freddy, the devoted son of Holy Mother Church, he'd be chaste on principle; till he couldn't bear it. I could just imagine him slipping off to some quiet tart, someone whose principles were past corruption; and then slipping into confession to collect his stint of purgatory for having failed to subdue the virility with which he was so well endowed. But the girls he met socially would be inviolate. His flirtation was something different. That was his disguise, his protection against the raised eyebrow, the clever malice, the leer behind the back with which society greets an affirmation of chastity.

'Well, let's find another sin to damn him,' I said. 'Anger, now. I imagine Freddy could lose his temper quite prettily.'

'I don't know. I've never seen it. Bullace is the one who'd say to his brother "Thou fool"—or rather to his cousin. Poor Freddy.' She sighed.

I gave her a look which unfortunately she saw.

'I'm not in love with him,' she said, simply.

'Why on earth not?'

She smiled. 'If I married Freddy I'd go mad. He's good, he's kind, he's generous, and he'd hurt me a thousand times a day, oh, not on purpose, just with his sharpness, his bigoted, cock-sure certainty that Freddy is right, nothing more to be said. I know he's insular, opinionated, self-satisfied. It's just that he's what I never had, never. A flirt.'

I looked at her serious austere face. Lovers, passions, a tragic marriage, the ideas suited her well. But flirtation, no; that I couldn't imagine.

'I was so plain and fat, all through my teens,' she went on. 'Boarding school in the war, you can imagine the food. And even now, you see—'

'You've a lovely figure,' I said. It came out with more warmth than I'd meant.

She pretended not to hear. 'And then just at the end, the services caught me. Needless to say how hideous I looked and felt in khaki. Then I went through the art school in a sort of serious-minded fog—nothing mattered except work. I didn't know then that I wasn't good enough to take that stand. I didn't even dress like an art student. They look so sweet now, all wispy and strange. I was just utility, missed all ways. Then I married, and it was too late.'

'For what?'

'To flirt,' she said, surprised.

How chaste she was! Few women, in my experience, consider that marriage puts an end to flirtation, for themselves; only for their husbands.

'All the same, Freddy should grow up,' I said.

'Give him time,' she pleaded, just as his mother had done: the Freddies of this world are always spoilt by women. 'He'll have his fling then settle down and be faithful to some pure creature. Hence the long and careful choosing. He'd have to revere a wife, Freddy, *Holy* matrimony, you see. He'll pick someone he can set up and venerate.'

'Then he'll be disillusioned.'

'Oh—you've been married, then?'

We looked at each other. She'd said enough. No need to enlarge on our shared experience of unhappiness.

'What a long time you've waited to ask me,' I said. 'Yes, I've been married.'

'Is your wife dead?'

'No. Divorced.'

'Oh. Have you any children?'

'We had a little girl. She was the one that died. She caught polio. That was ten years ago, before the vaccines.'

She said nothing. I saw her look at my hair, but she said nothing.

'And you?' I asked. 'No children?'

She shook her head. 'Perhaps it's just as well.' She hesitated. 'Why did you divorce your wife?'

'She preferred someone else. I couldn't blame her, at that time. To be exact, I didn't divorce her, she divorced me.'

She looked at me curiously, almost with abstraction. '*How?*' she said. 'How do you go about it, getting a divorce?'

To have lived secluded from all that muck, what wouldn't I have given!

'Adultery,' I said.

'I know—but how can you prove it?'

This strain of morbid curiosity surprised me. 'If you can't get someone willing to admit it, you employ a detective agency.'

'But what—'

'They'll bribe the maids and open doors and shine torches or take long distance shots with—'

'Don't!'

She sat down on an outcrop of rock and put her face in her hands. 'I couldn't,' she said, shuddering, 'I couldn't.'

Well, she didn't have to. That had all been taken out of her hands by the dispensation of providence. Then I realized what was disgusting her.

'Listen,' I said, 'that's not what happened to me. But you would ask.'

'I know,' she said, standing up. 'I'm sorry. It doesn't matter. It wasn't what you thought.'

We walked on in silence to join the others.

The sun was shining again, and Dart had summoned enough defiance to take out his camera. The girls were grouped at the water's edge, and Freddy cavorted behind Dart's back, waggling his fingers in his ears, allegedly to make the girls smile but in fact causing them to collapse with laughter. However, the photograph was taken in the end, and also one of the quiet Mike, Freddy's friend and foil.

'Now, then, Fred, one of you,' cried Dart, his Hoxton, or whatever it was, getting the better of him, to the discomfiture of Gillian.

'Wait,' said Freddy, 'I'm going to have this posed.'

He dashed up to a tuft of coltsfoot which grew near where we were standing and picked off a couple of flower heads.

'Freddy!' Corinna rebuked him.

'Why—it's only a dandelion,' he said.

'That's not a dandelion.'

'Not a dandelion?' he said, looking at it in astonishment. 'What is it then? A sweet pea?'

'You've never looked at a dandelion, Freddy,' said Corinna.

'I have! A dandelion is a plant with a transparent stem—about 16 gauge, steel wire—'

'What?'

'Well, that's how we engineers see things, you know, in sizes.'

'Everything?' I asked.

'That's right!' said Freddy with a wink. 'Females and all, we run them up against the standard gauge.'

And he rushed back to the stream, clutching his coltsfoot.

'Liar!' I said, softly.

Corinna smiled.

'You take a good look at people, don't you? I mean their characters.' She paused, looking thoughtful. 'Have you ever heard Freddy on the subject of women in trousers? "Are they *ashamed* of their femininity?" Doesn't he see that they're only emphasizing it?'

Of course he didn't see. He didn't really look at women. He looked at the skirt, the representation, the symbol, not at the disturbing biological facts of the sloping hips and tipped pelvis. If he'd looked he'd have been lost. They weren't fools, the church fathers, they put the blinkers on early. Forgive me, father, for I have sinned; given way to impure thoughts, looked on a woman to lust after her.

Freddy, Freddy. He knew the right answer to every question. No wonder he was bursting with *joie de vivre*. Life's fine when you're satisfied it's all for the best in the end. I wanted to snatch him, shake him, shout at him: Freddy, wake up, open your eyes, use your intelligence: how can you believe?

Oh, why? He was happy. Let him be. Besides, what would he have said in reply? I knew too well. He'd have seized me, shaken me, shouted at me: Nicholson, wake up, open your eyes, use your intelligence: how can you deny?

Meanwhile he was posing idiotically on one of the stepping stones, holding out the miserable coltsfoot at arm's length—as if that were likely to come out in the photograph; and the inevitable happened. His feet slipped on the wet stone, and in he went, not falling headlong, just staggering out of control for that one second, so that in the next he was standing in the bed of the stream with water swirling up to his calves.

The uncontrolled laughter on all sides was increased by the spectacle of his progress to the bank. He wouldn't hurry and cut short our entertainment, but lifted each foot out and shook it repeatedly before plunging it at the next step back in the water; accompanying this pantomime with the most ludicrous and exaggerated grimaces.

It amused me, in a way, to see how instinctively he went to Corinna when he reached the bank; the older one, the stand-in for mother. Certainly she made a great deal of fuss, giving him her flask to drink from, making him take off his socks, insisting that he was to drive straight back. And at the same time as he craved those admonitions and attentions, and accepted them, he was treating them with that verbal scorn which he believed to be demanded by manly convention; with 'Get off!' and 'Stop fussing, girl.'

I looked at her, standing beside him as he wrung out the bottoms of his trousers. No, she wasn't so chaste after all, with that half smile and those great eyes glancing over his loins and shoulders and neck and his hair, of course, his springing coal-black hair.

I went over to where the Darts were standing and talked to them; or tried to. I was struggling on about the possibility of having seen a trout in the stream when Gillian interrupted with an exclamation of surprise.

Across the river, in the space where cars were forbidden to park, among all the others a white Jaguar had pulled up, an X K tourer, with its red hood down. A man and a girl were sitting inside and the man was waving to us. He wore a soft cap pulled well forward, so it took me a few seconds to recognize Bullace.

I went over the stones before anyone else. It wasn't till I reached the other side and looked round that I realized no one else was coming anyway.

'Hullo!' said Dudley, expansively. 'Thought we'd see if we could join the party after all. Better late than never.'

His accent had never sounded more synthetic. I glanced at the girl beside him, and experienced a most curious shock. It was Judith.

'Well,' I said, recovering. 'You've certainly not missed this time. Where did you find it? Sheffield?'

'Manchester,' he said. 'Not a bad little packet, is it?' Not a bad little packet of money either. The car might not be new, but it wasn't more than two or three years old, and in immaculate condition, as they say.

'Freddy!' exclaimed Bullace suddenly. 'What *have* you been doing?'

I was wrong about no one else coming. Freddy was there beside me. He'd had to wait to put on his shoes, his lovely chestnut shoes, all spoilt and wetted.

'Fell in, Dud,' he said, with absent-minded simplicity.

Of course he was staring at the car. Poor Freddy. On his face you could see plainly that he was eclipsed at last in a field where it hurt. He'd been so proud of that tomato-red Consul, and till then Bullace had made do, God knows how, with an old Morris ten. But he had guts, Freddy; all a northerner's grit, plus an almost unnatural generosity.

'Smashing job,' he said. 'How d'you push it, Dud? All right for a ton?'

'Pretty good,' said Bullace complacently. 'Isn't it, Judith?'

She nodded, blushing. Well, I suppose it shouldn't have surprised me. A white Jag, a sunny day, the handsome Bullace beside her. She was only human.

Dart came across the river, and made a few awkward half-envious compliments.

'We ought to have a race,' Bullace said to me.

'Thank you, I won't contest your honours. Didn't you see one of those smashed on the road outside Sheffield last week?'

He laughed shortly. 'I don't suppose the chap knew how to handle it. Freddy—would you like to try?'

Judith uttered a little sound of alarm, and made to get out.

'What's the matter?' said Bullace, turning on her a superior smile. 'Don't you think he can manage?'

Her sweet face was screwed up in alarm and embarrassment. 'It's different,' she said in a whisper. 'If you're not used to them, these big sports cars—'

She stopped, almost choked with blushing.

'Some other time, Dud, many thanks,' said Freddy quietly.

Bullace smiled. 'Right then, that's a promise. As a matter of fact we'd better clear off, we're not supposed to park here. Just thought I'd show you, if I could. We might see you somewhere on the way back, if you can catch us. Otherwise, till tomorrow.'

He pushed the starter, demonstrated his efficiency in a neat turn, and drove off with a lot of noise that an X K doesn't need to make.

'Your cousin has the best of everything,' I observed to Freddy.

He looked at me, for once, quite straight and serious. 'He hasn't always,' he said. 'Let him be.'

Useless to protest that I didn't grudge Bullace his fortunes. Freddy was already on his way back, treating the stones this time with greater circumspection, creeping back to Corinna to comfort his wounded pride. I leaned against one of the cars and lit a cigarette.

It was nearly finished when Corinna came across the stream.

'What are you doing here?' she asked.

'Waiting to go,' I said, 'if you're quite through with Freddy.'

The look she gave me then. Joyful, triumphant, and aghast. How can a look be all that at once? I don't know. I know nothing, nothing. These moments, these glances, flash past too quickly for analysis. Besides, I turned away. One always turns away. If one didn't, all would be well.

—

It was better when we were back in the car, driving up the steep hills round Eyam and Monyash. That was our proper place, where we were used to being, where we'd come to know each other; together in a moving car. Ludicrous and pitiable state of affairs.

I nodded at the view to our left. 'Something for Dart, if he could persuade Gillian to let him waste his film.'

'It's easy to kick Colin,' she observed.

I ignored the rebuke. 'I hear he was a teacher before coming here.' I'd read, not heard, but it came to the same thing.

'Yes,' she said. 'He taught maths in a secondary modern somewhere down south. He thought there'd be more future for him in industry. Or rather Gillian thought, I expect. Industry! Assistant to Bullace. Anyway, poor Colin, he couldn't assist in a twopenny bun shop.'

'Easy to kick Colin,' I reminded her.

'It's a simple truth,' she said. 'How did he ever control a class?'

'Probably gave up teaching and talked about his hobby through the din. Do *you* belong to the camera club?' I knew she didn't.

'I'm not a blackleg!' she retorted. 'Cameras take the bread out of artists' mouths.'

'Mitchell doesn't share your scruples.'

She shrugged.

'Is he good, Mitchell? With the camera, I mean.'

'First rate. You should have seen his entry in the exhibition—well, he had two, but the prize one was the steam engine. Taken at night, all black, with the fire glowing and a shiny-faced driver peering out, clouds of steam drifting across—a proper professional turnout. He took it at Stafford station one wet night. He was proud of it too. He labelled it "Last Expiring Breath". He has a weakness for fancy titles. His other one was called "Bread and Butter". It was coloured, lovely colour, I must admit. An empty china bread plate.'

'I'm very stupid,' I said slowly, after a pause. 'You'll have to explain.'

'Why, don't you see? Pottery is his bread and butter. I thought you were supposed to revel in that sort of punning, crossword solver.'

'Sorry,' I said. 'I see now. What did the others put in?'

'Not bad, most of them, though no one in Mitchell's class. The stupid thing is that he's not the one with the best camera. Bullace has the Leica, needless to say. He showed some very superior views of Le Lavandou, just to let us know that he'd been there. Let's think, what else? Anthem—oh, you can imagine his, something in the Nature's Cathedral style. Colin did the harbour at Mevagissey.'

'And what foolery did Freddy think up for that occasion?'

There was a pause. 'I don't remember,' she said. She was looking away from me, and I knew she was lying.

We went on in silence till we passed yet another crash, not a bad one, just a matter of buckled wings and a litter of glass crunching on the road like sugar.

'A wonder it wasn't Bullace,' she said, 'showing off to his pick-up.'

I swallowed. 'Yes,' I said, lightly, 'appearances are deceptive, aren't they? Who would have thought it of Judith?'

'Judith?' she said. 'What are you talking about?'

'The little pick-up. You didn't think she went with the car, did you?'

She stared at me with her mouth slightly open, quite stupid with amazement. 'You don't mean Judith Sullivan?'

'Of course I do. What other Judith is there?'

'No,' she said promptly, 'you must have been mistaken. It must have been someone like her.'

'Listen, I was as close to her almost as I am to you. I heard him name her, I heard her answer. You were on the far side of the water, attending to—other things. Besides, she had a scarf round her head. That makes a difference, you know. I hardly recognized Bullace in his cap.'

'But it's impossible!' she protested weakly. 'Bullace—no, he just wouldn't have anything to do with her. A girl from the works, the switchboard girl! For him that would be equivalent to eating in the canteen.'

'He's just spent a lot on that car,' I said. 'Perhaps she's all he could afford.'

She was silent. I glanced at her quickly, to see that impatient compression of the lips.

'Well, who said pick-up first?' I asked.

'I didn't know it was Judith or I'd never have said it,' she retorted. 'You know she's not that sort of girl.'

'Sort of girl! She's a girl, that's enough. She's human, I suppose, and fallible.'

'All right,' said Corinna coolly, 'there's no need to be savage with me. You know you don't believe it anyway. You're just making a noise, like Freddy.'

Well, I'd be silent then. After a minute she got out the cigarettes, lit two and put one of them in my mouth.

'Here,' she said, 'take this, calm down. No need to send us both to a premature grave.'

—

Etruria. It fascinated me. I stopped by the lights at Cobridge, by the signpost that actually has the word on it; one way Leek, the other Etruria and Newcastle.

'Are you tired?' I asked her.

'Not particularly. Why?'

'I'd like to go down there, into the pit, see what it's like by day.'

In fact it was hardly day any longer. The pit was like a length of suiting; the dark vertical stripes of the chimneys interwoven with the grey of mist, dusk, and smoke; though far above could be seen, still, the tender sky of a spring evening.

We went down at a sightseer's crawl. On the left, red brick council houses, on the right, gantries and cables and the huge cone of a colliery tip and a bank of grass the colour of charcoal, where not even coltsfoot could grow; further down, spaces like bomb sites, rough with the rubble of slum clearance. Then in the floor of the pit, the pure industrial landscape of the iron and steel and the gas works and the ceramic colourists—black chimneys, level crossing without gates, heaps of slag and coke and scrap, a goods train clanking under a bridge, its engine pushing fat rolls of gritty steam into the sulphurous air. And through the middle of everything lay the Trent-Mersey canal, a motionless strip of water, black and glistening like a slug's back.

At the top of the hill on the Newcastle side, we stopped to look back. Miles above our heads a plane was cutting a perpendicular path into the sky, streaming golden vapour like sweat as it climbed in the sunshine we could no longer see.

'How marvellous to do that,' said Corinna.

'To fly up there?'

'To climb out of the muck, to be free, shake off the dirt.'

'All right till the port engine falls off,' I said, 'or whatever happens to jets.'

'Even so, you go out in a blaze instead of slowly rotting below.'

'You're hard on Etruria tonight,' I said. 'We shouldn't have come, we should have left it its illusory midnight charms. Facts aren't always worth the pains of getting to know them.'

She was silent. I turned back to the pit. 'Vallombrosa, vale of shadows. If only he could have foreseen, Wedgwood. Or Milton, for that matter.'

'What are you talking about now?' she said, with some impatience.

'One of Freddy's crossword favourites. You must know it, surely—

'Thick as autumnal leaves that strow the brooks
In Vallombrosa, where the Etrurian shades
High over-arched embower.'

'Embower!' she said derisively, nodding down at the pit. 'That's good. Can you see any trees? And I don't call the Trent-Mersey a brook.'

'You're hungry,' I said, and started the car.

She asked me in for a drink, blurted it out halfway to Endon, in great agitation, as if I were likely to mistake her invitation for soliciting.

So I saw without having to spy, for once, and inveigle myself, the inside of her home. It was much smaller than I'd thought, right at the top of the house; a living-room, two tiny boxes that were kitchen and bathroom, and presumably a bedroom that I didn't see.

The drink turned out to be a cascade of Scotch splashed into the glasses with a generous hand.

'I'll make some coffee,' she said, 'come and help me.'

Help her? To boil a kettle and spoon ground coffee into a pot. To lean against the narrow door of the pantry while she put two cups and saucers on a tray. Didn't she want me left in the living-room to look round it in my curious fashion?

I picked up one of the cups.

'That!' she said with a faint smile. 'Best Hanley.'

I raised my eyebrows.

'Hanley's mainly for earthenware,' she explained. 'China country is more towards Stoke and beyond.'

She went to a cupboard and fetched out a small matching teacup and saucer. 'Look at that, if you must.'

The saucer was covered, except for the centre, with a sharp design, black on white, as if a medley of fir trees and snow crystals had resolved itself into ordered formality.

The cup was milky white within, and plain black outside, so smooth and shining that the pattern of the saucer was reflected in reverse, like frost, on the sides.

I looked at the bottom of the cup. 'Good God!' I said. 'That's not Shentall's?' My conviction would have pleased Bullace.

She smiled. 'No, that's me. One of my failures.'

'Failures? It's beautiful.'

'That's not what the buyers thought. I meant it was a commercial failure. It never went beyond the sample stage.'

'How is it you've got this, then?' I asked, casually.

'Mr Luke gave it to me, just that piece. It was my first solo effort, you see. That was his way of saying diddums to baby, I suppose.'

'I see. Has he ever done it since?'

She laughed. 'I've never had a failure since. It didn't take me long to see what they wanted. Something graceful, pretty, and artistically negligible.'

'What would you like to do?' I asked her.

She was silent a moment. 'Paint—no, it wouldn't have to be paint. Put down somehow the things I see, I mean understand, think I see. Meanings, in fact.'

'The meaning of life,' I teased her. Flippant fool.

'Yes, to show that its meaning is that it has no meaning,' she said, not looking at me. 'Those complicated laws of nature, generation, all that endurance and struggle, all for nothing, for death. All of it, from the year dot, all the achievements, art and science equal, lavished on death. Futile. And yet if it weren't futile, I mean if it were the first stage of a master plan, to be completed in our next, it wouldn't be so moving. Well, it moves me, anyway,' she concluded shortly.

'Why don't you put them down, then, your perceptions of the heroic heartbreak?'

She smiled. 'Because I can't. If I could I would. That's the ridiculous, the really absurd part. I can see but I can't put down, not being in the Mantegna bracket.'

'Have you tried to put it down?' I said. 'Are you sure you can't?'

She banged the coffee pot on the tray. 'Look, I live isolated, very well. But give me credit for my training, at least. I know top art when I see it. And painting flowers to go round a teapot is just my level. That's why I do it, I suppose. I don't mind, it can't be helped, no use repining. Just that sometimes you get sick of mediocrity.'

I carried the tray for her into the living-room, and we sat down by the gas fire. What a room for her to live in! From each corner of the ceiling a brown hair-like crack crinkled towards the centre. The yellow distemper of the walls was marked with rectangular patches where pictures, no doubt too atrocious for her to bear, had formerly hung. We sat in brown armchairs, leather with velvet cushions, which matched the heavy sofa and concealed most of the faded carpet.

'If you're so sick of pottery, and Shentall's in particular,' I said, 'don't you think it's dishonest to go on working there?'

She stood up and took the glasses to refill them. 'How many people are heart and soul in their work?' she said. 'How can they be? There's not enough noble work in the world to go round.'

She was rattled by the word *dishonest*. I'd only said it to see her reaction. Well, without stirring from the seat, I could have shown her a far more ignoble job than painting teapots.

She opened the door of the cupboard where she kept

the whisky and this time I saw inside it. There was a great crowd of empty bottles, one untouched, and one half full from which we were drinking.

She saw my eyes, and smiled faintly. 'Time I cleared that out,' she said.

'How many years have they been there?'

She stared at me with an incredulous and ironical smile. ''That's about two months' drinking.'

I counted them quickly; fourteen altogether.

'I don't get drunk,' she said quietly. 'Not through virtue. It's something I inherit from my father, the ability to take drink.'

I wasn't shocked, as she seemed to think; not that way. I was only remembering, thinking of the bite out of her modest salary.

'Why?' I asked.

She shrugged. 'Some people take religion. I take that.'

'Couldn't you find something less—'

'Swinish?'

Expensive, I'd been going to say. I stood up and went across to her chair; only to take the empty glass from her. She shot back as if I were a serpent.

'Don't be afraid, Corinna,' I said.

She turned her head away from me.

'I am afraid,' she said. 'Oh, not of you. Afraid to leave Shentall's, because it's safe. Afraid to try and fail. Failure, commercial failure, means the garret, we agreed, didn't we? Anyway I couldn't do anything, I told you, I know my limitation. Talent.' She paused. 'Even so, staying at Shentall's, I'm afraid—yes, I'll tell you, but don't expect to be edified. I'm afraid of being seventy alone, worn out, not even able to work to take your mind off yourself, without friends, existing only as a nuisance to your landlord, in miserable furnished rooms, smaller and smaller, dirtier and dirtier, lingering on with nothing and no one, twenty years of it, perhaps, twenty years of weakness and cold, with three smoking coals in the grate, blankets heavy but not warm, stewed neck of mutton all gritty with bones, old clothes, long and shiny and threadbare and smelling of age, shoes your feet are too feeble to lift, yes, and a straw hat in the bitterest March, trembling with pleasure over a bunch of violets and then having to walk past the bus stop—you saw her in Sheffield, didn't you?'

'So that's why you wanted a drink.' I looked down at her ash-blonde head. 'Why should your future be like that?'

'What's to stop it? That's what happens to people who are alone and have no money. And I've none, I never had, never will have, apart from what I live on. If you knew you *don't* know—what I'd do to avoid that fate.'

'You could save the money you spend on drink,' I said.

'No. I need that to bear the present, the awful empty present.'

'Is it? Then why do you take such care of your hair, that lovely hair? Why are you so clean, so well-dressed, why don't you neglect yourself utterly if the present's no use to you?'

'To make up for my ugly youth,' she said, after a silence.

'You were never ugly, you couldn't have been. What about bones and eyes and mouth and chin and neck—'

'So you've given me what's known as the once-over.'

The once! She was too modest. 'Of course I have,' I said. 'Am I the only one? Don't other men look at you?'

'Do they? I don't know.'

'No, you don't,' I said angrily, 'you're so wrapped up in pining for youth and flirtation and Freddy. Freddy! You said you couldn't marry him, and you know you won't be asked.

You're wasting time, wasting yourself, wasting the assets that could assure this dreaded future, as much as anyone's future can be assured.'

She looked at me miserably. 'What do you want me to do, then?' she said.

Why didn't I tell her? There was too much to say, it was too important, too sudden, I was too grey, too worn, too base, it was hopeless. I was silent.

'Listen,' she said, after a moment or two, 'there's something I want to tell you. Only I don't know how—I can't.'

Her eyes reddened with tears. That was too much, the moment I could never stand. I bent down and took her hands.

'No, don't,' she said, pulling them away. 'Stop, go away. Please. It isn't fair.'

It hadn't been fair all along. I knew that better than she did. 'I'm sorry,' I said.

'No, not fair to *you*,' she cried. 'Not fair. Dishonest. You said dishonest just for that, because I don't like the work. Oh, if you knew—you'd never have taken me with you, spoilt me. I wish I hadn't let you. If you knew what I've done—'

If *she* knew what I'd done! Spoilt her! And all the time, in the middle of this, I had to remember who was paying me, and for what. The black and white saucer lay on the tray where I'd put it down, a reminder.

'Tell me what you've done, then, Corinna,' I said. 'It won't matter to me. I'll help you, I won't leave you in the ditch. Only tell me.'

She put her head in her hands. 'I can't. No, I can't. Too mean, too squalid—fraud and lying and dishonesty. Go away, please go away. That's all I want. You to go away.'

Why didn't I say it then, the truth, the only truth I cared about? But one never does say out at the right time.

'All right, I'll go, if you want me to,' I said. 'If you'd like me to come back, ring the hotel.'

She nodded. 'I'm sorry,' she said. 'Please go away.'

'Let me ring up later.'

'If you like.'

I left her. I didn't wait at the end of the road. Why should I have watched her, with that virtual confession still choking me like a catarrh. If you knew what I'd do to avoid that fate. *If you knew what I've done. Fraud and lying and dishonesty.*

Money. She needed money.

I had to tell Luke. I was paid to tell Luke. Corinna, after all. Corinna. I couldn't believe it. I didn't care anyway. No, that wasn't true. Even in that little time Shentall's had grafted me into their damned family. I felt it, the shock of that stab in the back; it hurt me too. It hurt.

—

I didn't tell him. What was there to tell, except her broken meaningless phrases? Even he wouldn't ask that for his money. In any case on the Monday morning he was in conference with some all-important scout of the Canadian market, and was not to be seen.

I sat in the library with my notes in front of me. Corinna. I'd tried to see her alone, but that, needless to say, she was careful not to allow. She wouldn't look at me. It was quite useless to wait for a glance from the suffering eyes. No, it wasn't just an accident in the disposition of the lids. She suffered, like all idealists. One glimpse of a Mantegna is their undoing. Corinna had judgement and intelligence and conscience. She set herself the most exacting standards, and suffered with proportionate intensity from her deficiencies, her faults, her graceful shallow talent. Wasn't that what she'd told me in her painful, muddled, unsought confidences? And at the end, in the plea to be released, in the confession of failure, hadn't she shown her innate honesty, by her very anguish at having ruined it, by her refusal to let me go on, in ignorance, to entangle myself with her? She didn't see that I too had my deceits, my fraud, lying, and dishonesty. The driving, the lunches, the dancing, these she took at their face value, their conventional meaning; that I was seeking her out for choice, for pleasure. She was wrong. And yet she wasn't wrong; that was the trouble.

I pushed away my notes and went out, to wander round the works. Perhaps because it was Monday morning and pouring with rain there seemed to be rows and tension everywhere. From the art room came the sound of voices raised in argument, all talking at once, cawing each other down like a lot of rooks. Through the open door of the accounts office I heard Dart protesting, Bullace chiding, and the clatter of a telephone banged into its rest. Even the normally placid works seemed on edge. Albert had had two smashes within ten minutes and in addition had sworn at one of the glost selectors.

Freddy passed me at a dangerous run, looking thoroughly put out.

'What is it?' I asked.

'A balls in number nine,' he shouted, over his shoulder.

Number nine. After a moment's thought I placed it; a small electric intermittent kiln, used for the firing of special on-glaze enamels and printing.

I wandered into the hall, where Judith sat as usual in her little golden box.

'Did you enjoy your ride yesterday?' I asked, as I went by.

'Yes, thank you,' she said, not raising her head. She sounded as if she were starting a cold; and sharp, unpleasant, painful thoughts as to how she might have got it ran through my mind.

I went back to the library, following Janice who was bringing my tea; not meaning to startle her, simply not thinking. My soft shoes made no sound at all. I walked round in front of her.

She sucked in her breath in a near shriek, her little arm jerked up, and the tea flew out of the cup to land with a thick splash in the middle of my notes.

She burst into tears, the violent tears of a highly-strung child who's always laughing. Then of course there was reassuring and comforting and mopping up of tears and tea and fetching of more. She was still sniffing when she brought the second cup.

'Do stop, Janice, there's a good girl,' I said. 'I told you it doesn't matter.'

'It's not that,' she said. 'Oh, I don't know. It's raining, and my hair'll come out and I'm going dancing tonight at Trentham. Everything's rotten today.'

Poor Janice. Spilt tea, and uncurled hair, and everything's rotten.

At twelve I went along to Mr Luke's office. He was still engaged.

'Will you tell him as soon as he's free that I want to see him?' I said to Miss Chapman.

She gave me a peculiar and slightly quelling look. A humble hack was not expected to lay down the law in such unseemly fashion.

Outside, wandering, I walked into Freddy.

'Hullo,' I said. 'Fixed number nine?'

He frowned, and for a moment showed a distinct likeness to Bullace. 'The silly blot forgot to switch on,' he said. 'Brassick'll have him on the carpet. Oven was loaded and the heat wasn't there. Panic and flap—must be a failure—send for Freddy! Never look at the switch, that's too simple. Still, there's no harm done, luckily, just a lot of time wasted. *My* time, too, and one of my juniors could have pressed a switch as well as me, I dare say! Would have to happen today. Another five minutes and I'd have been away all right. Now I might as well stay and have lunch here, on the cheap.'

'Where are you going?'

'Wolverhampton, staying the night.'

'Leave?'

'Get off! If I had two days' leave I'd go into Wales. Going to see some panels for the firm.'

'How's the crossword?'

'Well, with this flap I only got a quick look at breakfast.'

I had a brief vision of Freddy, paper in one hand, automatically spooning up milk and cornflakes heavily crusted with sugar.

'Tell you what, though, they've made a mistake,' he said. 'Nine down, I think, I haven't got it with me. "A little something is a dangerous thing"—I went to put knowledge and it won't fit.'

'Because it isn't right. Sorry, Freddy.'

He stared at me, disbelieving. 'What is it, then?'

'A little *learning* is a dangerous thing. Drink deep or taste not the Pierian Spring,' I added, to show him I knew what I was talking about.

'Yes, that fits,' he said. 'I think it sounds better my way. More true to life.'

'They're both true,' I said, 'but only one's right.'

We parted. On the way back to the library I saw Corinna coming out of the cloakroom at the end of the corridor. Catching sight of me, she turned aside, down the stairs. I caught up with her by the door.

'Where are you going?' I said.

She went out without answering, and ran across the yard to the earthenware slip house, with me splashing after her through the white puddles. I don't think she knew where she was going or what she was doing. She stopped, and leaned against the plate jigger, slightly out of breath from running. She looked tired and ill, and miserable.

The slip house was empty. I suppose as it was nearly time for lunch the men had gone to wash the clay off their hands.

'Corinna,' I said, 'won't you say now what it was you wanted to tell me?'

She shut her eyes and said nothing. If I press her, I thought, she'll break down, and then it will be over and done with. And yet I muffed, my nerve failed.

'Have you heard about number nine?' I said, hedging.

She began to laugh quietly; and I to sweat, wondering whether I could bring myself to slap her out of hysterics.

'What is it?' I asked sharply.

'You!' she said. 'Number nine!' She went on laughing in little gasps, no louder, no harder. 'The jargon, the assimilation—it's priceless.'

I didn't know what to say.

'Look,' she said, 'let's make a plate while old Joe's not here.'

It was the random wildness of overstrained nerves. Or else—it flashed through my mind—she had over-estimated her drinking capacity.

She picked up one of the lumps of clay lying ready cut

by the machine, put it on the wheel head and pressed the switch with her foot. The arm of the machine came down, spread the lump out to a flat disc known as a bat, then automatically raised itself.

'Now,' she said, 'we remove the bat from the head—like that—and we hurl it with all our strength on to the plate mould, in order to remove air bubbles—so!'

But of course she wasn't a plate-thrower, and instead of landing with a satisfying slap, the bat of grey clay missed, caught on the edge and hung down the side of the mould.

'Corinna! What *are* you doing?'

I turned round. Bullace was standing behind us.

'I'm making a plate,' said Corinna, gathering up the misshapen bat and rolling it into a ball.

'That amuses you, does it, to play mud pies in the slip house?'

She was modelling the clay into a head, digging holes for eyes, pulling out a nose and gashing a slit, with her nail, for a mouth. 'Look,' she said, holding it up. Then with her nail across the forehead she wrote *Dud* and put it back on the machine. Immediately the spreader came down, squashing the head to a pancake.

'Corinna, for God's sake stop fooling about with the machinery,' cried Bullace, kicking off the switch. 'Don't you realize that if you had an accident—'

'Oh, shut up,' she said, 'mind your own business.'

'It is my business. No one ought to—'

'Of course,' she said suddenly, 'everything's your business, I forgot. Dudley the pace-setter, the time-keeper, the soul and conscience of the works. God almighty, how you must think we'll go to rot when you've left, you conceited interfering busybody!'

'All right, Corinna,' said Bullace, heatedly, 'since you're in the mood for frankness, I'll tell you what you are. A scheming drink-sodden slut.'

Before I could move or speak she'd picked up the bat and flung it at him, full strength, slap, into his face. She couldn't miss. The soft grey plate stuck for a moment over his mouth and chin, a ludicrous, soggy, bandit's mask; folded thickly into his neck, rolled over his chest, breaking slightly at the edges, and fell to the ground, landing with a final insult on his shoes.

We stood still for a second or two, all of us. Then Bullace, without a word, put up his hand and began to pick pieces of clay off his tie and lapels. Corinna leaned against the plate jigger. I took her by the elbow. Poor Corinna. She turned round and dropped her head against my shoulder as if at last giving up a struggle. I put my arm round her.

Bullace kicked the clay off his shoes.

'Corinna,' he said, 'don't let me dash your matrimonial hopes, at this stage. But it might interest you to know that you're being embraced by a hired investigator, not a simple writer. Don't you think you might ask yourself if he has ulterior motives for his attentions?'

And with a short chilly smile at me he walked away.

I couldn't follow, couldn't do a thing, except stare blankly after him. He'd knocked me silly with his quick pitiless blow to the body, yes, right on the heart. I wasn't angry. I felt nothing but a sickening drop into disaster and loss that left me numb and speechless.

Corinna lifted her head and looked at my face. Well, it was something to be able to meet her eyes without the consciousness of deception. No need for her to ask if what Bullace had said were true; she could see that it was. She stood still for a moment, staring at me with her lips almost in a smile, and her greyish eyebrows lifted; an expression that seemed to say, *yes, this is the sort of thing one must expect.* Then she moved away from me and walked out of the slip house into the yard.

I went with her, in silence. We passed through the hall, and from a reserve of strength she managed to give Judith a particularly nice smile, as if to say to me *That for yesterday's vile insinuations.* She went upstairs, then up the second flight. She was going to Mr Luke.

He was free at last. In fact he was just coming out of his office into Miss Chapman's room; but one look at us was enough to stop him.

'Good morning,' he said. 'Yes, Miss Chapman, please go, it's past time.' He turned to Corinna. 'Come in, Mrs Wakefield.'

He held the door for her, and as she passed in he put his arm across to shut me out. 'Wait,' he murmured, and closed the door in my face.

Wishful thinking, to have imagined myself part of that family! I was the ultimate in outsiders. Miss Chapman was collecting gloves and handbag, too well-trained to appear to notice my exclusion.

Corinna. What would he say to her, what would he do? Oh, he'd be Luke; firm but gentle, more in sorrow than in anger. Obviously that sort of thing went down well. She'd gone to tell Luke, at last, what she wouldn't tell me. With the next woman to come my way in the course of work I should have to try paterfamilias tactics.

After about five minutes the door was opened by Luke. 'Come in,' he said.

She was sitting in the best armchair, smoking; white, but

quite composed. The two cups stood on Mr Luke's desk, the true and false Vinca. Of course he wouldn't have had to explain, as he had to me; just show them to her.

He nodded to me to sit down, which I was glad enough to do.

'Well, the chief thing now is to get hold of Bullace,' he began without preamble, 'and impress on him that he must keep his information to himself. Have you any idea how he got to know?'

'He's going to Brace Lanning, isn't he?' I said carefully, taking the conversational cue that was offered. 'You know yourself what I was doing there not long ago. At first when I heard about Bullace I didn't think it would matter, but now that I know him better I think he's probably spending his spare time acquainting himself with his new work, so that he can have it at his fingertips.' I should have liked to add, so that he can be free to keep his eye on everyone else, as he does here. 'Also I think he's probably found out what happened to his predecessor. He may have asked in order to see what promotion he might expect. Thereafter it's simple, for someone possessing a little patience and curiosity. He had two days off last week. Ask him if he went down to London.'

'Yes, I see,' said Luke. 'He's probably away to lunch by now. Mrs Wakefield, I wonder if you'd send someone to look, and if they should find him, to send him up. I'll wait. Meanwhile I'll ring the hotel. He's more likely to be there already.'

Corinna stood up and stubbed out her cigarette, or Luke's cigarette, in a porcelain ashtray.

'Don't hurry over lunch,' Luke went on. 'There's no need for you to be back before half past. You're sure you feel up to taking the visitors? Because Miss Ashe—'

'Thank you,' she said, 'I'm all right.'

She managed a faint smile and walked out; the smile for Mr Luke of course; for me not even a look.

As soon as she'd closed the door he put the cups away. 'She denies it, of course,' he said. 'I had to be tactful, apologize, hope she understood that we were forced to consider even the least likely possibilities. She took it very well.'

'Denies it?' I repeated. 'Then what did she come up here to say? *I* wasn't bringing her in to accuse her, you know.'

'Why,' he said, surprised, 'she wanted to know, of course, why I'd put you on to her, as she expressed it. So there was nothing I could do but tell her.' He paused. 'Did you think she was coming in to confess?'

'I don't know,' I said. 'I don't know anything. But I wish you hadn't sent her after Bullace. After a row like that they'd be better kept apart.' I didn't care if he was paying me; he was eight years younger.

'She didn't mention a row,' he said, 'just that Bullace had come out with—what you were.'

So I told him, sparing nothing. He looked at me in silence for a few moments. 'I see,' he said quietly. 'That was a most unfortunate episode, in every way. Do you want to go on? Or would you rather give up?'

'Don't you want to know any more who's passing out your designs?'

'You'll have to keep right beside her,' he said, looking down at the desk, 'now more than ever. After what Bullace said, you'll surely find that embarrassing?'

Embarrassing! That might express about a thousandth of it. 'I'll manage,' I said.

Again he gave me the half-disgusted look. 'It will also be distressing for her,' he said.

'You must be the humane killer, mustn't you? Well, it's a better role than mine. Whom I shall kiss, the same seize and bind fast.'

He looked down at his blotting-paper, and turned the porcelain seal handle between his fingers.

'Spare your disgust,' I said, 'I haven't kissed her.'

'You sound sorry.'

'I am.'

I stood up, and laid my hand on the smooth, gilded flower-sprigged inkstand. 'This,' I said, 'and the one in the library, and that seal you play with—aren't they all Shentall's?'

'Yes,' he said, 'part of my great-grandfather's experiments. Bone china got up to look like Sèvres.'

'Imitation,' I observed. 'He was the one who turned out the blue and white to nick Spode's market, wasn't he? The plates you hang in the hall.'

He looked at me, not unkindly. He was a patient man, Mr Luke; a potter. 'The ethics of pottery is treacherous ground,' he said. 'The difference between the inkstands and the plates and the Vinca cup is that great-grandfather didn't put the Sèvres mark or Spode's on the ware, but his own name.'

I went out. He was already lifting the phone.

Why did I have to meet her then, at the foot of the stairs? Why did she have to stop, and look me in the face?

'I'm going up to tell Mr Luke that Bullace has gone,' she said, 'the lodge-keeper saw him go out.'

Her voice was light, calm, and polite, as it had been on the first day when she showed me round the works.

'You don't have to explain as if you were giving an account of your movements,' I said. 'Anyway don't bother to go up. Luke's on the phone now. He'll speak to him at the hotel.'

'All right,' she said. 'Now I'm going to have lunch. You'd better escort me to the canteen.'

She didn't move, though. We stood for a moment in the quiet hall, where there was no one beside us but Miss Ashe behind the glass panel of the Enquiries cubicle, replacing Judith who'd gone home to lunch.

'Perhaps you don't want to come with me, now that your motives are no longer ulterior,' she said calmly. 'They were, weren't they?'

'Yes. No. Not all the time.'

'What do I do, take my choice?' She was silent for a moment. 'What made you think I'd do such a thing? Do I seem capable of stabbing Luke in the back? Am I that sort of person?'

'Don't you understand? There's no such thing as a sort of person. Anyone can do anything, at any time.' I put my hands on her shoulders. She didn't protest. 'Corinna,' I said, 'what was it you wanted to tell me last night, if not that you'd sold your designs twice over? What was it?'

She moved away and shook her head. 'It doesn't matter. It doesn't matter now.'

III
WHAT HAPPENED AFTER

Mr Luke stared into the ark.

'I had it stopped,' I told him. 'I'm sorry.'

'No,' he said, 'you did right.'

He looked up. His face was blank. Like Corinna's his shock was too great for agitation. He was silent for a minute, concentrating, pulling himself together; the leader, the head of the family. Younger than me.

'I've sent for the doctor,' he said. 'When Harry said accident, I told Miss Chapman to ring. He'll be here within five minutes.' He paused. 'We'll have to get him out.'

'Don't you think—you ought to leave him?'

The blank look went past me, discounting my words as panic gibberish, disappointed of my usefulness, turning to a more reliable support.

'Arthur.'

The man came from the press, a slip house worker, silent and calm.

'How can we do it?' said Luke, thinking aloud, not asking. 'Need we drain the ark? No, it's not very deep in there.

If we roll up our trousers and take off our shoes, we can go down the ladder and raise him. Joe can stand at the edge—'

'No need for you to go down, Mr Luke,' said Arthur, 'we'll do that.'

Luke was already unlacing his shoes. I bent down beside him.

'Listen, even if it were an accident, the police would have to come,' I whispered. 'Don't move him.'

Luke turned his head to me with a look of alarm, quickly suppressed. 'He's not to be left there,' he said, with utter finality.

I couldn't argue against the absolute sole lord of Shentall's. 'All right,' I said, resigned. 'I'll help you. You'll need all of three down there. Couldn't we find something to raise him with?'

One of the men was sent across to the packers for a length of rope while we took off our shoes and socks and rolled up our trousers; Mr Luke, Arthur and I. The head of the firm, the man from the filter press, and the outsider, all reduced to paddlers with pale feet and hairy legs. The other men in the slip house stood back, still silent, waiting for orders. Luke set them out like sentries, one to each door, to stop anyone from coming in, two to stand by the edge of the ark.

'Now,' he said, 'you and I, Arthur, down in the slip.' He turned to me. 'You stay on the ladder halfway, hold on with one hand and help with the other. You two take the rope, and both of you hold it. You won't have the whole weight, but there'll be extra heaviness in the clothes.'

I followed them down the ladder fixed to the brick wall of the ark, shivering at the iron rungs digging hard and cold against naked feet, and stopped just above the level of the slip. It was deeper than it looked from above, over the waders' knees, sloshing about as they moved.

Between them they raised the body from the paddles. But it was no good, I had to go down and help Luke hold it while Arthur passed the rope under the shoulders.

'Right,' said Luke. 'You get back on the ladder and for God's sake don't let go.'

I climbed out of the soft cold liquid, got a grip on the rungs, watched them as they lifted. He hadn't stiffened; his head fell back from Arthur's arm. As they raised him, his feet broke the surface, huge, they seemed, grey and glistening but immediately the slip ran off the well-waxed shoes, shrinking to little lines and blobs round the stitching and laces.

With strained reddening faces they moved him from the centre of the paddles and raised him as high as they could. I leaned down, clinging to the rung with my left hand till it hurt, put my right under his back where it sagged, clutched a lump of his slimy jacket, and pushed. The men at the top pulled on the rope and the body rose, dripping heavily, dragging against my shoulder, knocking into my face. I ducked. The men lifted the dangling legs clear of the edge of the ark, and laid the body on the floor. I climbed out, Luke and Arthur following.

A puddle of slip was beginning to spread round him as the men unfastened the ropes.

'Fetch something,' said Luke. 'Cover him.'

I took out my handkerchief, knelt down, closed his mouth, wiped his nose and forehead, and smoothed back his heavy hair. The grey squeezed out under my hand, leaving it streaked with black.

Someone gave us sacks to clean ourselves. They went to cover the body too, but at that moment the doctor arrived.

He was the one that always came. He nodded to Luke.

Luke, the head of the firm, barefoot, spattered, with a ghastly face. Arthur was pale too, and the men gathered round us, all the same. So, presumably, I looked also, pale, furrowed, sweating, with down-turned mouth, like a child about to be sick.

We finished drying our legs and put on our shoes and socks while the doctor went through his professional formalities, making sure that there was no life left in the corpse.

'How did this happen?' he asked, without looking up.

The only sound in the place was the splash of the water that dripped from the filter press.

'That's to say, was he inspecting your tank, or what?' The doctor frowned. His eye rested for a moment on the leather shoes; and enough of the clothes were left unsoaked to show that they weren't working overalls.

'No, he wouldn't have been inspecting it,' said Luke with an effort. 'Not officially. He must have gone down to look for some reason, and slipped, and stunned himself—and then drowned, I suppose.'

The doctor was silent, turning the head gently to one side, feeling it, wiping it with the handkerchief that I'd left on the floor, wiping round the left ear, pausing for a second as blood streaked the clay, marbling it reddish-brown on grey. He went on wiping, as carefully as I watched. There was no cut, no mark; the blood had come from inside the ear.

The doctor stood up, walked to the edge of the ark and looked down. 'I take it he wasn't moved at all till you took him out?' he said. 'How was he lying? On his back over the paddles, to judge from the state of his clothes.'

'Yes,' said Luke, 'near the centre, where the blades are close, lying hooked across two of them with his head hanging back and trailing in the slip.'

Arthur nodded confirmation.

'The paddles were turning at first,' I said, 'that's the only difference.'

'Who found him?' asked the doctor.

Luke looked at me. I shook my head. 'It was Corinna.'

'Where is she?'

'I put her in the rest room with one of the women from next door to stay with her.'

For a moment Luke's forehead was creased with an ordinary care. 'The visitors?'

'I sent for Miss Ashe to carry on. I'm sorry, there wasn't time to ask you.'

'And you don't know how it happened?' the doctor went on. 'How is it that none of these men saw him fall, or heard him?'

Silence, except for the drip from the press. I suddenly missed the men's disjointed whistling.

'Could have happened at lunch, Mr Luke,' murmured Arthur. 'Must have, when none of us was here.'

The doctor looked at his watch. 'Did you call me as soon as you found him?'

'Yes.'

'At ten to three,' said the doctor. 'And your lunch hour is from one to two. How is it that no one saw him lying there in that three quarters of an hour?'

In that pause even the press had to have stopped its splashing. 'The lid was down,' I said.

Luke's face was turned on me, blank with despair and wretchedness. He realized that he had to accept what I'd tried to tell him, what he wouldn't accept; the ineluctable flood that was about to engulf his firm, his family, his life.

The men's eyes turned on each other.

'Will one of you fetch some clean water?' the doctor went on, calmly, at last, as if nothing were amiss. 'I'll wash out his eyes, and then we must cover him. Mr Shentall—'

Mr Shentall. The formality of that address went through me like a draught. I knew what the doctor was doing as he drew Luke aside, speaking in a low voice—telling him the necessities, the inquest; the police.

I bent down and picked up my handkerchief. Luke was going, to the phone, I supposed. Arthur offered me a cigarette and I stood smoking it, by the ark, watching the doctor wash slip out of the eyes. He bent down close to the head, stayed for a few seconds, then looked up, frowning slightly, and signed to me to get down beside him.

'Would you mind confirming that I'm not suffering from imagination?' he said.

Suffering from imagination. True enough, true enough.

'Bend down close,' he said, 'get over his face, and take a deep sniff. No, wait a minute.' He opened the mouth.

I did as he asked, then sat back quickly.

'Well?' he said.

'I suppose he'd been drinking.'

'Thank you, that's what I thought,' said the doctor, shortly. 'That would account for a lot.'

'But not for the lid,' I said.

He gave me a quick look, then turned aside. A witness, on the spot, was necessary to him, to confirm his impression, but he was not going to be led into unprofessional speculation.

He closed the eyes. 'We'll leave it here,' he said to Arthur. 'It won't be in the way, will it?'

It. It. I lifted a strand of patchy hair from the face. Alcohol: affecting the sense of orientation, upsetting the balance, disturbing the centres of motor control. If after an hour and through the wet clay we could still smell it, to say he'd been drinking was not enough; he must have been drunk. But you'd never have got drunk, I thought, never, never. It was just a drink after lunch, the last superior lunch, successful, offensive, defensive. I remembered with nausea the name across the clay forehead, the squashed and flattened head. Dud. Dudley. Bullace.

The police came, naturally; the city police, quiet, considerate, fully aware of the disaster of an unpleasantness at Shentall's. How unobtrusively they shut you out! One minute you're in the centre of things, looking apprehensively at the schooled normality of their faces; the next you're behind their backs, by the wall, at a loss. Of course I made a brief and formal statement in Mr Luke's office. I suppose Corinna did the same, and Arthur, Joe, and Luke himself. The doctor, too, would say what he'd found.

As soon as I was free I went to the rest room. It was empty. I went into the works, to the benches where they brush down the dried ware with tow before firing. The woman I'd sent to stay with Corinna was in her usual place.

'Mrs Wakefield? She felt all right. She's gone back to work.'

So I had to go to the art room. Corinna was sitting at her table, painting. No, drawing; drawing on a coffee pot with a china-graph, a pencil which leaves a thick black line that can be wiped off the glaze with one stroke of the little finger. Drawing, drawing. The whole pot was covered with curling leaves and flowers and arabesques. Anthem was murmuring to Olive in the far corner. Mitchell wasn't there. Johns, sitting at his desk, caught my eye, shook his head deprecatingly and jerked it in the direction of the door. He was right. She was soothing herself in her own way.

I went back to the library, sat at my desk, smoking, waiting. At four, Janice came in as usual with my tea and two biscuits, setting down the cup with care after the morning's fiasco. Her face was pale.

'Oh, poor Mr Bullace,' she said.

The distress in her voice surprised me. 'Did you like him?' I asked.

She hesitated. 'Well—but he was only thirty. Poor Freddy! He'll be the one that's really sorry.'

'I'm sorry.'

She turned away. 'You didn't know him,' she said awkwardly.

'Doesn't stop me being sorry, just for the waste. Anyway, who did know him? Apart from Freddy.'

She looked round at me sadly and shook her head. Her eyes filled with tears. 'Drink your tea while it's hot,' she said.

—

At half past four Luke came in.

'It's all right,' he said, 'don't get up.' He pulled a chair to the other side of the desk and sat down. 'I came to thank you for keeping your head. You were very good, both of you, you and Mrs Wakefield.' He paused. 'I don't know what the police are thinking. They're very polite, of course, reassuring me that everything is a formality. But they've roped off the whole slip house and they're in there chalking marks and measuring—'

'In any case there has to be an inquest, and they have to present evidence.'

'In any case.' He looked at me. 'You said an accident. Did you mean it?'

'That was really part of the head-keeping.'

He sighed. 'I was afraid so. What I came to tell you was that I've had to explain to the police that you're not a writer, and why you're posing as one.'

'I know.'

'How?'

'When I made my statement they already knew who I was. Or rather, what.'

'Did they comment?'

'Not a word.'

'All the same, I felt it was proper to tell them, not leave them to find out, as you'll be going on with your investigation for me.' He frowned. 'Not that there's any connexion—'

'You think not? Bullace was a prier. He pried out my identity, he may have pried out something else.'

Luke rested his head on his hand. Head of the firm, younger than me. What did I know of responsibility?

'By the way, did you get through to Bullace at lunch?' I asked.

'No, it's strange, he must have gone elsewhere today, just this once. He wasn't in the canteen.'

'He may have been already in the ark.'

'No,' said Luke. 'He must have gone out, because apparently he'd been drinking. I heard the doctor tell them so. And in that case, you see, an accident could easily have happened. I must speak to the men in the slip house. One of them may be afraid to admit that he'd been careless with the ark door, and perhaps afraid too that no one will believe he saw nothing when he slipped it back on. Whereas with the turn of the paddles, if you were in a hurry and expecting nothing—'

'Did you ever know Bullace to be drunk?'

'No,' said Luke reluctantly, 'but he could have been, for

once. He'd had an unpleasant morning—mislaid a file from the office, or rather Dart had, but the responsibility was Bullace's. And as a culmination there was—'

He stopped short, looking as if he were trying to forget what he'd just thought of.

'The row with Corinna,' I finished for him.

'Yes,' he said, 'there was that.'

'What about the Press?'

He looked puzzled. 'What about it?'

'You'll be troubled by reporters—'

'Oh that,' he said. 'I thought you meant the filter press. I've rung our local paper and asked them to send someone round. I'll give them a statement.'

'Have you asked the police?'

He stared at me, staggered by the thought of having to ask permission to do something.

'I'm sorry,' I said, 'I think you should, even if only to check that what you say will tally with anything they may put out.'

'Well,' he said shortly, 'the paper comes out every evening, so there'll be nothing till tomorrow.'

'But they'll ring the country papers and the national dailies, and pass on the news, for what it's worth.'

'Exactly. I don't suppose an accident in a midlands pottery will rate more than a few lines, if that.'

'An accident,' I repeated. 'No, I suppose not, provided the police don't add any riders. Has anyone thought about getting in touch with Freddy?'

'That's another headache,' said Luke. 'I rang the firm he's visiting but of course he hadn't arrived. I left a message that he was to ring back as soon as he showed up, and I hope they don't fail to give it to him, otherwise there'll be hell's delight ringing round all the hotels till we find him. I don't want him to learn it from the papers.'

'What about Mrs Lumberdine?'

'I've sent round Mrs Massey, the welfare officer, to break it to her. I'll ring up later.' He paused. 'She brought him up for years, Bullace, I mean.'

'I know. Have they taken the body out of the slip house yet?'

'Yes, away to the mortuary. I suppose they'll have to examine it.' He stood up. 'Go off if you'd like to,' he said,.'You've made your statement, and they know where to find you if they want anything more. Mrs Wakefield too, tell her. Unless you'd rather not.'

'I'll tell her,' I said.

I waited another ten minutes before putting away my notes and going to the art room. By that time it was quarter past five anyway, and the others were packing up; but Corinna still sat drawing, running a Greek key pattern round the rim of a dinner plate.

I went over to her and touched her shoulder. 'Home now, Corinna.'

She raised her head, looked at the clock, then at me. 'It isn't time,' she said.

'Luke said it was.'

I waited in the hall. The cubicle seemed less bright than usual. After a moment I realized that the light was being soaked up by the dark head and navy blue suit of Miss Ashe, who was seated at the switchboard.

I walked across and slid back the panel. 'I'm sorry I had to call on you so abruptly this afternoon,' I said.

'Oh, don't give it a thought, please,' she begged. 'What a dreadful thing! Poor Mr Luke, he looks quite ill, and I don't wonder, it gave me a terrible turn myself. Thank goodness I didn't hear about it till I'd finished taking the visitors round. I've put through a dozen calls wrong, at least, I was so upset.'

'Where's Judith?'

'I sent her home. She's got a shocking cold—turn to flu I'd never be surprised—and she was in such a state too when she heard the news, between one and the other she could hardly hold up. In fact I got Mr Roach to run her home. What a terrible day!'

'Yes,' I said, 'terrible.'

Judith, Bullace. Only yesterday.

I said good night to Miss Ashe. Corinna was coming down the stairs. We went together into the yard. Why did the weather have to be so perverse? The rain and clouds of the earlier day had been dried and rolled back by a gusty wind. At last even Stoke's veil was tattered. The sun sparkled on the waiting cars. Down at the end of the line I saw it, longer and lower and more daring than the others, the white and shining Jag. Only yesterday, Judith and Bullace. Bullace of the synthetic accent, Bullace the pusher, the prier, the kicker-away of ladders, Bullace, interfering, offensive, defensive, Bullace, Dudley; dead.

I put back the hood because she looked so ghastly and I thought the air would do her good. We didn't speak. Indeed, driving through Stoke to Hanley, into the central web of streets choked with traffic and bus queues, I couldn't even spare her a glance; until, as we were pulling up to let a stream of pedestrians over their crossing, there was a sudden movement beside me. I looked round in time to see her head go down on her knees.

'Hold on,' I said quickly, 'I must get across, then we'll stop.'

'No, go on,' she cried urgently, 'please, please, quickly, go on. I'm not ill.'

Her voice was muffled but not faint. Some woman's inconsistency, I thought, and let the car go forward, heading for Leek New Road.

After a minute or two we had to stop again, at lights. 'Corinna?' I said.

She raised her head and sat back. Her hand moved to her jacket pocket, then checked. She closed her eyes.

'Don't do that,' I said, as we went on, 'you'll see the ark all the time. Look at the road, take your mind off it.'

She shook her head, obediently opening her eyes all the same. 'It isn't that,' she said weakly. She drew in a short trembling breath. 'I've just seen my husband.'

Hysteria, delusion, they never crossed my mind. I'd heard the literal truth. I pulled in to the kerb and stopped. 'So that's it,' I said.

She nodded and was silent.

'No wonder no one knew how he died,' I went on after a moment. 'I thought you were an extreme case of silent grief.'

'Don't,' she said. 'I tried to tell you.'

I thought of all my scruples, my sorrow at deceiving her. 'Well, now we're quits,' I said. 'You're not divorced, of course. That explains your curiosity at Dovedale, on how to go about it.'

'No. I left him, that's all.'

'How often do you see him?'

'Never. I didn't think he knew—where I was.'

'Why should you think so now? People can come to Stoke-on-Trent, I suppose, without having you in mind.'

She turned sideways in the seat, snuggled down in it and

closed her eyes, like a child coming home to the suburbs after a day by the sea. She needed a woolly rabbit to cuddle in her folded arms, and the picture would have been complete. There was nothing for me to do; nothing, at least, that I would allow. I started the car and drove on.

When we reached Endon I had to wake her. I went in, uninvited though not forbidden, holding her arm to support her in the long climb to the top floor, four flights. I sat her down in one of the brown armchairs and poured her a drink. Perhaps it wasn't the best thing for her; but she wanted it. I had one myself. After all, there was enough.

'Suppose he comes here?' she said, in a low voice.

'Are you afraid of him?'

'Not in that way. He wasn't rough.' She paused and drank. 'Anyway, I have to go out, to the Art School.'

'You can't go,' I said, decidedly. 'In this state, after today? Don't argue, you're not going. I'll ring the school and tell them you're not well.'

'Gillian,' she said feebly.

'What about her?'

'She waits for me afterwards. We go on the bus together. She doesn't give lessons, she takes them, commercial Spanish.'

'What's her number?'

'That's the point, they're not on the phone. I must go.'

'For Gillian?'

'I can't let her stand about waiting.'

I had to be patient. She really wasn't well. 'All right,' I said. 'I'll drive over and tell her. It won't take twenty minutes. Don't worry, I'll come back. Give me the key, I'll let myself in. Then you needn't answer the doorbell if it should ring.'

She handed me the key without a word.

—

Dart's quiet road was sheltered from the wind, which made its presence felt only in the faintly sulphurous air which its gusts had stirred up from the pit. And as I waited in front of the glass-panelled Victorian door, vacantly returning the belligerent stare of a mealy-breasted thrush that stood guard over a worm on the plot of grass, I began to feel tired.

It was Dart who opened the door to me. He looked as though my presence on his doorstep was slightly more than a surprise. I explained about Corinna.

'Oh,' he said, 'thanks a lot for coming, it was pretty decent of you, but Gillian always eats out and goes straight on to the classes. It doesn't matter, I'll nip down afterwards and meet her.'

He seemed even more harassed than usual.

'Of course, Corinna's very upset,' I said. 'You've heard, I suppose, about Bullace?'

'Yes, oh, yes,' he said. 'Dreadful—'

He was more than harassed, he was agitated. His glance went past me, to the road.

'She was the first to see him, you know,' I insisted, 'lying there in the ark, drowned, as I suppose he must have been.'

'Terrible,' he said, meeting my eyes for a second with open anxiety.

There was a cruel pause; cruel because I needn't have prolonged it. I had every reason to go back to Endon. Dart was in agony. If I waited a few more seconds—

'Sorry I can't ask you in,' he said, all of a rush. 'The fact is I'm expecting a visitor any minute.'

I knew it. I had only to wait to let him crack, to let his plaintive desire to be socially acceptable thrust him into one of his peculiar gaucheries. Easy to kick Colin, I remembered.

'I have to go anyway,' I said, not without shame.

He looked desperately up the road. 'Perhaps we could have a drink together tomorrow lunch time.'

'With pleasure,' I said, and at last released him.

I turned the car in the road and drove round the nearest corner, where I'd noticed a telephone box. I rang Corinna. There was no answer. The phone rasped on and on in my ear. For a moment I felt panic; then I realized that she was afraid to pick it up, that she wanted to pretend to be out. She couldn't know who was calling.

I went back to the car, reversed, moved to the end of the road and stopped, to let a car across, a plum-custard Vauxhall with squashy springs. I had a glimpse of what was behind the wheel—a white sweater, a scarf, candy floss hair, a mouth; and instinctively I watched, instead of driving on; a Cotton's, not a natural, instinct. She stopped outside Dart's house.

A narrow shave, I thought. If that was the sort of visitor he received while Gillian was at evening classes, no wonder he'd been agitated when I appeared. I shrugged, and drove at last round the corner, leaving Dart and his visitor behind me.

—

There were no lights at Corinna's windows. I ran upstairs, whistling. She was sitting where I'd left her, in the brown armchair, with the empty glass beside her, sitting in dusk in the shabby room.

'Why the darkness?' I asked, flicking on the lights.

She screwed up her eyes. 'I didn't want anyone to see that I was in.'

'You could have drawn the curtains.'

'They don't meet in the middle. It doesn't matter now that you're back.'

That was something, I suppose. I laid my hand on hers. 'You're cold. Even afraid of the glow of the fire? You'd better have something to eat.'

She shuddered. 'I couldn't.'

'I could, I'm afraid.'

She looked at me with a shadow of bitterness. 'Are you staying the night?'

'If you want me to.' I banged the sofa. 'I could sleep on this.'

She heaved herself out of the chair. 'Once and for all, I did not sell Luke's designs.'

'I know you didn't,' I said patiently. 'You've said so, that's enough, I believe you.'

'Then why are you clinging to me like this?'

Clinging to her! The thought! 'You'd be afraid if I left you here alone, wouldn't you?'

She nodded.

I bent down and lit the gas fire. 'Well, that's why I offer to stay. If it will help.'

In her face I saw the unquenchable human longing to believe that all is about to be well, alternating with doubt, incredulity, and reservations; an expression that called for the touch of her adored Mantegna to pin it in an allegorical drawing; hope leading experience blindfold.

'It will help,' she said, after a minute. 'The thing is, there's only one spare blanket.' And she looked at me with her eyebrows knitted and her forehead so wrinkled that if anxious frowns had been my gauge of events I should have thought that nothing, in all that ghastly day, had moved her to such anguish as there being only one spare blanket.

I recalled her little shocked sleep in the car, and, from earlier, the tablets, the hands pressed into the pelvic girdle.

'I think you'd better go to bed, Corinna,' I said.

'Yes, I'd like to. But what about—'

I took her by the shoulders and sat her down in the chair. 'Where's the hot water bottle?' I asked.

'In the kitchen,' she said, lying back, 'on the hook inside the cupboard door.'

—

How strange, yet how mustily familiar, like coming home after a long holiday, to light the geyser, run the bath, fill the hot water bottle, put on the gas fire, turn down the bed—to do these things for a menstruating woman was the fabric of marriage, one of its few memories that was not unhappy but quiet, neutral, steadying in its ordinariness. The kitchen brought me back to the present, the kitchen of a single person—the packet of soup, the small loaf, the tin of fruit.

She came in and stood watching me when she'd taken her bath. Her hair straggled on the collar of an old pink flannel dressing-gown, carefully buttoned up to the neck.

'You're used to cooking, aren't you?' she said.

'I live alone.'

'You might have lived in rooms, or had a housekeeper.'

'I wasn't born to servants,' I said, lifting a tray off a small enamel-topped cupboard. 'Go to bed, or you'll catch cold. You're going to have some soup—yes, you must. I'll bring it in to you.'

She looked at me, startled, not knowing whether to swoon at my self-control or doubt my virility, I suppose; but she went off to the bedroom with her usual meekness.

When you live alone you're either in bed or out of it, you can't bring yourself a cup of tea, or breakfast; so there's no call for bedjackets. She'd put on a grey cardigan, over which the collar of her nightdress was caught up like a ruff, faded pink cotton dotted with blue flowers, like a child's. She saved her money for the clothes that showed. They're all the same.

I put the tray on her knees.

'Have you had yours?' she asked.

'Yes, I couldn't wait for you, I'm sorry. May I stay in here while you eat that?'

She nodded. I moved one of the two hard chairs to the foot of the bed, sat down, and made myself look chastely round the small sparsely-furnished room.

'How long since you left him?' I said.

'Six years. When I came to Stoke. I saw the job advertised, I knew it was my chance to go, and I took it.'

'What was it? Women?'

'Partly.'

'What did he do for a living?'

'Anything. Anything that might make money he'd turn his hand to, if it came his way. He had to have money. Not to hoard. To spend, to be lavish with, even to give away—not through generosity, but to show off. Everything had to show, with him. He had to have the flashiest car, the biggest TV, the most expensive clothes—'

'And a beautiful wife.'

She sighed. 'I've told you, I was plain and dull in those days.'

'Well then, he had an eye for a winner.'

'Oh yes, he had that. He could always tell when a line would sell.'

'Line in what?'

'Dresses. The rag trade was his mainstay. That's how I came to know him, through working on textile designs.' She paused. 'I'd never met anyone like him. So quick, so full of energy, so decided. And he could be flattering. Only I didn't realize, of course, that it was so easy to him, and so shallow. Or didn't choose to realize. I wanted him, all right,' she said, with a faint flush, 'and I wanted to get away from home. Well, I was away, but not far enough for my liking. So when he proposed marriage I was only too glad to accept without asking why. Not very noble, was it? One way and another I got what I deserved. He didn't particularly want me, you see, as I discovered to my consternation. He wanted an assistant, a partner, a good designer that he didn't have to pay good designer's rates and could use as some income tax fiddle, I don't know what, I never understood it. Marriage to him was a speculation, an investment, purely a business matter. But even if it hadn't been, we should have come to grief. We were too different. I thought it would do me good. I thought he'd transform my life and character. But he only got on my nerves.'

I stood up and took the tray from her. 'I know,' I said, 'that was my mistake. Like should wed like, but it's hard not to fall for your opposite. What sort of a man was he to look at?'

'Oh—tall, dark, well set up, muscular. Handsome. That was what knocked me so, I suppose.'

'It still does, doesn't it? Think of Freddy.'

She turned her head away from me. 'I don't love Freddy,' she said, 'I've never loved anyone. Really to know someone and still respect them, to trust them, to feel affection as well as passion, that's what I've never had.'

'Don't you think it's hoping too much, to combine all that for one person?'

'No, I don't think so,' she said. 'It's possible, easily possible.'

I stood there like a waiter, holding the tray, looking at her averted head; and the front doorbell rang twice.

'Don't go, don't answer,' she said quickly. 'Please don't.'

I put down the tray, took her hand, and placed it on my outstretched arm. 'I may not have the obviously *bien musclé* air you so much admire,' I said, 'but he won't come upstairs if you don't want him to. Don't be afraid. Isn't this what I was supposed to stay for?'

I went downstairs, trying not to be tense, thinking of all manner of things to say, not to mention various harmless tackling techniques. I opened the door.

There were two men standing outside, two men in raincoats and soft hats. Behind them, parked in the drive beside the Alpine, was a black car with a uniformed driver.

Already.

—

I took them upstairs. I should have liked to warn her, but how could I call out *Corinna, get dressed, here's a detective inspector come to see you?*

No, there was nothing to do, nothing to say but the truth. I put them in the living-room.

'Mrs Wakefield's in bed,' I said, addressing the inspector. Should I try to explain that a little? No. 'I'll tell her you're here. Sit down.'

'Thank you,' he said. They stayed standing, both of them. I went into the bedroom.

'You've let him in,' she whispered, with a most anguished reproach.

'It isn't your husband, Corinna,' I said, 'it's the county C.I.D.'

She sat up against the pillows. 'Did they say what they want?'

'No, but it will be about Bullace.'

'All right, I'll get up. Tell them I shan't be a minute. Wait—don't go, will you, unless they make you.'

'Make me?' I said. 'They investigate crime, not moral welfare.'

'Oh you're so clever,' she said, her voice breaking, 'and so pigheaded and blind. Just like Freddy.'

I picked her dressing-gown off the floor and threw it on the bed. 'I'm nothing like Freddy,' I said with a bitterness that took me by surprise. 'If only I were!'

I went to the living-room, told them briefly that she was coming, and retired to the kitchen before they could show me the door.

As there was no hot water, I put on a kettle to boil, collected the washing up, and lit a cigarette. Poor Luke! Imagining that it would get by as an accident; reassured by the politeness of the Stoke police. Well, they'd got to work in the roped-off slip house, added up their chalk marks and measurements into a neat little sum, looked the problem over to judge the size of it, and quietly handed it to the C.I.D. to solve.

I washed up the dishes and put them away where I'd found them, gathered Corinna's hairpins off the table and picked up her jacket, which she'd dropped on a chair.

I took it into the bedroom, found a hanger in the cupboard, and hooking it over the handle of the door smoothed my hand down the soft suède, something I'd wanted to do in other circumstances, but which, lacking the appeal of a Freddy, I had to confine to an empty gesture in solitude; and in the lower left-hand pocket my hand struck on something hard, as if it might have been her hip bone. Though in consideration of the fact that Corinna was by no means sparely built, that would probably take some finding, I reflected, putting my hand in the pocket. It was her flask. She'd had it all the time. I unscrewed the cap, put the flask to my mouth, and tipped it back. A disappointing trickle ran cold over my lips. It was empty. That, I supposed, was what she'd remembered, when she checked herself taking the much-needed swig. I left it out, so that she shouldn't forget to fill it, and wandered restlessly into the bathroom, where I practised lighting the gas geyser, to make sure there was no danger of its blowing out on her. On and off, on and off—I don't know how long I stood there moving the tap before I was aware of someone standing in the door.

The inspector was watching me. I saw with a shock since he had taken off his hat, that he was almost bald.

'If you could spare a minute,' he said, 'before you have your bath.'

'I wasn't going to have a bath,' I said. 'Not yet.'

We went into the kitchen, just the two of us. He looked round in the way they do, summing it up, putting marks in his mental file on Corinna, noticing, probably, the signs of my domestic activities. Luckily I hadn't put on an apron.

He led off with routine formalities—having to ask me a few questions in connexion with the discovery of the body of Dudley Bullace, and so on. I half listened, waiting for the questions themselves.

'You were with Mrs Wakefield, I understand, when she made this discovery in the slip house this afternoon,' he said.

'Not exactly. I was a few steps away. I went up to her because I could see something was wrong.'

'Of course, that's what I meant by with her, just loosely.'

He wouldn't speak loosely. He'd have read my statement. He'd have seen Luke.

'How did you know there was anything wrong?' he asked.

'From her face.'

'Yes. How was she looking? Frightened? Faint?'

'Shocked. I mean dazed shock.'

'Were you shocked when you saw it?'

'Yes, of course.'

'It was you who gave all the orders, wasn't it? Stopped the machinery, sent for Mr Shentall, packed off the visitors, and dealt with Mrs Wakefield.'

'Yes,' I said, wondering if it would have been better to have fainted myself.

'What were your relations with the deceased? Friendly?'

'Not particularly.'

'Did you quarrel?'

I hesitated, I couldn't help it; just long enough to guess that Luke, probably unwillingly, had told him of the episode in the slip house.

'No,' I said, 'we didn't quarrel.' That was true, strictly speaking.

'Do you know where he was in the habit of lunching?'

'At the North Staffs.'

'Did you ever join him?'

'No.'

'I thought you might have done, as you're staying there. Where do you usually lunch?'

'In the canteen, during the week. At weekends at the hotel. But Bullace doesn't—didn't—'

'Mrs Wakefield tells me it's a good canteen,' he interrupted.

I nodded. I saw the next question coming.

'What was on the menu today?'

Yes, it had come, not quite as I'd expected. 'I wasn't there today,' I said.

'Where did you have lunch then?'

'I didn't. I wasn't hungry.'

'How did you pass the lunch hour?'

'I went out. I walked along and looked at the Trent.'

He gave me a stare; and well he might. The smug and silver Trent. Shakespeare never saw it round the back of Victoria Road.

'Why didn't you go to the canteen as usual?'

'I've told you,' I said. 'I wasn't hungry.' I wondered briefly whether he'd discovered my absence from anyone but myself. In any case it was pointless to go on with such evasions. The only thing to do was to tell the truth, bit by bit. 'All right,' I said, 'it was because I didn't want to seem to hang on Mrs Wakefield's heels.'

'Yes,' he said, encouragingly, much as a priest might slip the word into a pause in the penitent's recital. 'You're referring to your employment by Mr Shentall as a private investigator? But Mrs Wakefield, I understand, already knew by lunch time what your position was.'

'I didn't want to force it down her throat.'

'Had you no personal reasons for wanting to avoid her, all of a sudden?'

'I've no wish to avoid her, as you can see.'

'"Matrimonial hopes",' he quoted suddenly. 'Sorry to put it so bluntly, but that phrase has been used recently, I believe. Surely at that point you felt some indignation towards the deceased?'

Luke, Luke! Did you have to tell him all of it, every humiliating word? But he couldn't have helped himself, information would have been filched from him by painless subtleties.

'I just felt numb at the time,' I said, 'overwhelmed because of what he'd revealed to Mrs Wakefield.'

'In fact the loss of your anonymity was more disturbing to you than any personal references.'

'I'm not anonymous.'

'The loss of your semi-disguise.'

I was silent.

'If the deceased—'

'Bullace.'

'If the deceased had spread what he'd learnt round the works, Mr Shentall could hardly have continued to employ you.'

'Me, or anyone, in that capacity.'

The inspector paused for a moment or two. 'There's a Sunbeam Alpine parked outside. Is it yours?'

'Yes.'

'Very nice. New model, isn't it?'

'Yes.'

He smiled faintly. 'It must cost a bit to run. Well, I expect we'll be seeing it around. No, don't come down. We'll see ourselves out.'

We. I'd forgotten the assistant. He was standing in the door of the kitchen; had been, I suppose, all the time. I heard them go downstairs, waited for the slam of the door, then went into the living-room.

She looked like someone I'd never met; so much smaller, on account of her flat slippers and the hair hanging straight down to her shoulders. She'd put on her skirt and the grey cardigan.

'What did they ask?' I said.

'If I'd quarrelled with Bullace.'

'What did you tell them?'

'About the bat, of course, this morning, the clay bat, and why I threw it, and what he said.'

'All of what he said? Every word? Including what he said afterwards?'

She nodded, looking miserable.

So they'd heard it from herself, not from Luke; perhaps from Luke as well.

'They asked why I'd lifted the ark door,' she said.

'And why did you?'

'It was just something to do. I wasn't thinking.' She paused. 'They asked about you. Stupid things. Whether you'd had tea or not after lunch today. Not that I could tell them, I wasn't there.'

'Corinna! Neither was I.'

We stared at each other.

'Why didn't you go in?' I asked.

'Because I thought you'd come after me.'

I sat down on the end of the sofa. She was right, she was justified, I deserved all she could say; but how I wished she hadn't said it. I was just too tired. Every extra ten years, and I could give her ten years, count hard against the ability to take sleepless nights and days of shocks.

I pulled myself together. 'Well. Between your desire to

avoid me and my delicate refusal to inflict my presence, we've landed ourselves in a pretty mess. Either of us could have been in the slip house with Bullace. He wasn't at the hotel for lunch, you see. Luke rang, and he wasn't there.' I paused. 'Where were you, Corinna?'

Her eyes turned on me, troubled but unwavering. 'I took a bus up to Basford and looked at Etruria.'

'And I walked by the Trent. Do you realize how difficult it would be to prove the truth of what we've just said?'

'Does it matter?'

'I think so.'

'It is true,' she said.

'I believe you. The trouble is, the police can't permit themselves the human weakness of an act of faith. They have to know, to have proof, and they bother about inconvenient things like motives.' I was silent for a moment. 'Do they know yet about your husband?'

She shook her head.

'You'd better tell them. They're sure to find out. They dig up everything, you know.'

She sat down on the sofa. 'We're in the pit,' she said in a low voice, 'down in the muck and filth, slipping in deeper and deeper.'

'Shall I throw you a straw to clutch?'

She was silent for a minute. 'No,' she said at last, 'you'll only get dragged in too.'

'I thought you said we were both in the pit,' I murmured.

How tired I was. I could have put down my head and gone to sleep at that moment.

'Listen,' she said. 'I must tell you. My husband—'

'Go on,' I sighed, 'tell me something new, then.'

'He's not in Stoke for nothing.'

'Perhaps he's going to seek you out to ask for a divorce.'

'He'd have done that long ago if he'd wanted it. He doesn't.'

'Why not? Religion?'

'No, oh no. He just doesn't need to divorce me because, I suppose, he's found he doesn't need a wife. Marriage as a speculation failed, and he always used to boast he never made the same mistake twice. He won't be lonely, that's certain. He never was. Divorce would make no difference to him.'

'But to you it might.'

'That's why he won't bother. He's punishing me for having left him. He was like that. You were all right till you showed weakness. Then he could never resist the joke of seeing you squirm. I imagine if he ever thinks of me at all it will be with amusement at the thought of my early and lifelong widowhood.'

'But you could divorce *him*, you simpleton,' I said. 'Why don't you? You can't plead poverty, in these days of legal aid.'

'You forget I did the deserting. Oh, besides, raking it all up—'

'Suppose you wanted to marry again?' I said, trying to sound casual.

She looked away from me. 'I'd think long and hard before I did that, after my experience with Victor.'

'What?'

'That was his name.'

Victor. The rag trade. Ladies' Wear.

'Corinna—did he have a car?'

'No, he was just standing on the pavement by the shops. Oh, I see. I thought you meant this afternoon. Yes, he had several. Not all at once. He kept changing them. He knew a lot about cars. Hence my knowledge, that surprised you. I wasn't all that interested in the design, just picked it up from him.'

'Corinna, before I distracted you by mentioning divorce, you were going to say something about him, you even began. You said he wasn't in Stoke for nothing. What were you thinking?'

'I told you we were in the pit. At least, I am.' She turned her grey eyes on me. 'It's this, you see. The reason, the real, the last reason I left him was that when I worked in Manchester—we both did—oh, it sounds so priggish, try to understand—well, he tried to get me to steal from work. Designs. Mine, and other people's as well. So that he could get the cottons printed cheap abroad and import them and make them up and undercut. You see?'

'Indeed I see. Did you tell Mr Luke this morning?'

'No. Because although it passed through my head, the minute he told me about Vinca, I couldn't see how there could be a connexion. I didn't think Victor knew where I was, let alone what work I was doing. I still don't understand. But as soon as I saw him in Stoke, I knew. It couldn't be coincidence. I knew I must be mixed up in it after all, I couldn't escape, it was partly my fault that the designs had gone, no, not my fault, but through me somehow. And you were right, you and Mr Luke, I was the weak point in Shentall's, though I didn't know it. Today,' she cried, 'why did he have to come today?'

'Don't tell me you still love this worthy husband?' I said, hurt by the despair in her voice.

'I never loved him, I told you so. You can't get down to my level. You don't know me. You don't know.'

I took her by the elbow—it was all I ever seemed to do to

her—and helped her to her feet. 'I know when you've had enough,' I said. 'Go on, Corinna, back to bed. I'll stay here, don't be afraid. You needn't lock the door. And in the morning you'll have to go to Mr Luke and tell him what you've told me. Yes, you must, Corinna. You must tell him.'

And the police, I added to myself. And the police.

—

'It doesn't make any difference,' said Luke when she'd gone. 'We can't blame her for having married rashly, and we'll need to prove a connexion between our piracy and her husband's unfortunate ways in the past. Anyway—'

'What's a poached design beside a violent death?' I finished.

He nodded. 'I'd give away the next dozen, complimentary, if I could have the C.I.D. out of the works. Did you know they were here?'

'They spoke to me last night.'

'So soon? I had to tell them—or strictly speaking to confirm what the city police had told them—about you, and why you were here. They didn't seem to have any objection to your carrying on, but they did say we were bound to pass on anything we might uncover in our private investigations. I can't help feeling that in any case you'll be kept under observation.'

'No doubt. Did you tell them about Corinna's row with Bullace in the slip house?'

'No,' he said, looking down. 'I didn't mention Corinna except to say that she was the designer of Vinca. They asked that.'

I sighed. 'Only it was Corinna they were coming to see, last night. I just happened to be there.'

'Corinna? Why should they go to her?'

'Because they're not so well informed as either of us on the design piracy. They simply know that it exists, and to them therefore, as to us in the beginning, Corinna is the obvious line to follow, if only to get the obvious quickly cleared out of the way. If trouble already exists, it's something for them to bite on, a way of making a start, a possible lead.'

'Bullace may have died by accident,' said Luke.

'He may,' I said with a sigh for the Shentall obstinacy. 'Everything is possible. Now listen. Several other things transpired last night that Corinna didn't tell you, either because she doesn't know, or because she doesn't see their significance.'

He listened. He didn't like what I had to tell him, but he had to put up with it. When I'd finished he sat for a moment playing with the porcelain seal.

'Then it looks as if we're too late,' he said at last. 'We'd better tell the police.'

'No, wait. Not yet. Let me have till the end of the day.'

He looked at me doubtfully. 'Wouldn't that count as obstructing?'

I sighed. 'We *will* tell them, when there's something definite to tell.'

—

I went along to the library, from sheer force of habit. Janice was bringing my tea.

'Already?' I asked her.

She looked at me with astonishment. 'It's time.'

I glanced at my watch. Yes, it was time. I'd forgotten how

late I'd arrived, finally arrived, that is, because after dropping Corinna at the works I'd had to go on to the hotel to shave and generally make myself presentable and then I'd gone with Corinna to see Luke.

'Poor Mr Bullace's car,' said Janice, 'it's still outside in the yard. Who's going to see to it?'

'Freddy, I suppose, when he comes back.'

'Poor Freddy!' she repeated. 'D'you think he knows yet?'

'Yes,' I said. Poor Freddy. Badly knocked up, in Luke's words. He'd be at home now, with his mother. Luke had sent him off for a couple of days.

They'd had to go round the hotels, after all, the Wolverhampton police—not that it took them long; Freddy was in the best. He'd had a tyre burst outside Stafford and had arrived too late to call on the firm that afternoon. But it hadn't been left to the police to break the news. They were merely asked to tell him to ring Luke urgently; as he did. Luke wouldn't shirk what he considered to be his duty. I think if I'd been in his place I'd have been glad to spare myself. However, I was not a paterfamilias; and had little hope of becoming one.

When Janice had gone I scribbled at my notes for a couple of hours, my innocuous notes relating the rise of the firm of Shentall. There was nothing else for me to do, or perhaps there was but I was too tired or not bright enough to see it. I was at full stop until the middle shift gatekeeper came to work at two o'clock. He was the one I wanted to speak to, no one else. What they might be saying in the works, about Bullace, about the ark, didn't concern me; that was an affair for the police.

Just before lunch Dart put his head round the door.

'Hullo,' he said, slouching into the room. 'Thought I'd

find you here. About our drink—how about having lunch out together? I've got to go into Hanley. I know a nice little pub where they do you a good sandwich. If that's all right with you.'

He drew a small circle on the floor with the toe of his shoe, staring moodily at the ground as if its polished surface filled him with a mixture of disgust and *ennui*. Any excuse I might have made he looked as if he would have been only too relieved to accept. But I made none.

I went across to the art room.

'Corinna,' I said, 'are you going to the canteen?'

She nodded.

'I'll be out. I promised Dart I'd have a drink with him.'

'Have you seen the police?' she asked, without looking at me.

'No, not this morning. Have you?'

She shook her head. 'They don't seem to be here. I wondered why.'

'Bullace didn't spend all his life in the works. They'll want to make outside enquiries.'

She turned away, and went on laying thin streaks of olive green paint over a lime-coloured leaf. 'I suppose so,' she said.

—

We went into Hanley, Dart and I, in the feeble car, to the pub where they did you a good sandwich. My head ached. I was tired. I'd hardly slept in the night, doubled up on that brown sofa, and between fatigue and drinking and the warmth of the pub, I was beginning to move in a dream. Dart too seemed to look on his surroundings with a faintly incredulous air. He wanted to pay for everything, the whole lunch, all the drinks, muttering some unimaginable embarrassments about having turned me off the doorstep. However, that I managed to prevent.

'Why did you leave teaching?' I asked him. The inconsequence was too slow, too lazy to startle. It wasn't meant to.

'Who told you?' he asked, in similarly remote curiosity.

'Corinna.'

'Ah yes. Of course.' He paused for a moment. 'She's a good sort,' he said; without longing, without admiration, with only a plaintive resentment that the good sorts of this world were utterly beyond his reach; as they were, of course, since he thought so. And what would have been the use of telling him not to think so? Characters, unhappily, can't be rigged with an assurance. He swilled the last two inches of beer round the bottom of his glass, staring into it with an expression of distaste, his lips twisted and slightly sneering, a twitch, a petty nausea, evidently for his thoughts, not for the beer.

'Why?' I repeated.

The soft brown eyes lifted. 'Why what?'

'Leave teaching.'

He shrugged. 'I wasn't much good. They're quite friendly outside, these kids, but in class they just wouldn't listen. They do to some people, but they wouldn't to me.'

Because there was nothing in him to respect. And no one can blame children for not feeling pity, that highly conscious application of experience.

'Besides,' he went on, 'there weren't the prospects.'

Prospects. He didn't mention the one crucial word. Gillian.

We finished our lunch, at last, and went out.

'Not bad, is it?' he said. 'I come here quite often.'

'Yesterday?'

'No,' he said, surprised. 'I was in the canteen as usual. Though there was hardly anyone on our table. Freddy missed you. He had a whole pack of crossword to get through.'

We walked down the cobbled back streets towards the centre of Hanley, in the sunshine that drew reddish-brown lights, even now, from bricks which on dull days seemed black. A fat little kiln was puffing an almost invisible smoke, a mere quiver of heat across the bluish sky. The air was quite warm. When we reached the shops he went into a grocer's and bought a pork pie and some frozen peas.

'My tea,' he explained. 'Gillian has another class tonight.'

His car was parked by the museum, as usual. I sat down in the front seat. He started the engine, hesitated, then switched off.

'I've forgotten something,' he said, 'do you mind waiting? Shan't be a tick.'

And he went off, up the slope towards the market place.

It was stuffy inside the car. After half a minute I got out and stood looking vacantly at the lines of daffodils splitting into bloom by the museum entrance, and a policeman strolling past, calmly sunning his uniform. Dart couldn't have gone far, for after a few minutes he came loping back to the car, looking rather taken aback to find me outside.

'Forgot to get some aspirins,' he explained, awkwardly, half pulling the pink box out of his pocket.

I nodded without interest. Why tell me? I hadn't asked. And there was a chemist outside the very door of Shentall's, on the corner of Rush Street.

It was just on two when we reached the yard, and the middle shift gatekeeper had arrived. I could see him in the lodge, bent over the table, leaning on his elbows, reading a paper. Having parted from Dart, I went across and tapped on the door.

'Hullo,' he said, looking up. 'Seen this?'

He placed his finger on the inner page of the evening paper; not the front page, which was given over to national and international news—for it was a local paper but not parochial. The paragraph was of about third importance in the lay out, more or less equal with the construction of a children's playground at Tunstall. All hail the power of Shentall's name, I thought; for the restraint was remarkable in the light of the paragraph's final line, on which the gate-keeper's finger insistently pressed: *Police have stated that the possibility of foul play has not been ruled out.*

I raised my eyes, and met his, very dark brown, almost black, set in a sharp, swarthy face.

'Foul play,' he repeated incredulously; as if to add, *here, at Shentall's.*

I shrugged. 'Even in the best regulated families. Were you on this shift yesterday? Did anyone leave late?'

He began to say something, then stopped, looking at me with doubt and suspicion.

'It's all right, nothing to do with *this*.' I tapped the paper. 'Mr Luke wants to know, that's all.' At this stage, it hardly mattered if I cited him as my authority. Besides, the name worked like a charm.

'Oh well,' he said, 'there was Mr Luke himself, of course, he was here till all hours, what with the police and the comings and goings. Miss Chapman stayed too, though not so late as he did. And Miss Ashe didn't go till about six.' He paused to recollect. 'That's all. Everyone was glad to get away, I should think.'

I thanked him. Instead of going back to the works I walked out of the side gate into Canaan Street, dodged through the traffic to the other side of the road and took a bus into Hanley; a heavy double-decker with slippery leather seats that seemed too low, and round the windows the muted advertisements of a self-contained town.

I got down at the museum and walked towards the market place. It was like being back at Cotton's—going into certain shops, asking the old Cotton-type questions compounded of truth, guess, and suggestion; a formula which rarely failed, and didn't now.

When I'd found what I wanted I went round the corner to the G.P.O. and looked up an address in the Manchester directory, then into one of the telephone booths, to dial the number of the Northern Security General Finance Company.

'I want to speak to Mr J. D. Lawrence,' I said, 'I've some information about a car.' I gave the registration number.

'One moment, please.'

I waited, staring through the panes at the clerk behind the stamp counter, who was tearing neat segments off the lovely purple sheet.

'Hullo,' said the voice; the voice of a junior girl. 'We do have the registration on our files, but Mr Lawrence isn't at this office, he's the area representative. He has his own office in Stafford.'

I asked for this number, put down the phone, lifted it again, dialled for the operator and repeated my request to another young girl at the end of the line in Stafford.

'Mr Lawrence is out,' she said, 'he's dealing with that at the moment, I think. Would you like to leave a message?'

I replaced the phone without answering and pushed open the door. At the moment. That meant today, a working day. Either, therefore, a call in the evening, or a letter delivered, as opposed to a mere reminding card. I walked into the street and took a bus back to Shentall's.

Luke was engaged. Business had to struggle on in the face of calamity. I asked Miss Chapman for a sheet of paper and an envelope; and in a form that Luke would be able to understand, but which would give away nothing to Miss Chapman in the unlikely event of her being driven by curiosity improperly to open it, I wrote out what I had to tell and what I wanted him to do. I sealed it, and asked her to give it to him as soon as he was free, in case I hadn't by then returned. She nodded calmly. The hierarchy of Shentall's was shattered by foul play. In face of that disruption the humblest hireling, acting out of station, could draw no quelling stare.

I went down to the yard. It would be unwise, I decided, to ask Corinna for what I wanted. I would discover for myself; behind her back, as I'd discovered so much.

The car was at the far end of the line, a fact which reminded me how late I'd driven into the works that morning; to reach it I had to pass the earthenware slip house. A man in a raincoat was standing by the entrance, but the rope cordon had gone.

I walked across. 'May I come in now?' I asked.

'I should think so,' he said, standing aside.

They hadn't taken away all the barriers; the ark and its environs were still roped off. On the floor, beginning to dry out in patches to a whitish powder, the large shapeless puddle of slip still showed where we had laid him down. That it hadn't dried altogether was probably due to the damp atmosphere which persisted in spite of the twenty-four hours' rest. I wondered how badly and how soon the closure of the slip house was going to affect earthenware production. How silent it was, uncannily silent, like the silence, the absence, of the police. I knew what that was; the lull, the pause, while Dudley was cut up; the calm before the storm.

I closed my eyes. In a way I wished I were on the inside, talking it over with them, knowing what they knew; whether, for example, there were traces of alcohol in his blood and if so to what extent.

Alcohol. Why should he have drunk? Why, apart from the unheeding drinking of grossness, boredom or blind conviviality, did people drink? To escape from an unendurable present, to raze flat in disgust and humiliation the rubble of shattered self-esteem. I thought of Corinna, a battlefield of loneliness and austerity; Dart at Freddy's party, surrounded by hopelessly unattainable good sorts, brooding on the atom and other woes. But Bullace?

I remembered *him* at the party; the sudden smile at Freddy, the way he'd taken my unkindness, in silence, with a flinch that even then had shamed me and now made me smart in those most futile regrets inflicted by death. There was something in Bullace, something, encrusted though it was with his offensive pushing ways—and if he was kicking away the ladder it had to be remembered that the ladder, early in his life, had let him down. Mother running off with a neighbour is no inspiration to stick to the bosom of the family. Offensive defensive. That was what Corinna had said. Corinna was the only one, apart from generous Freddy, to utter a grudging word in his defence.

'Deep in thought?' said a voice.

I opened my eyes. The inspector was standing beside me.

'Trying to solve our problem for us?' he said.

'No,' I said. 'Mine, just mine.'

I went out to the car and drove to Endon; in my pocket I still had the key to her flat.

—

I started with the bedroom. In the cupboard there was nothing but a suitcase, two handbags and her clothes; not very many of them, though more than some women could make do with. I noticed the absence of a winter coat. The chest of drawers was equally unfruitful; gloves, scarves, handkerchiefs, stockings, underwear, sweaters, and finally household linen.

I went into the living-room and began to search, galled by the lack of time that hampered my opportunity to take stock of her through her possessions. I could do no more than glance at what I turned out and slam it back to its place; about eighteen months of *Harper's*, stacks of paperbacks, the big Phaidon Mantegna, writing paper, annual notice of tax code, medical card. No letters, no bills—why should she have either? The rent probably included electricity and there was a meter for gas, I'd discovered to the cost of all my shillings. No bank books; probably in her handbag. No passport, no marriage lines, no insurance policies, no certificates of training; possibly all in the bank. But at home there was such an utter lack of documents as to emphasize, in the age of paper forms, the loneliness of her life. Above all she had no photographs, no souvenirs, nothing to link her with the past.

I turned to the wall cupboard. It was built similarly to the one in the bedroom, with one shelf at the top on which were her drawing materials, paper, water colours, charcoal, pastels; and below, in the hanging space, a faded canvas deck chair, some empty bottles, and a tartan rug which could have supplemented my bedding if I'd known it was there. There was also a large flat container, about a yard square, made of cardboard glued to strips of canvas that formed sides and base. I pulled it out of the cupboard, untied the tapes that closed the top flap and looked inside. It was full of papers. I put in my hand and drew them out, the whole uneven collection.

They were her drawings, of course. On top of the pile lay a torn-edged piece of cartridge paper on which, sketched in soft pencil, was the old woman from Sheffield, bent double, in her black straw hat, her feet like lumps of coal under the long coat, her vacant watery smile turned down on the twist of paper held in her hand.

As a drawing it was more than competent, it was really quite good; but as what I knew she wanted to express, it didn't even approach succeeding. I turned it over and looked at the next.

I recognized myself, after a moment, my own head and shoulders. She was good at likeness. But when had I ever let her take mine? Perhaps in those evenings when we'd sat together in the art room she hadn't spent all the time at work. The pose, head on hand, the downward glance, suggested that the subject might have been reading or writing. Good at likeness! Was I so gouged, so furrowed, and so grey? I stood up and stared at my reflection in the mirror that hung above the fireplace. If anything the drawing flattered.

I turned away and began to go through the rest. Occasionally I came across another face, none that I knew. There were a few people at work in pottery, charcoal sketches of parts of Stoke, one quite good water-colour which must have been done from Shentall's roof, and lots of oddments such as lamp-posts, scraps of masonry, and kilns. But most of the drawings were try-outs of designs for pottery and presumably in the case of large sheets of pattern for textiles, relics of some years back. The papers gave off a smell that was a mixture of must and chocolate as I turned them over, faster and faster, looking for what I wanted. I didn't find it; or not in the form I'd hoped. One only of all the collection I set aside.

A man. His head, shoulders and half a back. He was asleep, or at any rate lying down, his left arm crooked over a pillow, his face hidden in his arm. I laughed. At least, it was meant as a laugh. Tall, dark, *bien musclé*. She'd got that over all right, although the tallness could only be imputed from the width of the shoulders. Perhaps she would have gone on to finish, full length, if he hadn't woken or turned over. But the muscles were there, shaded in with devoted sensuousness, and the dark armpit and the thick hair pushed up by the bend of the elbow.

Victor. Victor as he must have been ten or eleven years ago. For this would have been drawn in the earliest stage of their life together, perhaps even the honeymoon stage, when he was still complaisant and she still overwhelmed, before he found her too exacting and escaped to the routine of bright professional liaisons that constitutes what's known as a good time; before she began to suffer, really to suffer.

I put the drawing down on top of the others. It was a striking testament to an intense infatuation; it confirmed, to me, that Freddy was miles out in alleging Corinna's coldness; it furnished, if I'd needed them, proofs of her physical preferences; but for purposes of identification it was useless. I tied the tapes of the folder. Why had she kept it? Had she forgotten that it was there? I doubted that. It stood out from the other work in the file, it was easily the best. And that, probably, was why she kept it; because it was a good drawing. I put the folder back in the cupboard, banged shut the door and went into the kitchen: an unlikely place to keep photographs, but I looked all the same, rattling and crashing among the drawers and cupboards. It was useless; there were none. Apart from textile patterns and old sketches, there was in the whole flat only one backward glance to a personal past: Victor, the husband, the raven.

I ran down the four flights of stairs, slammed the door, got into the car and pushed the starter. It wasn't only that I was in a hurry. I was angry. No, not angry, nothing so elevated. I was jealous, simply jealous, that he'd wasted and humiliated what I so hopelessly wanted; in short, that he'd had her and I hadn't.

I drove through to Newcastle, up Basford bank, where Corinna had passed her miserable lunch hour the day before, and turned into Dart's road.

There was a car outside his house. A blue A 40, the same sort of car as J. D. Lawrence, area representative, had driven away from Hanley car park seventeen days ago. Although I hadn't at that time been able to see the number, I didn't think it too rash to assume, all circumstances considered, that this was the same car. In which case, where was Lawrence? For I drove past slowly enough to see that there was no one inside, nor any sign of him standing about the road. All right, he was in the house. But who let him in? Little Tommy Thin. Only I thought I'd left little Tommy safe in the accounts department before coming on this particular jaunt.

I drove round the corner, out of sight, into the side road with the telephone box. Pennies. A thousand curses,

I'd only enough for one call. But one would be enough to prove a point, by default or elimination. Not to Shentall's; for at such a time an anonymous call abandoned without explanation would certainly cause alarm with all its unpredictable repercussions. I rang Tiller's, the machine tool people out at Longton. What had she said she was? A secretary. Probably she meant a shorthand typist; or even just a typist.

'I want to speak to Mrs Dart,' I said.

'Mr Phillips' secretary, you mean? One moment, please.'

I waited, my malice duly slapped down. The pause was brief.

'I'm sorry, Mrs Dart has gone. She always leaves early on Tuesdays.'

'Thank you,' I said, and put down the phone.

I stood at the end of the side turning, sheltered by the garden fence of the corner house. From there I could just see the Darts' front door. The car was still outside. I waited. The fence beside me smelt of creosote, a lovely smell which, if it rose high enough, might meet its cousin fume from the tar tanks of Etruria, and the two could mate in the air like birds—or were they only trying to, when, on the wing, they hurtled and fluttered together?

Only a few minutes passed before the door was opened. He came out, the same man, J. D. Lawrence. I recognized the dark greased hair and, even from a distance, his high colour. The door shut so quickly behind him I wonder it didn't clip the heel off his shoe; however, he didn't appear to be hobbling. I waited till he'd driven out of sight, then I left the fence and walked up to the house.

I rang the bell. There was no answer. The second time I kept my finger on the bell push for about a quarter of a minute, without result. Opening the letter-box, I bent down and put my mouth to it.

'Gillian!' I shouted, 'I know you're in. Come and open the door or I'll call the police.'

Looking through the box, I saw her slender ankles running down the stairs. I straightened up just as she flung open the door.

'You!' she said, stepping back.

I walked in and closed the door after me.

'Shouting about the police like that!' She faced me, livid with rage. 'What do you want?'

'I want to know whether your husband went into Sheffield either last Saturday or the one before or both.'

'I don't know,' she said quickly. 'I don't know anything. What's it to do with you?'

I said nothing.

'Listen,' she went on, 'I didn't know about this. It's nothing at all to do with me, you understand.'

'What do you mean by "this" and "it"?' I said. 'All I asked was whether or not he went to Sheffield. Can't you say simply yes or no?'

'No. I don't know. I didn't go with him. I only know he said he was going.'

'Last Saturday or a week past?'

'This last.' She swallowed, staring at me with hostility. 'And don't stand there trying to pretend you don't know what's going on. As if you'd come here just by chance the minute that other man's round the corner. I suppose you've been spying for Shentall all this time? Going over the books to see how much is missing. Well, just understand this. Whatever Colin's done, stupid silly fool, I'm not responsible.'

'Aren't you?' I said.

'I tell you I didn't know till just now,' she said rapidly. 'He never said anything, not a word.'

I walked past her into the kitchen.

'Do you mind!' she cried.

'Not at all,' I said, with the silly flippancy that had always exasperated Stella, my wife. I put my hand on the washing-machine. 'Ninety pounds,' I said. 'Nearly two months of Colin's net salary.'

'If that's all you want to say would you mind going? I'm in a hurry.'

'Why? Your classes don't begin till seven-thirty.'

'Mind your own business!'

'Just now you'd concluded it was my business,' I said. 'And since you're off as early as this every Tuesday why can't you find time to put a casserole in the oven instead of leaving him to treat himself to cold pie and a packet of peas?'

I knew she wanted to scream at me, but couldn't, choked with rage.

'Get out,' she managed, in a husky squeak, 'go on, get out.'

I put my hand on the door. 'One more question. What is it, exactly, that you think Colin's done?'

I didn't wait for her answer. Her face told me enough. She almost squinted in panic. To give her her due, she said nothing; however, to take it away again, perhaps that was less from loyalty than from fear.

'All right,' I said quietly, 'I'm going. I think you're imagining too much, you know.'

That was all I could say, even to her. I had no wish to be numbered among the judges of this world; although so many times, my resolution failing, I'd fallen into the part, and should again.

As soon as I'd shut the door I heard her run upstairs.

It was twenty to five. I could wait for a little before going back, so I walked round the corner, sat in the car, and lit a cigarette. For years now that had been my life, to sit or stand, waiting and smoking. How long would it go on?

At five to five a taxi passed the end of the side road. I started the car and moved along to the corner in time to see Gillian hurrying down the path, holding two blue suitcases. She hadn't wasted any time. She must have been watching for the taxi's arrival. How had she called it when they weren't on the phone?

She could be going to one place only, with cases. All the same I followed, at a reasonable distance, down the bank into Etruria, by Hartshill, to Stoke station. The Manchester-Euston train left at five sixteen.

She was paying the taxi driver as I pulled in beside Wedgwood's statue. I waited till she had gone to the ticket office, went inside, and stood behind her. She booked to Euston, single, first class. I moved to where she'd left the two suitcases by the wall. Putting her change in her handbag as she turned from the window, she didn't see me till she was right up against me.

'Where are you off to?' I said. 'Home to mother?'

She recovered herself, setting her bright lips in a nasty line.

'How long have you had this planned?' I went on.

'I haven't planned it,' she said tightly, 'I've just come.'

'How did you get a taxi unless by arranging one beforehand?'

'You're not quite so clever,' she said maliciously. 'I used Mrs Gosling's phone, next door.' She bent down and picked up the cases. 'And don't try sending Colin to stop me. It won't do any good.'

'I shouldn't dream of interfering with his happiness,' I said. *'Bon voyage!'*

She sent me one last look of loathing, over her shoulder, and walked through the barrier.

—

I had to nerve myself to go along to the art room. It was the drawing, the thought of the drawing, that unsettled me. Not the drawing of me, that was something I had to accept as best I could, with a shrug if possible. The other one.

I opened the door. She was sharpening a pencil, talking to Mitchell; and when she saw me she came across.

'I'm afraid I'll have to stay rather late this evening,' I said. 'Would you wait for me at the hotel? It shouldn't be for too long. Have you any money?'

'Yes,' she said, reaching for her handbag. 'Do you want some?'

She made me smile, in spite of everything. 'No, thanks,' I said, 'that was just to make sure you can buy yourself a drink.'

'What's the matter?' she asked quietly.

'Nothing much. I want to finish some work in the library.'

She compressed her lips impatiently at what she knew to be untrue. 'I meant what's the matter with you?'

'Nothing, nothing at all,' I said shortly. 'I'll see you at the hotel, then, as soon as I can.'

And I rushed out before she had a chance to say or see anything more. Either she was getting uncomfortably perceptive or I was losing command of myself to an alarming degree. Probably both.

I went to Luke, who was free at last.

'I suppose you've seen the paper,' I said. 'Foul play—that'll definitely make the national press tomorrow, in some form or other. As it isn't a matter of a woman or a child it probably won't rate for much, especially since the mode of death wasn't particularly gruesome. I mean the body wasn't mutilated.' The place of disposal might have a bizarre appeal, but that was a suggestion from which I refrained, not wishing to add to Luke's distresses.

'Do you know how he died, then?' said Luke.

'Only by guessing, from what I saw. He was bleeding from the ear, so I suppose he had a skull fracture round the back of his head somewhere. Someone must have hit hard.'

'Not necessarily as hard as all that,' said Luke. 'The inspector told me this afternoon. He had one of these thin skulls, you see.' He paused. 'And to my mind that brings back all the possibility of accident. After all he could so easily have slipped—even have fallen in the ark itself and struck his head on the paddles—it's true the slip house swears to a man that the door wasn't—'

'Listen, if the police have publicly mentioned foul play, knowing the man had a fractured skull, you can be sure they've considered accident and ruled it out. Still, that's not our affair. Let's leave it to the police. Forget it,' I added, without much conviction. 'Where are the prototypes of Isfahan?'

'We're *not* calling it that, remember,' said Luke. 'They're back in the art room as usual—I mean where anyone would expect them to be.'

'So much the better. I've asked her to wait for me at the hotel, and in present circumstances I doubt if anyone else will want to work after hours. But in case they do—'

'I'll see to that,' he said. He glanced at his watch. 'It's

nearly time. I suggest we let the cleaners finish. They always start up here first, and I'll tell them to be quick. Then we'll wait in the library.'

'Is it possible to lock the other door of the art room, the one that leads to the paint shop?'

'Yes. I don't know which key it is, but I know which set. I'll take them along to Anthem, he'll know.'

'In that case we've only the one entrance to watch, and there's an excellent view of that from the library. You didn't give me my headquarters without reason, did you?'

So we waited, hidden behind the half-closed door, I with my eye to the crack of the hinge. It was always quiet in the library. Why should the silence have been different, more intense, simply because it was past office hours? It was a psychological, subjective difference, caused by the knowledge that the place was deserted. Occasionally I'd stare at Luke's pale, freckled, expressionless face, and thank the fate that had kept a Shentall at the head of the firm instead of Brassick, a Hansell or a Tombey. There was nothing wrong with the directors, but Luke was Luke.

We didn't hear the footsteps till about half past six. They were very quiet, no more than a faint squeak of crêpe rubber soles on the polished floor of the corridor. They approached. They stopped. I held my breath. We'd been seen, or sensed, standing behind the door, he'd be creeping away and I couldn't look out to make sure, the chance was slipping out of our hands.

No. The door of the art room opened and closed, quietly, but we heard it. Luke made a slight movement. I put up my hand to stop him.

'Wait,' I whispered, 'you want your tangible proof.'

I forced myself to count a hundred, then making a sign

to Luke to stay where he was, went on tiptoe across the corridor. There was no sound from inside the art room. I counted fifty, and bent down to look through the keyhole, with no more than a faint tremor for my debased life. In any case it was a waste of time and conscience. Whatever was going on was beyond the range of my limited vision. I beckoned to Luke, and stood up. My stomach tightened. Luke put his hand on the door, raised his eyebrows. I nodded, and he opened the door.

I was on his heels, ready. What for? Violence? From that clumsy, cow-eyed, shambling, self-despising fellow creature?

'Good evening, Dart,' said Luke quietly. And then he came to a halt, helpless before the fact. The model of Isfahan, the plate, was propped against a board at the back of the bench.

It's the surprise that shows, always, just for the first moments, before alarm or fear, the sheer staggered astonishment at being caught; blank faces, slack mouths. I walked forward and took the camera out of Dart's hands.

Silence. I'd moved. It was up to Luke to speak. Besides, it was easy for him, doubly easy. He was prepared, and the offender was an outsider.

Dart sat down suddenly on Corinna's chair. 'Oh, all right,' he said. He sounded fed up, that was all. 'Go on, don't hang about, get it over.'

Luke made a gesture towards the camera in my hands. 'Why?' he asked, in his gentle way.

'Money, wasn't it?' I said quickly. 'Money for the car. You got into difficulty over payments very early. That was when you passed out Vinca. And now this latest—'

Dart stared at me. 'How do you know?'

'It's my business to know,' I said shortly; and remembering how he'd wanted to stand me all the drinks at lunch, I turned away.

'But why pick on Mrs Wakefield?' said Luke.

To find him capable of guile surprised me. He knew very well why Mrs Wakefield.

'What do you have against her?' he went on.

A muscle began to flutter in Dart's cheek. 'Nothing,' he said. 'I didn't pick on her.'

'Who did?' I asked. 'Victor?'

He swallowed, looked as if he would like to cry out at the unfairness of my knowing; but thinking better of it, just nodded.

'Well then,' I went on, 'why did *he* pick on her?'

'She's the best designer.'

'How did he know?'

Dart shrugged, with the clumsy violence that had always marked his movements. 'He said he'd seen her work.'

Luke and I exchanged glances. It sounded like the truth, as far as Dart was concerned. He appeared to know nothing of Victor's relationship to Corinna.

'Didn't you ever wonder how a garage owner would dispose of pottery designs?' I asked.

'He told me. He had a finger in the clothing trade. He had contacts through foreign cottons.'

That tallied too. 'I suppose you bought this car with a low deposit and had to make special credit arrangements with him, in person. When you came unstuck for the payment you went to him and tried to sell it back?'

'I tried other places,' said Dart, 'only prices were falling all the time, and none of them would give me enough to cover the rest of the payments.'

The old, familiar, commonplace history. I remembered Corinna's words: you were all right till you showed weakness, then he couldn't resist the joke of seeing you squirm. And if ever anyone visibly squirmed, Dart did.

'So you went to him, and instead of buying it back he proposed a deal,' I went on. 'You were to hand over a Shentall design, and—what?'

'He'd give me the money for the next instalment,' muttered Dart.

'Just for the next instalment? How much?'

'Twenty-four pounds.'

The price of a jacket and trousers. The cost of maintaining for one year a small domestic cat.

Luke's light eyes turned on him in disbelief. 'Do you mean that for twenty-four pounds—'

'Well, if you haven't got it, you haven't,' said Dart, irritably, with that same air as I'd seen in the pub—the twisted mouth, the kicking foot, like a sulky child. It wasn't the whine or cringe of self-pity, just a dull resentful disgust for circumstances and his inability to get clear of them, disgust for himself, that was too weak to possess the dignity of utter humility; a wriggle rather than a writhe.

'When you made this personal credit arrangement with—Victor,' I said, 'I mean when you bought the car, you told him your occupation and place of work, I expect, perhaps you were asked. Did he mention Corinna, even then?'

'Yes, he asked if a Corinna Wakefield still worked here. That's when he said he'd seen some of her designs.'

'But didn't mention any by name?'

Dart shook his head.

'I see. So you took Vinca nearly a year ago. You've had the car about eighteen months, and I suppose you were given two years to pay. That means you must owe another five or six instalments. Why didn't you sell it this time? However much you lost you'd have made enough to pay off the debt.'

'But I wouldn't have had a car.'

'You'd have had enough left to put a deposit on another, a smaller one.'

'But Gillian—'

'Wouldn't have liked a smaller car,' I finished for him.

He picked up a paper clip and began to straighten it with sharp nervous movements of his fingers. 'Besides,' he muttered, 'I'd done it once. There didn't seem any point in not doing it again. I needed the money.'

'Couldn't you have borrowed?' said Luke.

'Who from?' said Dart, moodily.

'Friends, relations. Isn't there anyone who would have helped you out?'

Dart laughed shortly. 'My relations need helping out themselves. And I wouldn't ask Gillian's, obviously.'

'The bank,' Luke said. 'Surely you could have arranged an overdraft?'

'I've already got one. I've never been out of the red since I came to Stoke.'

'But *how*?' Luke persisted. 'You earn a fair living and something more. Your wife works.'

Dart fidgeted with the paper clip. 'Yes—but we had a lot to do—the mortgage on the house, the furniture—we're still paying for some of the bedroom stuff and the kitchen and the TV and washing-machine. And of course there was the car and the cost of running it. Then Gill's sister got married the other month. That meant a present to think of, and going down south for the weekend.'

'But look here,' said Luke, rather sharply, 'if you knew

you couldn't cope with these commitments why undertake them? Furniture, yes, that I can understand. But why the luxuries? The washing-machine, for example?'

Dart jerked his head, in no particular direction.

'Gillian went out. She couldn't manage hand laundry after a day's work.'

'And the car? and the TV?'

'You have to have these things,' cried Dart. 'If you don't, people look at you like a poor relation.'

'You'd rather steal?'

'That wasn't stealing,' he muttered. 'Ten to one they'd have copied the design anyway, when it came out. They just got the chance earlier, that's all.'

'All right,' I said, seeing Luke completely at a loss for words. 'Let's go back to what happened, as opposed to why. You found you were short of money, and at first you just put off paying the instalment on the car, hoping to straighten out your finances by juggling the various claims in turn, is that right? But when you found Lawrence's card in the car window and realized that they were starting to press for it, you had to think of Victor again. Did you try to get in touch with him straight away, that very Saturday? By phone, perhaps, because Freddy's party stopped you from going to Sheffield. But when you rang he was away for the weekend. Well—but why have you waited so long before doing anything more?'

'You've been busy, haven't you,' said Dart bitterly. 'You know so much, work it out for yourself.'

'I suppose you were waiting for Mrs Wakefield's new design to be passed?' said Luke.

'As a matter of fact, I wasn't. Everyone was pleased with it, I'd have banked on its going through. He's been away, that's all. I couldn't get in touch.'

'Till last Saturday?' I said. 'You went to Sheffield then, didn't you?'

He nodded. 'He said he had to come to Stoke on business on Monday.'

'What business?'

'Didn't say. I suppose to pick up a car. Anyway—' Dart stopped, scowling. 'I couldn't do it last night, of course. The police were here, all over the place.'

'So was I,' Luke put in.

'In any case, hadn't you forgotten your flash bulbs?' I said. 'You had to buy some in Hanley today, didn't you? With the aspirins.'

There was a cup on the table beside him, a white glazed cup. He snatched it up, sprang to his feet and hurled it at the opposite wall, full force, throwing in from the boundary. It smashed with the brilliant ring of bone china, the fragments falling on the bench as our hands shot out to hold him, Luke's and mine.

'You know bloody everything, don't you?' he shouted. 'Tell me something else, go on.'

Your wife's left you, I thought, that's something I know. You ruined yourself for her, and she's left you in the dirt and run off to mother.

Dart sat down. Disgust consumed him, a dejection worse than before.

'All *right*,' he said wearily, his voice trembling. 'I'm not violent. You needn't stand there like that, waiting to pounce.' He paused, swallowed. 'I used two flashes at home last night on a couple of shots of a vase of freesias. I was going to put them in for the club exhibition if they'd come out good enough. That's all. I thought I'd better replace them in case I needed more tonight than I had with me.'

'I see. Is he calling again this evening, Victor?'

'No. He was only in Stoke for the day. They're going by post—I mean, that was the arrangement.'

'And he was to send you money on receiving them?' I paused. 'What's he like to look at, this Victor? Tall, dark?' I nearly added *bien musclé*.

'That's right. A bit like Freddy, in fact, only taller.'

Of course. The favoured type. I should have seen him if I'd waited. He would have got out of the back of the plum-custard Vauxhall driven by the blonde who had so effectively caught my debased eyes that they looked for no one else.

'Did you tell him what had happened here in the afternoon to Bullace? What did he have to say to that?'

Dart shrugged. 'Just a sort of string of exclamations. How you would if you heard something staggering.'

'So he seemed staggered?'

'Well, of course he did. Even a bit alarmed, come to think, I can't see why.'

'Can't you?' I said. 'You know Bullace had his finger on everyone in the works. Why should you think your side activities were going to pass unnoticed? What's this file you mislaid yesterday morning, the one Bullace was so upset about? Are you sure you haven't been working the books for your own benefit, as well as lifting the designs? And are you sure Bullace hadn't inconveniently discovered one or other or both? Bullace went after cars in Sheffield, don't forget, and he was a great one for following up little clues, as I know to my cost. No, I don't think I can blame Victor for his alarms. Trouble breeds trouble.'

Dart stood up. 'I didn't fiddle the books for the very reason that I knew Bullace would find out,' he said, quite steadily. 'And I didn't kill Bullace.'

'No one said you did,' I reminded him.

'All the same,' said Luke quickly, 'you realize we shall have to tell this to the police.'

'I'll tell them myself,' said Dart. He'd turned terribly pale. His soft brown eyes turned from Luke to me, desperate to convince. 'I did not kill Bullace,' he repeated, 'I did *not* kill Bullace.'

—

'Then who did?' said Luke, when we were alone again.

'I don't know,' I said, 'and I'm not concerned. I don't even wonder. My part's finished. After the inquest, I can go.'

I stared out of the window. The inspector had come, with his sergeant, had taken Dart off to make the statement he insisted on giving, in his anxiety to clear himself of a possible charge of murder. It was over, the affair of the designs, on which I'd spent my time and thought; and though I'd been right in that money was at the root of it, though I'd been prepared, yet all I felt was disappointment, anti-climax, a sense of *is that all*? I knew, I'd experienced years of it in Cotton's; the monotonous similarity between all the categories of misdeed, the narrowness of their basic motives, the limpness of most of their conclusions.

'Are you going to prosecute Dart?' I asked.

'No,' said Luke. 'I told him he'll have to go, of course—well, he's already gone. I had the unpleasant task of dismissing him while you were phoning the inspector.' He paused. 'It's so stupid—if he'd even come to me, in the last resort, I'd have made some arrangement. God above! Twenty-four pounds! Not even for the sheer necessities of life, for frills—'

'For things you've had from birth and taken for granted,' I said. 'When have you known a tap not gush hot water at a touch? Has there ever been a time when there wasn't a Bentley for you to step into?'

He was silent.

'Tougher characters than Dart crack under the pressure. Advertising and producers on all sides attacking with greed, vanity, envy, snobbery, patronage—oh, don't look so indignant. I don't mean you. Pottery's among the cleanest and most dignified of rackets. You just push your sales on a straight appeal to the eye. But you heard what Dart said. "You have to have these things." *Have* to. Obligation. England the great mercantile nation, rolling in prosperity, measures poverty against a new list of basic possessions. And it's no longer a pity to be poor, a misfortune, it's a disgrace, a stigma, a reflection on your character, a condition you daren't permit to be seen, like syphilis. Perhaps I exaggerate.'

'You do,' said Luke shortly. He opened a cupboard in the bottom of his desk, took out two glasses and a bottle of Scotch, poured, and gave one to me.

I drank, and looking at the large measure that still remained in the glass, thought of Corinna.

'What about Wakefield?' I asked. 'Are you going to chase him?'

'I don't know,' said Luke thoughtfully. 'I'll have to take advice, get some more information about him. The solicitors can do that,' he concluded hastily. As if I'd have wanted to touch it.

'We'll have to tell Mrs Wakefield,' he went on. 'She'll take it hard, I'm afraid, not that it's in any way her fault. She can ignore the whole affair, as far as I'm concerned.'

'Can you imagine that?'

He was silent.

'You're going to lose your white hope from the art room,' I said. 'She won't want to stay.'

'I suppose not,' he said sadly. 'Quite apart from her personal feelings, she'd be afraid of some sort of vendetta, perhaps, on her husband's part, whether we prosecute or not. After all there must have been spite behind his picking on her. It couldn't have been simply that she was the best artist, even if he really thought so.'

'On the other hand I don't think he'd have bothered unless the chance had been flung at him. He's essentially an opportunist, I'd say.'

'He'd bothered to find out where she was working. Dart didn't have to tell him that.'

'If your wife leaves you, you *do* bother to find out where she's gone, at first, if you can, however little you care. Just for the convenience of the thing. He's probably known for some years and left her alone.'

'Still she'd do better to leave, make a fresh start somewhere,' said Luke. 'She'd really need to change her name.'

'She would,' I said. 'Talking of fresh starts—I'd like to know what expediency forced Wakefield to shift from Manchester to Sheffield. Something grubby, I don't doubt.'

I put down the glass and shook my head as he went to refill it. 'I'm going to drive her home now. Shall I tell her, or do you want to?'

'You're welcome,' he said wryly. 'Listen—this awful business of Bullace—'

'That's for the police.'

'I know. But if in thinking about it you should have any ideas—'

'I shan't. I wash my hands of it.'

He smiled faintly. 'Be careful. Posterity hasn't much to say for Pontius Pilate.'

'No,' I said, 'but he rates one up on Judas.'

—

Corinna was waiting for me in the hotel lounge, looking at a back number of *Pottery and Glass*.

'Hullo,' I said, 'didn't you have a drink?'

'Yes, two.'

'Want another?'

She shook her head.

'Listen, I can't face another night on that brown sofa. Why don't you stay here? You'll feel better.'

'You think he's still in Stoke?' she said.

'No. I don't believe he's concerned with you at all. It's simply that if you stay here you may feel more at ease. We could have dinner now, then I'll run you out to Endon to collect whatever you want. Wouldn't you rather do that?'

'Perhaps,' she said, 'just for this evening. But let's go home first.'

I sighed quietly. I was hungry, I wanted to wash off the filth of a day in Stoke, and I was tired. However, we went out to the car.

We'd got as far as the council estate at Abbey Hulton before she said what I knew she'd been longing to say.

'Where have you been all this time?' she asked. 'What were you doing? It wasn't—about Bullace?'

'No. At least I don't think so. Just keeping to my own line.'

'You mean my designs,' she said bitterly.

'That's right.' I paused. 'You won't be seeing Dart from now on.'

'Colin?' she cried. 'Not Colin, surely not. You don't mean he was taking them?'

I told her. All of it, the connexion with Victor, everything. She had to know sooner or later; and it was easier for me to tell her in the car, while I could keep my eyes fixed on the road ahead, and didn't have to see her flinch.

'Poor Colin,' she said, when I'd finished. 'What will he do?'

I shrugged. Poor Colin. They look at you like a poor relation. He *was* the poor relation, and he couldn't take it. Perhaps if he'd stayed single he'd have been content, he'd have had enough. Gillian was his undoing. Gillian with her cold, bored, restlessness of envy and discontent.

'Gillian!' I said. 'Money for Gillian who's run off and left him at the first breeze of trouble, just because he's fallen behind with the car payments. If she knew the rest—*when* she knows!'

'Naturally you condemn a wife for not sticking to her husband,' said Corinna, not very steadily, 'for better or worse, through thick and thin, honesty and dishonesty.'

'Why do women always find a personal meaning in every remark? You know I'm not equating your case and hers. What Dart did she drove him to. Your husband was trying to force you to steal.'

I paused. I thought I might as well go on, having said so much. 'You could divorce him, you know, I'm sure you could, in spite of your desertion. Cruelty, probably—'

She shook her head.

'Why not? Can't you face publicity? You'll have to anyway, if Luke prosecutes. You'd be free. You could start again.'

'No,' she said, 'you can never be free, there's always the past to trip you up somehow. It's the thought of the past that kills you.'

I was silent. To me it was the thought of the all too short future.

'When you had lunch with Colin today,' she said, after a minute, 'did you know what you were going to do?'

'That's right. He that dippeth his hand in the dish.'

'I see,' she said. 'Thirty pieces of silver wouldn't take you very far, would they? What will you do now—go off and make some more out of someone else's petty crimes and weakness and failings?'

'Would you rather have taken the rap for something you didn't do? You were Luke's first choice of suspect.'

'And yours.'

I said nothing. We were too tired, that was the trouble, both of us too tired to cope with our circumstances.

I turned into the drive at Endon, and pulled up outside her door. She slipped out quickly, and stood digging in her pockets one after the other. I remembered that I still had her key, and held it out to her.

'There's no need to come up,' she said. 'In fact I'm staying here. I'm not afraid of Victor. He's only a grubby crooked small-time sharp dealer, not a criminal.'

'Small-time grubs can make mistakes, in the heat of the moment, or in panic.'

'Mistakes,' she said, 'but not murder, if that's what you're thinking.'

'All right. Stay, then, if you want to. Let him in if he calls, be reconciled. Perhaps you'll get a chance to finish your drawing.'

She looked at me blankly.

'You know,' I said, 'the pillow, the elbow, the *bien musclé* shoulders.'

She went back against the wall as if a gust of wind had

slapped her, flat, in one movement. I got out of the car, fumbling with the door, silently swearing at myself, willing to have bitten my tongue if that would have done any good. The sight of her face made me stand still. It was quite composed, but it had changed in the way a landscape changes without moving as a cloud covers the sun. Something was wrong, far more wrong than the outrages of my jealousy.

'Corinna,' I began.

She looked at me with a faint flicker in her eyes. I recognized it. Fear.

She pulled herself away from the wall, turned the key in the lock and went in, leaving the door open. I followed her up the stairs, four flights without stopping, at a run, into the living-room. She went to the cupboard, took the folder, untied the tapes, pulled out the drawings, parted them about three-quarters of the way through, and began to flick through the last of the pile. I watched her stupidly, breathing fast, my mind all awash, not even capable of telling her that I'd left it on top, at the front. She reached the end of the pile and turned back to the beginning. And there, the first, was the old woman from Sheffield.

I stepped forward. She'd turned it over already, searching through the rest, flicking them over carelessly, clumsily, tearing a couple of corners, not stopping once to look at me. Only at the end, when she was back where she'd started, did she raise her head.

'You've taken it,' she said, her voice catching.

'No. I left it on top of the pile. That's where it was at four o'clock. I didn't take it, Corinna.'

She was silent for a moment, looking at me, almost cowering, as if against an awaited blow. Her face was bent away from the light; grey, it looked, with greenish shadows. For one moment we seemed about equal in age.

'Who did?' she said.

For it was gone, the portrait of the sleeper. And so was another, which she appeared not to have missed; the portrait of me.

—

It wasn't over. Nothing was over. Why did I lie to Luke, fooling myself that I'd wash my hands, wouldn't think, wouldn't wonder who'd killed him and why? I woke at five, with my mind churning the same questions as when I'd fallen asleep, as if it hadn't stopped all night, the same ideas, same vocabulary—blackmail, pressure, threats, exposure, murder. The same old slides of memory insisted—Bullace's clothes, Bullace's Jag, the Leica, the lunches, Le Lavandou, all of which had to be paid for, Bullace looking for cars in Sheffield, Bullace so adept at forging links, quite my equal at that, no doubt, and with longer to work at it. And then, ineluctably, I'd see the blonde in the plum-custard Vauxhall. Bigamy, sir, is a crime. Bigamy.

At that point I had to stop, refusing to face the next half-glimpsed possibility. Only after a few minutes I'd start all over again, trying to build cases and answers. Elaborate, unlikely, artificial cases and answers too. Oh, they were ritual gestures, stock deferences to the situation of death by foul play; imaginings that I knew to be useless but still couldn't stop. Useless. For I felt that the reason for this death, this fractured skull, this violence so terribly foreign to the calm of pottery, would be found not in tortured chains of coincidence and motive but in something simple, as simple as my equation of the piracy with money; simple, but beyond me this time to formulate, because I knew nothing. Not the hour of his death, nor the strength of the blow, nor its place, nor the weapon. The police knew, they had the information, they would use it. It was their business, now, not mine, to find out who had killed Bullace. But I wished, how I wished, that I hadn't walked by the Trent; and that she hadn't stared down on Etrurian shades.

Corinna. Five doors along the corridor she was sleeping. She'd come back with me, after all, ashy-faced, silent, barely able to eat so how could she sleep? Perhaps, after the four aspirins I'd made her take, she'd drifted off, sleeping as she had been when I took her tea after my night on the brown sofa, on her side, with her grey-blonde head curled forward and her knees drawn up, trying to return to the womb.

Poor Corinna, no use! We were out in the floor of the pit, both of us, a morass in which she'd been struggling for thirty-five years and I for ten more; a morass of futility and aimlessness in which people clung to tussocks of faith, hope and charity to prevent themselves drowning, formed habits on their tussocks, paddled energetically, some with their eyes shut, to give themselves the illusion of purposeful motion. I too. I had my weakness of hope, my dream of escape. To work for Shentall, perhaps, part of the calm family helping to make and distribute objects of use decorated to give a pure and harmless pleasure; and after work to return to Corinna. Corinna. Yes, I'd forgo the work, the better life, the death with less dishonour; I'd forgo it willingly if only I could keep her.

—

It was utterly hopeless, of course. I thought of that throughout our almost silent breakfast. The wrongs I'd done her, wrongs of thought and judgement, suspicions, intrusions, those were things she surely couldn't forgive. And then, as I drove the short distance to work, I kept imagining before my eyes the grey furrowed face, looking down, as if reading or writing—me, worn and scarred by a life that had left me nothing good to offer. Hopeless. There was nothing for it but to prepare to live through the sufferings of the teens, only this time conscious of losing against time.

I stopped in the yard, and sat for a moment or two looking at her.

'I'm sorry I went through the drawings,' I said. 'I wanted to see if I could find a photograph of your husband. We might have needed one, to identify him. I didn't ask first because—'

Why go on?

She ground the stub of her cigarette in the ashtray. 'I don't know what to think,' she said miserably, 'I don't know what to do.'

'Nor do I.'

Two men passed us, on their way to the stores. They smiled and nodded. They would have done anyway, but there was a quality of awareness in the smiles that showed they would broaden to grins as soon as we were behind them. That we were arriving together hadn't escaped their notice, and they wouldn't be slow to draw inferences.

We went upstairs together, all the same. And at the top the inspector was waiting.

'Good morning, Mrs Wakefield,' he said politely, and immediately turned to me. 'I'd like a word with you, Mr Nicholson,' he said, taking my arm.

I saw Corinna's face, bright with alarm, beseeching me. She wanted to say something. But it was too late, the inspector was drawing me aside.

We went into the library. He'd put some of his things on my desk—gloves, and a scarf and a large buff envelope.

'Sit down,' he said, taking my own chair for himself. I pulled one of the hard ones to the opposite side of the desk.

'Mr Shentall was telling me of the work you've done for him in this business of the young man Dart,' he said. 'You know, it would be a great help to us, if you, as an observant person who was here all the time and *at* the time—'

'I don't know that I—'

'Near enough, near enough,' he said easily, again as if I didn't know that *near enough* wouldn't do in a case of foul play, or come to that in any case. 'It would help, if you could cast your mind back, just think of anything at all out of the ordinary that happened.'

I laughed shortly. 'Such as Mrs Wakefield slinging a clay bat in Bullace's face.'

'You know I don't mean that sort of thing. Little slips in routine, anything that might be puzzling you, anything that you feel or felt or remember feeling was wrong. You should know how important trifles can be. It's odd in a way, the fence that divides us. Yet we both have the same sort of job.' He frowned. 'You should know what gets turned up when you start digging. You lose the quality of surprise, don't you?'

I wasn't in the mood for exchanging amiable platitudes.

'For example,' he said, 'Mrs Wakefield and this—intimacy.'

'At last!' I said sarcastically. 'I've been waiting for this ever since I opened the door to you the other evening when she was in bed. Intimacy! How you police love that word. You're always so anxious to assume it. No use assuring you,

I suppose, that I was only acting as combined nurse and father figure.'

There was something wrong with the way he was looking, something disconcerting; and in the second before he spoke I saw it. Kindness. Unprofessional kindness, regret, pity.

'Not with you,' he said quietly, 'intimacy with Bullace.'

It was no worse, no worse than I'd done to scores of people in the course of earning a living. Not a tenth as bad. True? Oh yes, true. Tall, dark, *bien musclé*. As in the drawing.

'The drawing,' I said.

He picked up the buff envelope, took out a sheet of paper, unfolded it and laid it face upward on the desk. I looked just long enough to see the black hair pushed up in the crook of the elbow.

'*You* took them, then,' I said. 'I hope you had a warrant.'

He ignored it, beneath reproof.

'You frightened her taking it like that,' I went on. 'Why did you have to? It might have been drawn from imagination. It means nothing—at least, not what you said.'

'No,' he agreed, 'a mere drawing is no proof. There's one of you, for example, not quite in the same style, it's true. You deny any improper relationship with her, and I'm inclined to believe you.'

'Am I in the envelope too?'

He took out the second sheet and put it down, turning it so that I could see. Collar, tie, lapels meticulously drawn in; strictly, formally, fully clothed. Not the sort of drawing from which one would deduce great passages of love and passion between the artist and the subject: not, as the inspector put it, in quite the same style.

'Again, you spent a night in her flat,' he went on, 'but not with her. And I'm still prepared to believe you.'

I noted the slight difference between being inclined and being prepared.

'But if you were in the habit of passing the night there, I think you'll admit it wouldn't be only a policeman's mind that would doubt your protestation of innocence. And that was Bullace's habit, at one time.' He looked hard at me. 'She didn't tell you?'

'Why should she?'

'Yet she showed you the picture?'

'No. I found it myself, alone, looking through the flat—just before you must have come to do the same thing. I thought it was her husband. How naïve.'

'So you had no idea about Bullace?'

'No. I didn't know. And it makes no difference to me. I mean to what I think of Mrs Wakefield.'

'That's not quite the point, is it? Could Mrs Wakefield know that it wouldn't make any difference? Besides, in the circumstances, there were other things—and Bullace might have known them—that would certainly have made a difference to you. That her husband was still alive, for example. When did you first learn that?'

'Monday evening. She told me. How did you know about it? Oh, Luke, of course, you've been talking to Luke, and he told you Wakefield's connexion with the Dart business. Well—what is it supposed to have meant to me, that Corinna was still married?'

'You couldn't marry her yourself, to put it bluntly.'

Pointless to protest. I deceived no one. Not Bullace, not Luke, nor the men going to the stores, nor the inspector. They all saw the truth. And I saw, all too clearly, where their thoughts could lead them.

I stood up. 'I'm going to see her.'

He smiled faintly. 'I shan't stop you.' He picked up the drawing, the one of me. 'It's good, you know. Makes you look rather too old, looking down like that. She should have shown the eyes to liven it up.'

I tapped the sleeper's hair. 'Thank you,' I said. 'I can't compete.'

I went to the door and opened it.

'You don't have to compete, do you,' he said quietly, 'now he's dead.'

It stopped me for a moment. They were there, were they? Without answering I went out, not straight to the art room, along to the top of the stairs, just to steady myself for a moment. I'd been so intent on not being surprised, in there with the inspector, that I had to let it stagger me now, as it did. I don't know why. Wasn't I always preaching *nil admirari*? Anyone can do anything at any time. There's no such thing as a sort of girl. That's what I'd said to Corinna on the subject of Bullace and Judith. Judith. Something stirred, unpleasantly, at the back of my mind, and I suppressed it in a panic. Bullace and *Corinna*, that was the subject. Oh, what I'd told him was true. It didn't make any difference to me, apart from the pang of envy that I discounted. All the same, it took time to get used to the idea. It took time.

I went back to the art room. She was sitting at her table, not yet working, simply straightening some papers. I suppose the others were there, Johns, Mitchell, Olive, and Anthem, but I didn't notice them. Perhaps she was expecting me, for she stood up at once, before I'd signed to her to come outside.

'Does he want to speak to me?' she asked, closing the door behind her.

'No. I do.'

We went into the showroom, right to the far corner, behind one of the tall, dresser-like cases full of what was called dinner-ware. The door communicating with the library was shut, and if the inspector had still been on the other side he could have heard nothing through its thickness. We were in about the most private place, at that time, on the whole works.

'What did he want?' she asked, not looking at me.

'Chiefly to tell me something.'

'What?'

I took her chin in my hand and turned her face towards me so that short of closing her eyes she couldn't look away. 'Guess,' I said.

The muscles under her chin moved against my fingers as she swallowed. 'That I slept with Bullace.'

I nodded. She stared up at me without flinching, puzzled, even, as if she were trying to see my reaction.

'How did they find out?' she asked.

'The inspector took the drawing.'

'But that could have been anyone, they couldn't have recognized him. You didn't. You thought it was Victor.'

'He won't have inferred it from the drawing. That was just a lucky find. Someone will have said something to put him on the track.'

'But no one knew, no one.'

'There's always someone who knows. The police haven't been sitting idle since Monday afternoon, they've been unearthing Bullace's home life. They'd only need to ask questions about women—as they would—and someone would have seen, noticed, however little. Even here there'll be people who know, or who have guessed.'

I remembered the lodge-keeper: what's it to do with

anyone, his private life? We're all in glass houses. And Johns; her private life's her own, still waters run deep.

'Did you sleep with him properly?' I asked. 'Or just fields and cars stuff?'

She tried to move her chin, but I held it tight. 'Don't tell yourself it's none of my business,' I said. 'You're in a nasty position with the police on account of Bullace, and so am I. Now tell me.'

She swallowed, but she kept her chin still and looked at me steadily. 'He used to come to the flat,' she said.

'Often?'

'Fairly often. Not for a long time now.'

'Ever go away together?'

'No.'

'When did you quarrel?'

'Never. Apart from Monday morning in the slip house, if you count that. He just stopped coming. No explanation. Just stopped. I suppose—he began to earn more, and could afford someone, and thought it safer. Perhaps he even found someone who really liked him.'

'Didn't you?'

'I didn't *dis*like him or I could never have touched him. It was just that he was lonely and so was I, he'd cut himself off from his past and his family, and so had I. That's all. We weren't friends, so how could we quarrel? We hardly spoke, ever. At work we were no different. No one could have known.'

'Then how did it happen, if you were so silent? The first time.'

'It was quite—ordinary and commonplace. We were working late, just the two of us, and we happened to meet in the corridor outside the art room. Even then we didn't say anything, just stood there looking at each other. Then he put out his hands—oh, I don't know how it happened. Not then and there, of course, I couldn't.'

'Some men have all the luck,' I said, 'they just put out their hands and over you go! Mitchell, no. He made the pass but he has the misfortune to be fat and freckled, not the favoured type.'

'Oh—even that absurd embarrassing episode you've had to grub up,' she said wretchedly.

'Even that. Everything about you. Or so I thought. I couldn't see wood for trees, could I? Well—how did you arrange to meet. By phone? Letter?'

'No. He used to find some excuse to come into the art room, easy enough for him, and he'd stand behind me, not speak, not touch me. And I'd nod, or shake my head as the case might be.'

And she expected that to pass unnoticed! Johns wasn't so blind, evidently. I looked at her. She was smiling faintly, a smile that nearly made me double up with jealousy, the smile of a remembered pleasure. 'And when you nodded, and he came, that made you happy?' I said.

'Not happy, pleased.' Her chin moved. Colour came into her cheeks, but she kept her eyes on me, though they brightened with the heat of blushing. 'I used to enjoy it, that's all. And then, when I'd left my husband for so long—can't you understand?'

'Yes, of course. But you liked the power too, being a woman. Bullace, the almighty, reduced to the same abject condition as any other man—that must have pleased you.'

'He wasn't always offensive,' she said quietly. 'Sometimes when he was off his guard with no one to see him, or no one that mattered, he could be—'

'The next best thing to his cousin.'

'Oh, you!' she cried. 'I've told you I didn't love him, and I don't love Freddy.'

'Did he know that your husband was still alive?'

'No.'

'That means you didn't tell him. He might have found out for himself.'

'He never mentioned it. He would have done.'

'Corinna,' I said, 'you have such a truthful glance.'

'But I *am* telling the truth,' she protested.

'I know. That's what I mean. I believe you.'

The point was, would the police see inalienable honesty in those grey, beautifully shaped eyes? Or would they see only a woman, passing out of youth, without money, without friends, without a future, but with a past, playing her last chance, accepting, perhaps reluctantly, a grey-haired insurance policy, prepared to risk bigamy, quarrelling with the ex-love, the possibly well-informed ex-love—

'Did you kill Bullace?' I asked her.

'Why do you have to be so flippant?' she said angrily.

'I wasn't. I wanted to know. How long since he stopped coming?'

'Just over a year.'

'I thought you said a long time?'

She looked at me. 'It seemed long,' she said.

All the weaknesses of pity came over me, weak knees, trembling hands, stomach fluttering on some internal glove stretcher. I let go her chin. 'I wish you'd told me yourself,' I said.

'I would have done if I'd known what to think of you,' she said. 'And I would have told you about Victor—I nearly managed it on Sunday evening after Dovedale. But when

I found out what you were doing I didn't know whether it mattered to you if I was married or not, whether it was any of your business, whether you were pursuing me for love or money—I mean the money Luke pays you. There, you asked, I had to say it. And I don't know even now. It's no use looking like that. Oh yes, Dart took the designs, so it's all cleared up and finished and we're on the straight. But yesterday you were having lunch with Dart, knowing what you planned to do to him in a few hours. If you're capable of that, how am I to be sure? How can I believe a word you say? It's no use, I just can't trust you.'

She walked away, round the show-case, out of the room, not hurrying, knowing she wouldn't be followed, that I stood there stricken and confounded by that frightful cold indictment.

The truth. She must have seen the truth, everyone else had—the inspector, the men going to the stores, just in the way I looked at her, without a word spoken. Perhaps she did see it. The trouble was that she didn't dare believe it. Nothing I could say would convince her. Well—was there anything I could do?

Yes, possibly. I could try to lift her out of the floor of the pit.

I walked out of the showroom. How everything played into their hands, Luke's and the inspector's; each of them asking me to scour my mind for what I could remember, each for their different reasons, yet with such closeness in time and manner as to suggest collusion. Well, I would think, would apply the mind that they made so much of, for what it was worth; not for their sakes, not for the family, society, honesty, justice; only for Corinna.

Corinna. Too late now to ask her—but I had the feeling

that she hadn't told me the truth; not perhaps a deliberate lie, but somewhere, at some time, a trivial matter unresolved, a lack of frankness. It probably didn't matter; it might be fancy. Yet in our plight we ought to strip everything to its bones.

I leaned over the banister of the stairs and looked into the hall. The light in the switchboard cubicle was reflected brightly off a yellow sweater. Judith was back, recovered from the cold that hadn't, as Miss Ashe predicted, turned to flu. Judith. Again my mind stirred, this time more insistently.

Fortunately the inspector hadn't taken over the library as a permanent base. I went back, sat at the desk and put a clean sheet of paper in front of me, so that I could write down, if I remembered them, the slips of routine, the things that puzzled me; and that was as far as it went, because as I was taking out my pen Luke appeared in the door. He was holding something in his hand, but I couldn't see what it was as he walked forward.

'You're here, then,' he said.

'I've been here since nine. I was talking to the inspector.'

He put what he was carrying on the desk. A camera. Dart's camera.

'I've taken out the film,' he said. 'I don't suppose he'd finished by any means, but I'll have it developed. It's all we need. We can't keep this, it wouldn't be right. But I don't care to send it through the post, it might be damaged.'

I laughed shortly. 'You should visit a slaughter house, see a real humane killer in action. I'm sure you'd be interested. Well, why put it on my desk? I suppose you want me to take it out to him, on the principle that one more dip in the dirt won't make any difference to me.' I paused. 'I take it the police let him go last night?'

'Yes, the inspector told me. I asked him if he thought it was safe, he seemed to think it was.'

Lord Almighty Shentall, asking the C.I.D. if they quite knew what they were doing!

'They'll have someone watching him, I expect,' I said, 'at least till everything's blown over. All right, I'll take the camera. I feel for him. Fellow outsider, you see. You must get a certain satisfaction out of being proved right—that it wasn't one of your own people, only the Cockney from Camberwell with his cow's eyes and apologetic shamble.' I picked up the camera. 'I hope he's still there. He may have gone chasing after his wife. Or swallowed a hundred aspirins.'

Luke turned to me, aghast. 'I'll come with you—'

'I don't really imagine he's done either. Not Dart. He's certainly a fool if he's gone after Gillian. He should count his blessings. No, you go into conference with Brassick, join him in his agitation about short time in the earthenware biscuit. By the way, who's seeing to the accounts, now that you've lost both Bullace and Dart?'

'There's young Massey, and Margaret knows the work very well. They'll run it themselves till we can get new staff.' He looked at me suddenly. 'Why? Have you any experience of accounting?'

'Only with false entries. I'd soon have you bankrupt.'

'That's a pity,' he said, 'a great pity.'

—

Dart opened the door to me. He was wearing a dark red cotton dressing-gown over pyjamas. He was fresh, shaved, his brown hair neatly combed.

'You!' he said, looking surprised. 'What do you want?'

I held out the camera.

'Oh, that,' he said. 'I wondered if I was going to get it back. Thanks.' He made a gesture of opening the already open door. 'Come in.'

I hesitated.

'Come on,' he urged, with a rather melancholy grin, 'men of leisure now, both of us.'

'I can't stay long,' I said.

He closed the door and led me into the kitchen. 'Just finished breakfast,' he said, whisking a plate off the table. 'Sit down. Have a cup of tea. It's still fresh. Cigarette?'

I must have looked stupefied. He shrugged. 'No use going in sackcloth now, is it? Once it's done, it's done. I start all over again, that's all.'

'What will you do? Teach?'

He poured out some tea for me, pushed the ashtray into the middle of the table, so that we shared it, and sat down astride a chair, the back between his knees. 'I can't very well go back without references from here,' he said. 'Oh, I'll find something. One of these jobs labouring, on a nuclear power station site. I'd make more in a week than I do here in a fortnight. If they're building any power stations just now. I could save up and go to Canada. I've got a cousin out there.'

'What about Gillian?' I said reluctantly. It would have been unnatural not to ask, it seemed to me.

'She's gone home. I found a note when I came in.' He laughed, a short mirthless snort.

'I'm sorry,' I said, embarrassed by the situation, and by having to utter that particular lie.

'I'm not,' he said.

It shook me to hear him so calm, even though I privately considered his loss a matter for felicitation. When my wife had left me I'd spent the whole of Easter weekend in a stupor; not of pain, after two years of freezing warfare, but of shock, disbelief. But then Dart and Gillian had had no child, even if only for a few years, to make them sometimes remember, pause, and regret.

'You did it all for Gillian,' I said. 'Gillian had to have the washing-machine, Gillian wouldn't have liked a smaller car—'

'Yes,' he said, 'I did it for her. If I hadn't she'd have nagged my arse off.'

'I see. You were buying peace, not love.'

'More or less. Only I didn't get it, even so.' He paused. 'The trouble was, we never had any trouble. I mean, some people strike it really hard—they get ill, they can't work, they have kids to feed and clothe, they become redundant, get evicted or their rents raised, all sorts of things. If anything like that had happened to us, well, that would have been an end to it. I mean, when you're up against real hard facts it's no good fretting for this and that and kidding yourself you can't do without. You have to. Like the war. Not that I can talk, I only dimly remember the end part. I suppose you were in it?'

'I suppose so,' I said. 'Why that awed look of deference? I didn't choose my year of birth any more than you did. Go on.'

'Well, I don't know—now, when you see things in the shops and other people's houses, and it seems so easy, there just wasn't any excuse I could put forward for not getting them. If I ever said "We can't afford it" she'd say, "Why?" It didn't carry conviction, somehow, to say we hadn't the money. Because in a way we had. I suppose that's what they mean by the nation going soft. The curse of materialism, the evils of prosperity.' His mouth grinned his scorn and envy of people who vented such statements.

It filled me with depression, the screaming banality of the Dart ménage: the weak, disgusted husband, the cold, covetous wife: the knowledge that there were so many thousands of Colins and Gillians. And what was Dart's solution? A war, apparently, with its slaughter, maiming, anguish, waste, futility, meanness, greed, rottenness, lies, hypocrisy, blindness, hate. I laughed. 'How old are you?'

'Twenty-six.'

'Well, I'm forty-four, and divorced, so do you mind if I trade on that seniority to ask something you don't have to answer? When did you stop loving Gillian, and how?'

He pushed his cigarette stub backwards and forwards in the ashtray. 'Well, I didn't ever, really, so I couldn't stop.'

'Why did you marry her, then? Not for money. Not because you had to, was it?'

He shook his head. 'She wasn't pregnant, if that's what you mean. I'd never touched her, just taken her out a bit—and then, I don't know how to this day, the situation suddenly seemed to be that she expected me to propose. I hadn't really thought of it. But then I felt I ought, if I'd somehow given her cause to believe I would. Besides, if you don't get married, people imagine you're after choirboys or something. They don't seem to understand you can be just not over keen on women. I find women boring, except for a few. To tell the truth I think sex is overrated—all right occasionally, once every month or so, perhaps.' He looked at me with a sudden grin. 'I bet you can't understand that.'

I shrugged. 'I can as a communication, not as an experience.'

He nodded. 'That's what I thought. Still, it suited Gillian

all right. In fact it'll suit her even better to be quit altogether. I expect she'll write to me asking about a divorce. She can have it with pleasure if she'll come up here and see to selling this lot.' He made a clumsy gesture round the kitchen. 'I don't know why I went to such lengths to keep it all going. Habit, I suppose, appearances. What a life!'

I stood up; there was the camera, on the draining-board, next to the eggy plate; the reminder that he, talking and smoking with me so calmly, was the one I'd spent my time searching out, the one who'd misappropriated Vinca, made the attempt on Isfahan. Was it natural, that matter-of-fact, almost cheerful calm? Even free from Gillian, could he really mind so little? It was defence, perhaps, against a situation he simply couldn't believe. Later, caught in the bleak toils of divorce and creditors, he'd wake up. In the meantime he slept late and fried eggs for breakfast. I was seized again by a sense of faded anti-climax. Dart, petty banal Dart, was overshadowed even in his disgrace by the coincidence of Bullace's death.

'You're not worried about the business of Bullace?' I asked.

'Why should I be?' he said, surprised. 'It's nothing to do with me. Poor sod.'

'Did you like him?'

'Don't think anyone did. Even Corinna, though she was the only one who ever made any excuse for him.' He paused. 'I'm sorry it had to be Corinna—about the designs. Does she know?'

I nodded.

He pulled a face. 'Probably can't understand it, being so straight herself.'

'Straight?'

'Honest. Don't you get that impression from the way she looks at you? With Gillian you were for ever having to pass things over in silence to keep the peace, outrageous remarks like Stoke being provincial, and worse. And when Corinna had to, she always used to flush and look the other way. And that was just silent acquiescence, after all, a sort of passive lie.'

It was there. The trivial lie that had worried me, the unsettled question, the tiny seed too remote from all our troubles to have raised its shooting stalk till now, days later, when I had the camera under my eyes and in my ears Dart saying that Corinna couldn't face you with a lie. In itself it was unimportant; but because it was between me and Corinna I had to know; to discover the fragment of truth which Corinna faced with such reluctance that on Sunday afternoon in the car between Eyam and Monyash she couldn't bring herself to utter it.

'What did Freddy enter for the camera club exhibition?' I asked.

He stared at me, bewildered by the inconsequence. Then he gave his short, snorting chuckle.

'Daft!' he said. 'That's my only regret about having to leave—no Fred to liven things up. Funny you should mention that, though. Bullace wasn't half mad with him. It was a photo of the switchboard.'

'Of Judith?'

'No, that was the point, the cubicle was empty, taken from outside through the glass panel. Problem picture, see. Quite good, it was, better than Fred usually achieves. Coloured. Bullace thought Fred was making a fool of himself or the club, I suppose, and he didn't like it, being a cousin of one and a member of the other. Still he wasn't president, for a wonder, so he had to give way to Mitch. *He* roared his head off when he saw it, the title tickled him. Know what he called it, old Fred? *A beautiful golden frame.* The oak round the window came out yellowish, like it is, in fact. Clown!'

—

Did I say goodbye to Dart? Yes, I remembered something about being sorry; and Dart saying it was only what I was paid to do, and perhaps all for the best anyway, meaning Gillian, I suppose. And then I must have walked out, sat down, let in the clutch and driven to the end of the road, overlooking Etruria, the pit, shades and clouds of grey. Automatically I would have done all that, the way they place the ware on the trolleys, thinking and talking of something else, but never missing a pin.

Escape. What seduction, the mere thought. Go and fetch her, run away, together, hide, forget, start again. I had money, enough for that. But if she wouldn't come? Beg, implore, threaten, coerce. Blackmail her with pictures of old age, grimy, lonely, poverty-stricken, the dreaded future of her imagination. Bar no holds, no weapons, hit below the belt, only get her clear before it was too late, before they found out, as they would. They'd work it out, better than I could. I hadn't worked it out, I only knew, by instinct, at last, recognized the vein of simplicity that I'd sought and accidentally struck. In fact it would work out. I didn't want to see, but I could. They were falling into a pattern, infernal pattern, the little slips of routine, the things that puzzled me.

But would they work it out?

They didn't know the slips, the fragments. Only I knew them, only I saw them, only I was there. Unless I were to tell them how could they ever work it out?

Good. Leave it. Say nothing. Poor Bullace, poor Dudley, only thirty. Yes, but there must have been a reason; so say nothing. *Ideas? I'm sorry, I've tried. Nothing.*

No. I couldn't do that. They might conclude—oh, easily, I couldn't blame them, in the circumstances—that someone else had done it. The wrong one. They like to have a solution, it makes the files look better. The wrong one? They wouldn't do that. Wouldn't they? Not on purpose, perhaps, but they might. The wrong one suffering. And, in the circumstances, how easy to imagine who the wrong one might be. So I couldn't run away. A last hope flickered in my mind. I might be wrong, it was all a mistake. But I knew I wasn't. There was no hope, no hope of anything in this life.

I pressed the starter. The car moved towards Etruria, the floor of the pit. And as it sang down the bank I sang quietly with it, something I remembered from childhood, something my father used to sing, with loud derision, in his Tyneside accent; a piece of sentimental tripe from an Edwardian lower middle-class parlour.

If those lips could only speak;
If those eyes could only see;
If only those beautiful golden tresses
Were there in reality;
Could I only take your hand,
As I did when you took my name!
But it's only a beautiful picture
In a beautiful golden frame.

I'd parked the car in the yard, just stepped out, when I saw Mitchell. Old fat Mitch, wandering mysteriously round the works, as usual.

'Hullo,' he said, 'just arrived? You don't usually keep such Bohemian hours.'

'Listen,' I said, ignoring politeness in my urgency, 'Dart said there was hardly anyone at our table in the canteen on Monday, apart from him and Freddy. Were you there? And if so can you remember—'

'Sorry, I wasn't. I had to do a bit of shopping so I nipped into the Bluebird café for a snack. Why, what's up? Are you playing private detectives? Mind they don't nab you for obstruction.' He paused. A look approaching seriousness came into his freckled face. 'As a matter of fact, there's something I wonder if I ought to tell them. But who wants to be the sort of stupid self-important ass who runs round braying that he's got a vital clue? It's nothing really. I don't see that it could matter, and anyway they probably know. Just that I saw Bullace that lunch time.'

'Saw him?'

'Well, you see what I mean, that's all there is. Except that it was in the Bluebird, and it's not the sort of place I'd expect him to go for lunch, in fact I *know* where he usually went. Still, it's near the end of the month, perhaps he was short of cash.'

'Was he alone?'

'Yes, but he may have been meeting someone. I was downstairs at the snack counter, he was going up to the restaurant. Well, what do you think? Should I go and tell them?'

'I should wait a bit,' I said, trembling at what I was doing. 'As you say, they may know. It may not matter.'

'Yes, probably wisest,' he said. 'I say, you look rather under the weather. Feeling all right?'

'Tired,' I said, 'that's all. By the way, is this café licensed?'

He laughed. 'Not even for ginger beer.'

I'd asked him enough. I went out of the yard by the works gate and asked a passer-by where I could find the Bluebird.

Bath Street, Hanley. I took a bus.

Corinna. Bullace. I remembered the scene in the slip house, the acrid exchanges, like blows, delivered crudely, without finesse, just to hurt. *Conceited interfering busybody. Scheming drink-sodden slut.* One good pain deserves another. But Bullace had wanted her once, badly enough to go and beg with his eyes and his outstretched hand. Oh, we happened to be working late and we happened to meet! That sort of meeting, with that result, doesn't just happen. One or both of them must have wished and hoped, at whatever level of consciousness. Then was it so easy for him, even when he'd finished with her, to see her leaning on someone else? And was it so easy for her to be abandoned? I knew it wasn't. *We didn't love each other: we hardly spoke: we were lonely.* Yes, but also—*I enjoyed it: it seems a* long *time.* To be chosen, then rejected; to hear him coldly rebuking her for misusing the machinery, as if she were just another girl from the works, as if he'd never stood behind her silently asking for favour, charity, as if they'd never measured their naked length together, as if he'd never, alone with her, rested for once or twice off his guard; and finally to look at what she'd lost beside what in future she believed she'd have to make do with, the black hair and the grey—no, it wouldn't have been easy for her to reconcile herself to that.

I got off the bus at the museum and cut through to Bath Street. The Bluebird was a pleasant little place, optimistically painted pale blue, in the face of a small kiln across the road; very clean inside, with many green plants in pots hung round the walls, and flowers in vases, pottery vases, on every table of the restaurant upstairs, carefully arranged flowers, none faded, though it was Wednesday, mid-week. A door with *Ladies* written on it, no matching *Gentlemen*; they presumably had to be continent. Two women sat at one table, three at another, glancing at me with passing curiosity. Feminine, the Bluebird was overridingly feminine. What would Bullace have done there, alone?

There was a waitress, which was fortunate, just one, which was even better. I asked for coffee, lighting a cigarette in an illogical attempt to counter the effeminacy of the order.

I glanced at the card clipped to the side of the ashtray, my eye caught by the words *bread and butter pudding*. That northern favourite! Homely food, called by its own name. The waitress brought my coffee. She was young, and her face was pleasant, not pretty, but bright and lively—the proprietor of the Bluebird wouldn't have chosen a crumby slattern to wait on the customers; and I turned on her a charm that Corinna would never have suspected in me; would never have believed.

'I feel out of place,' I murmured, glancing at the other tables. 'I suppose most of your customers are women?'

'Round this time,' she said. 'A lot of gentlemen from the town hall and the offices come in for lunch.' She put down my cup and turned away, discreetly, well trained.

'Wait a minute,' I said, too anxious to be subtle or cautious. 'Are you the only waitress? Did you serve at lunch on Monday?'

A flicker of doubt and alarm passed across her eyes. My heart sank. 'Can you remember seeing a well-dressed man of about thirty?' I went on in a low voice. 'Handsome, tall, dark-haired.'

She looked round nervously, and I knew for certain that I was too late. 'Are you another detective?' she whispered.

Of course they'd have gone the rounds of eating places, systematically.

'That's right,' I said. 'I didn't know the inspector had already sent someone. There seems to have been a misunderstanding.'

I saw disbelief in her face, and realized that a Stoke detective would speak with a Stoke voice. 'I'm a private detective,' I said, my thought flashing for a second on Mitchell. 'The inspector asked me to help him. It's all right, you can ring them up if you want to make sure.' I prayed that she wouldn't.

'It isn't that,' she whispered, 'but I hope there won't be any trouble.'

'Don't worry, I'm sure there won't. If someone's been here, I needn't stay. Unless you've remembered anything else since he left?'

She shook her head. 'Well—only that the lady didn't seem very happy. If that's anything. Only he seemed more interested in the lady, the detective who came in this morning.'

Oh Christ. 'He must have come early.'

'Yes, first thing.'

'Had you seen either of them before, the dark man and the fair woman? It *was* fair, wasn't it?'

'That's right, long fair hair done up at the back. No, they hadn't been in before. I'd have remembered them, they made such a nice-looking couple. If only she'd been a bit more cheerful. Aren't you going to drink your coffee? You might as well, you'll have to pay.'

I gave her half-a-crown. 'No time,' I said, 'keep it.'

I ran downstairs, into the street, looking round automatically for the car, till I remembered I'd come by bus.

No time. They were ahead of me, of course. I couldn't compete. I wasn't trying. I was only afraid that without my fragments of knowledge, the slips of routine, the things that had puzzled me, they might make up a different pattern, lay their hands on the wrong person.

I should have to tell them. Now? Yes, now, before the mistake was even made. The wrong person mustn't suffer. That was to say, suffer the penalty. Because as to pure suffering, I could see that everyone was going to be in, wrong persons and right. All of us.

—

'What it boils down to is this,' said Luke. 'An empty cubicle, an empty flask, and the fact that a man who'd had no chance to get drunk reeked of alcohol after almost an hour in the slip. How could you have smelt it on his breath—I mean in his mouth—when it was full of clay? But I distinctly remember that the doctor said he was drunk.'

'The doctor, not the police,' I said. 'He came to a hasty conclusion, that's all. Doctors are only qualified medical students.'

'All right. We'll see.'

'Wait!' I said, seeing his hand go to the phone. 'What are you doing? I'm tired of telling you this is something for the police, not just a domestic matter of your designs. Suppose I'm right? Do you want to be accessory—'

'I don't propose to shield anyone,' he said. 'They'll go to the police as soon as I've seen them. Or I shall. But I'm seeing them first. They work for me.'

'Yes, and your duty's to give them a fair return in money and conditions, not to be their father confessor. They won't thank you.'

'I'm not concerned whether they thank me. If you think it's none of my business, why did you tell me?'

'Christ, I wish I hadn't!'

Why had I? Because the inspector was gone, he wasn't there when I wanted him, because in my fear of a mistake I rushed to confide my knowledge to a second party, a witness, in case anything should have happened to me. What could have happened to me? And why should I have imagined that they would make a mistake? Now, in the cold sweat that covered me, the horror at Luke's decision, how wild my earlier panic seemed. Why did I have to tell him? Wasn't it, finally, out of some muddled, misguided sense of loyalty, the pull of the Shentall family? Because, just as he said of the others, I worked for him?

'You haven't paid me yet,' I said, following my thought aloud. 'Why do you think I don't take money till it's over? So that I can say what I like, so that I can refuse, so that I'm not bound to do what I don't want, so that I can be free.'

'No one is free,' said Luke, lifting his phone; not the office phone, the outside line. I watched him dial, heard him speak the equivocal message, marvelled again at the Shentall obstinacy.

'Have it your way, then,' I said, as he put down the phone. 'I'm going.'

'I'd like you to stay,' he said.

No, it wasn't simply obstinacy, I was wrong. He didn't want to do it. He was forcing himself to carry out what he believed to be his duty, to stand by the ones who for eight hours of the day were his responsibility. He was prepared to act alone; but he hoped, though he wouldn't ask for help. That was what I saw in his anxious pale blue eyes. *You're older, you started it, you brought it on me. Help me.*

'All right,' I said, feeling tired out. 'At least ring the police, see if you can't get a message to the inspector, ask him to come out as soon as he can. Make arrangements with Miss Chapman outside. And send for—the others. You can do that on the call box, can't you, it won't matter.'

We sat in his office and laid our slight plans, pausing involuntarily to stare at each other with disbelief. He rang the police. He went into Miss Chapman's office, while I sat staring at the grey-green walls with their white moulding, listening to his voice giving orders, distant, as in a dream. Even when he came back and spoke twice into his desk, I couldn't believe the people he called would really come; not till I heard the knock on the door.

Corinna was first. She hadn't so far to walk, just along the corridor and up one flight of stairs. Oh, it was all right for Luke, he could be busy placing a chair, *saying good morning, Mrs Wakefield.* I went to the window, and looked at the greys of Stoke. *If you're capable of that, how can I be sure? I can't trust you. How can I believe a word you say?* That was what had started it. I'd wanted to help Corinna, to get her out of the ugly mess, to prove in a way she could believe beyond doubt, that I'd do anything for her. And this was the happy result of my labours. This.

The second knock, soft and hesitant. My heart beat fit to choke me. A yellow cardigan, a green tartan skirt, fair hair swept up as usual in a neat bun. Judith. Judith Agnes. Sweet virtuous gentle virgin, standing uncertainly on the threshold, pale, heavy-eyed, still suffering from the cold that hadn't turned to flu, looking from one to the other, fastening timidly on Corinna for feminine support.

The eyes! They moved in a sort of chain reaction. Corinna's to Judith, puzzled and surprised, to Luke, questioning, to me, alarmed. Luke's to me, horrified at having come to the point of no return, begging for help, beseeching me to take it, all of it, on my hardened dirt-worn shoulders.

I turned my back on Luke and Corinna, and attacked, like a brave and experienced soldier, the weakest point.

'Judith,' I said, 'you go home to lunch, don't you?'

'Yes, sir.'

'Don't call me sir.' Till then she never had. 'Did you go home on Monday?'

She stared at me, her poor face struck with horror. She couldn't speak, but she was truthful. She shook her head.

'You went out to lunch with Bullace, at the Bluebird, didn't you? Did you have anything to drink?'

'Coffee,' she whispered.

'No, I mean alcohol. Not there, afterwards, perhaps?'

'No.'

I saw tears filling her eyes.

'Did you love him?' I asked.

Luke moved, protesting. Judith shook her head.

'You just happened to go out to lunch with him. He stopped and had a few drinks afterwards, even if you didn't? No? But all the same when you got back to the works he took you in the slip house and made a pass at you, and you pushed him—'

'No!' she cried. 'No!'

Corinna was on her feet, her hands pressed against the lower half of her face, covering it, so that her grey eyes, horrified and sickened, stared over the tips of her fingers.

'Leave her,' she cried. 'Stop it. Leave her alone. Judith, it's all right, be quiet, you needn't say anything.' She stopped, and swallowed. 'I did it.'

Silence.

'Listen, I'll tell you what happened,' she went on rapidly. 'I'd had that scene with him, when I threw the bat, and I thought—all sorts of things. That he might tell everyone I'd slept with him, how he didn't come any more, how I wanted him, I didn't stop wanting him. I went for a walk, that's true. And when I came back I saw them together in the slip house. I was jealous, after Dovedale, you see, yes, jealous, and I went in. There was no one there, it was just before the end of lunch. I went up and—'

She had to stop. Her voice failed for a moment.

'I didn't mean to,' she went on, breathlessly. 'We argued, I pushed him, and he slipped. He hit his head somehow—'

She closed her eyes.

I attacked her in her weakness. 'Was Judith there?'

She nodded. 'That's why—she's so upset.'

'*Were* you there, Judith?' I asked.

She nodded, weeping.

'And is it true, what Corinna's said?'

'Leave her,' cried Corinna, 'can't you see?'

'All right,' I said, 'you can tell me yourself if it's true. Look at me. Now. He hit his head, you didn't notice where. Leave that, then. You thought at first you'd knocked him out, that's all, you didn't know he had one of these ultra-delicate skulls. So you took out your flask and poured whisky down his throat to revive him. That's right, isn't it?'

Judith moaned.

Corinna stared at me, her eyes wild with anxiety. 'Yes,' she said. 'Yes.'

'And when you realized he was dead you dumped him in the ark. How? He must have weighed all of thirteen stone.'

'Somehow—I had to. I dragged him.'

'Did Judith help you?'

She gripped the back of the chair with her hands and leaned on it, bent over like a woman in labour, it struck me. 'No,' she whispered. 'I did it alone. I sent her away.'

'And why did you put him in the ark?'

'I couldn't think. It was panic. To hide, to delay—'

'Then why did you lift the lid of the ark not an hour later?'

'I don't know,' she whispered, 'I couldn't help it, I had to see.'

'What were you wearing when you pushed him?'

A long pause.

'My skirt and jacket,' she said at last.

'Of course, you had the whisky to hand, in the pocket. When you'd finished, where did you put the flask?'

'Back, I suppose. I don't remember.'

'I do. At half past two in the cloakroom you wanted a drink before joining the visitors. Your jacket was on the rail. You dipped in all the pockets, they were empty. Then you remembered something, and gave up looking.'

'I must have put it down, left it there, in the slip house.'

'But you've got it now.'

'I picked it up afterwards.'

'When? Not when you took the visitors round. I was watching you all the time. And afterwards there wouldn't have been a chance, the police would have found it.'

'No, it must have been somewhere else. In the art room, yes, I wanted a drink.'

'When?'

'After—'

'After pushing him in the ark? Between say, two, and two-thirty?'

'Yes.'

'Did you go into the art room wearing your jacket?'

'I don't know.'

'If you took the flask into the art room, you either had it in your pocket or carried it in your hand. Which?'

'I can't remember. Pocket.'

'The jacket was in the cloakroom at two-thirty.'

'I took it off when I'd had the drink.'

'Why didn't you put the flask back in the pocket then?'

'I don't know. I wasn't thinking.'

'When you wanted a drink in the cloakroom you remembered that you'd left the flask in the art room. That was what made you pause, and give up looking?'

'Yes. That the flask wasn't there.'

'It was only across the corridor. Why didn't you slip in and fetch it?'

'There wasn't time. I couldn't be bothered.'

'Did you have a drink afterwards, when you went back from the rest room and sat drawing on the coffee pot?'

'Yes.'

'And put the flask in the jacket again before going home?'

'Yes.'

'But on the way home, when you saw your husband, you went to take out the flask and you stopped in just the same way. Remembering it wasn't there, weren't you? *Believing* it wasn't. In fact it was. I found it afterwards, when I hung up the jacket in your bedroom. But you didn't know, because you hadn't put it back in the pocket. Weren't you surprised to find it standing on the chest of drawers, and weren't you even more surprised to find it empty?'

She put her head in her hands.

'You're confusing her,' said Luke sharply.

'I couldn't confuse her if she were telling the truth,' I said.

'But she isn't. She's improvising an explanation. Very sound, very credible, but not true.'

Two soft buzzes sounded on Luke's desk. The arrangement with Miss Chapman.

Luke sent me a distress signal. I nodded, and his hand moved on the desk.

That's all it was. A matter of buzzes and lights and flicked switches, and a yawning silence as the door opened.

Freddy. Oh, Freddy.

That was all I thought; just that. So I didn't realize for a second that it was what Corinna had said. She took a couple of steps towards him and stopped, looking at him. Then at last, at last, she began to cry, not, like Judith, in sobs of anguish and fear and love; silently; letting the tears run out instead of the long hold back, tears for the hopelessness of her gesture, for the life that was ruined, for the waste that self-sacrifice couldn't annul.

He was gone. The frame was still there, the hair, the neat clothes, the features. You might have said pale, tired, not haggard or wasted or aged. But he was gone, the fountain of life; quenched, dowsed, spent, *épuisé*.

He looked at Corinna as if she were at the far end of a telescope, with a faint attempt at a smile. 'Don't cry, Corinna love,' he said, 'it's all right.'

He was like a sick parent calming a frightened child. It's all right, nothing to worry about, run along. He took her by the elbow, the old gesture, and pushed her towards me. He'd seen, too, and even now remembered, that I was the one who wanted her.

I took her. She twitched away, and went to the wall by the fire and leaned against it.

'I was coming,' said Freddy, turning to Luke. 'Then to

the police. There were things I had to settle, took time. My savings, the house—I had to make sure my mother could get it all. I didn't know the law, the position, if things get confiscated. I'm sorry, Judith, it wasn't fair on you to have to hang on so long.'

She lifted her face, not minding about the wet blotches, the red swollen eyes, trying to be controlled now that he was there. 'It didn't matter,' she said.

'Judith hasn't said a word,' Luke cut in quickly. 'No one suggested, or mentioned—'

'Only Corinna,' I said, 'trying to tell us she killed your cousin.'

He stared across the room, at the back of the ash-blonde head. 'Corinna?' he said, bewildered. He turned to Luke. 'But you *know*. You knew when you rang, asked me to come in. You didn't say, but I could tell. Not just conscience working.'

Conscience. Only a Catholic says it so familiarly, and yet so seriously. He was looking at me now, questioning.

'You?' he said. 'You know. How?'

'I'm not a writer, Freddy,' I said, 'just good at crosswords and other puzzles.'

'He was looking into something for me privately,' said Luke, who wouldn't let down anyone who worked for him. 'Something to do with the firm, finished now.'

'I happened to be here,' I said. 'I thought about it, I remembered things, I asked questions, I guessed an outline, not details. That's all. I don't *know*. I only believe.'

He knew the difference, he, the Catholic, acknowledged the nicety with a slight nod. 'I killed him,' he said.

Luke moved forward, on the course of duty. This was the point where one cleared out the women.

Seeing his intention, Judith jumped up.

'Freddy,' she cried urgently, 'I only went out with him in the car on Sunday because he said we were going to find you. And I didn't want to have lunch, only there was no excuse, it seemed so rude, he'd taken me out. That's the truth.'

'I know, Judith,' he said. 'It doesn't matter.'

'And I never thought,' she went on, crying helplessly. 'You know what I mean. You never said anything, only that photograph that everyone laughed at. And with all the other girls—'

'They were different,' he said. He looked round, swallowing the misery of having to speak while three people listened, because it was all the time he had left. 'I didn't want to treat you like them. I wanted to marry you.'

'Oh Freddy, so did I!' she cried. 'Why didn't you say, why didn't you say?'

He put his arms round her, a gesture, without energy, and shook his head. He didn't know, unreflecting Freddy, who'd thought he knew all the answers.

They were there, shut in one room, the four from Shentall's who meant most to me. Patient, dutiful Luke, Freddy and Judith Agnes, resting their heads against each other's for the first time, learning the lesson of not speaking out; and Corinna, leaning against the wall, alone.

'Mrs Wakefield,' said Luke, reluctantly. 'And Judith. I'm sorry. You'd better come with me now. I'll take you through to the dining-room. You can—'

What could they? Dry each other's tears?

Freddy moved his arms. 'Go on, Judith,' he said. 'I'll see you again. There'll be a time, if you want. Thanks for hanging on. I'm sorry.'

'It didn't matter,' she whispered, 'you didn't mean to.'

Not a kiss, not even a touch of hands. They moved apart, trying to put it all in their eyes, Judith even managing a smile. She was so young, she could snatch hope from a moment of his gratitude.

Luke took Corinna's arm and drew her away from the wall. Freddy looked at her with surprise; he'd forgotten her.

'Corinna,' he said, puzzled. 'It wouldn't have been much of a life, for me, would it, the one you offered? You don't think I'd have let you do it—even if anyone had believed you.'

She shook her head, not bothering to look up; so that he could only go on staring, perplexed, as Luke took them out, through his own washroom from which by a passage they could reach the directors' dining-room. Judith's loyalty, hanging on in silence, suffering all her fright and horror alone rather than let him down, *that* Freddy could understand; but not Corinna. He wouldn't be with the judges who would damn her with the word quixotic, pontificating their mercantile commonsense. He was generous, he'd thank her for trying, for her love; but he couldn't really take her measure, could only stare bewildered at her because she offered herself without hope of success, knowing it was futile, but still persisting.

'Corinna,' he repeated blankly, to me, or to himself. 'Why?'

'Because she thought you were worth more than her,' I said. 'Because she loved the idea of you. Because she's good, the best sort of good, struggling on her own without a book of rules, not for a reward, knowing there's no reward, only this life as it is—'

What was the point? He wouldn't consider, he couldn't, that she was therefore admirable; only that she was mistaken.

We were divided by the unbridgable gulf between faith and despair, optimism and pessimism.

'I was afraid of a mistake,' I went on, changing abruptly. 'I was afraid they'd think she'd done it.'

'Why?' he asked, with a dull surprise.

No need to tell him about her and Bullace. 'Different things,' I said. 'Otherwise I'd have said nothing, no, not even if they'd got nowhere with it. I'm sorry.'

He shook his head. 'I'd have gone to the police. Don't you believe me?'

'Yes. Of course.'

'Then don't look so harrowed. It's all right. You haven't done anything.'

That generosity! Natural plus supernatural. Just as I'd seen it in Dovedale, and had thought it was the white Jag that had knocked him, when Judith was sitting there next to Bullace. I pulled out my cigarettes and offered them, the agnostic's exchange for a draft on heavenly grace.

'Did you really burst a tyre outside Stafford?' I asked, picking up Luke's lighter.

'No. I got beyond Stone then I pulled on the verge and sat thinking. Not thinking, no, I don't know. Just sat.' He put the cigarette between his lips, but hardly drew on it. 'If I'd been five minutes earlier,' he said, 'or if I could have gone off in the morning, like I should, if there hadn't been that trouble in number nine. Only I was just going when I saw them.'

'Bullace and Judith?'

He nodded. 'Coming in together through the works gate. I don't know where they'd been.'

'They'd had lunch at the Bluebird in Hanley.'

'Good Lord.' He paused. 'Yes. It's the sort of place that suits Judith.'

'Also conveniently out of the way of the works. Bullace wasn't likely to be seen there with the girl from the switchboard. That's not me, Freddy, you know it isn't. But it was what he thought.'

He looked at me as Dart had looked, hurt by the unfairness of my knowing what he'd thought was private.

'I told you I'm good at puzzles,' I said. 'Things people say, stale crumbs of information. That photograph you entered—*A Beautiful Golden Frame*. There were two ways of looking at it, seriously or not. That was your idea, a declaration with a defence. Most people took it as a joke, just because it came from you, but you couldn't deceive the cousin who'd been brought up with you like a brother. Could you? And the reason he was so furious about the picture, wasn't it that he thought you were letting yourself down, that she wasn't good enough for you? Without regard to what she was like, just because her father was a welder.'

'But *his* father, *my* father—oh, what does it matter! He had these pigheaded wrong ideas—he wanted to push up to the top of the middle class. Well, why couldn't he let me be? I was all right where I was.'

'He wanted to do you good. Give him credit.'

'Good? Disowning all your people that brought you up and gave you everything?'

'He didn't see it as you do.'

'He was wrong.'

'Are you so invincibly right, beyond error?'

The cigarette went up to his mouth, shaking between his fingers. From now on his confidence would always founder on one memory.

'Listen,' he said, 'after the picture business it all went quiet for a couple of months, nothing more said, either side. So when I saw him with her at Dovedale I didn't realize. I thought he'd sort of looked at her for the first time on account of me, and seen how wrong he'd been about her. That's what I thought had happened, even on the Monday when I saw them together. Only then he grinned at me—I don't know how, I can't explain. If you knew him the way I do you'd understand. They weren't in the car, they were walking, been on the bus to Hanley, I suppose. When he saw me he changed direction, towards the slip house, and I knew. You see, you won't have heard it, it's gone out now, but about a year ago there was a catch-phrase in the works, a fashion, you know how these things go. If you asked anyone, the men, where they were going, they'd say *going to lay Susie in the slip house*. I don't know how it started, there isn't a Susie, it didn't mean anything. But I knew from his grin he was thinking of that, and meaning me to think of it, and then, just to make sure, he called out *You didn't know her middle name was Susie*. Well, I went after them. Not because I thought he meant to do it, I knew he was just talking, but because I saw he wasn't serious with her, I saw why he was taking her out.'

'To show she didn't care for you,' I said. 'To disillusion you, prove she wasn't worth all your veneration, that she was just a piece like the others, flattered by an accent and a Jag, to show he could beat you with the push and the veneer that you refused to share. He couldn't, and he probably knew it, but he could try to make you think so.'

I saw Luke come back as I spoke, alone. He stood by the door of the washroom, looking at us in silence.

'Yes,' said Freddy, 'all that, only muddled, in a rush. It made me hot. I went in the slip house and the minute he saw me he caught hold of her and tried to give her a kiss. He wouldn't have done, I'm sure he wouldn't, why did I have to go in? She pulled back and struggled, and I ran up. He said *Come to her rescue, all part of the game,* and then something else. I can't remember, I didn't hear it. I pulled her away and I hit him, just up, under the chin, it hurt me, I hit so hard. I knocked him out anyway, I think. I'm strong, I know that. He went back straight, didn't stagger, just fell dead weight backwards. And his head—his head hit the iron frame of the press. It made a noise—you wouldn't think, would you? You hear it, thick, smack, like a box dropping.'

He began to shiver. He looked as we'd all looked when we lifted Bullace out. He had the same down-turned mouth; but his eyes were more sickened, they had the bright concentrated horror of someone right on the edge of what they can stand. I pushed him down on the chair Luke had set for Corinna.

'I knew when I saw him lying there,' he went on. 'I knew inside, but on top I made myself think he was stunned. I couldn't remember why I'd hit him, it didn't seem to matter. I called him and shook him and rubbed his face. I had Corinna's flask. She gave it to me in Dovedale when I got my feet wet and I'd forgotten to give it back. I poured some whisky down—oh, hell!'

He swallowed, surprised at the cigarette stub trembling with his fingers. It must have been burning him. He looked round, lost, unable to think what to do. I passed him Luke's ashtray.

'It kept running out,' he said, 'down his neck and on his clothes. My hand hurt where I'd hit him, kept shaking. There wasn't all that in the flask, about a quarter. I drained it, I was so mad, trying to revive him. And yet I knew he was dead. His eyes. They were open. I knew it was no good. I told Judith to run off, gave her the flask to slip in Corinna's pocket and say nothing—I don't know if she ever—'

'She did. She slipped up to the cloakroom just at half past two, when she'd seen Corinna go along the landing to join the visitors. I remember finding the cubicle empty, wondering where she'd gone.' And I remembered seeing the white handkerchief rolled into a ball; not knowing then that it was wet with her tears of fright.

'Judith!' he said. 'She's good. It wasn't fair, to happen to her. When she'd gone I couldn't think. I knew the men would be back from lunch any minute. It wasn't that I meant to get out of it. Only I couldn't believe what I'd done straight away. Couldn't even breathe properly, all thick in the throat. So I thought—the ark, just for a bit of time, to think. I pulled back the trap and put my hands under his shoulders—we were right close—and dragged him. Then I pushed—'

Such an awful cry broke out of him, violent, abrupt, the horrified repulsion of his memory. His hands flew up, squeezing the sides of his head.

'I couldn't touch him, see, I couldn't bear to, not his face. His mouth—I had to leave it open, and his eyes, and he dropped on the paddles, into the slip—'

'Freddy!' Luke jumped forward, sticking desperately to duty, to help.

I put my hand on Freddy's shoulder, not that I needed to feel, I could see him shaking, with the great long shudders that look as if they come from outside, stripping through the muscles like a ninety mile gale.

'Sorry,' he gasped, 'I can't—can't help it.' Even then he tried to repudiate and deny this weakness, this failure in the masculine convention. 'Only it was Dud. I killed him, I don't know why. There was nothing. Murdered for nothing.'

'Freddy, that wasn't murder,' said Luke urgently. 'That was an accident, manslaughter at worst. Everyone's going to come forward and swear, and stand by you, you know that, Freddy.'

He twisted himself round and flung his face in his arms, hooked across the back of the chair. I saw with a shock the thick black hair pushed up in the crook of his elbow, the image of his cousin.

'He's dead,' he said, through his shudders. 'Not there, ever again. He was the only one. No one to talk to. And I hit him, the last thing ever.'

'Freddy,' muttered Luke with difficulty, sticking on duty as he saw it, 'you're a Catholic. You believe in life after death—'

'Now!' he cried out. 'I want him now, tell him I didn't mean it, I'm sorry. I didn't care what he'd done, leaving home, going away, getting things wrong, mistakes. It doesn't matter. I don't care. He was good. I never told him, never thanked him. He made my boats go, he held me on the donkey, he'd give me his bus fare and walk, every day, even winter, so's I could have twopenn'orth of lime juice nibs. I can't tell him I remember, he'll never know, only that I hit him, I killed him, Dud.'

Freddy. Poor spoilt Freddy. Spoilt by so much love, so much faith, a life without pain, without trouble, without doubt, spoilt so that he wasn't prepared for the major shock of betrayal, jealousy, disillusion and anger, spoilt so that the book of rules was so much straw in the flood, so that he crashed on the first rocks. Was it his fault? Yes. No. No one's. One could analyse, assign a blame here, an *if only* there; but what would be the use? Life can't be cured, must be endured.

There was nothing to do for him now, nothing to say, no way of bringing back the cousin, the blood brother, the masculine stay in a feminine family; nothing to offer in place of the bond of a shared childhood, the deep involuntary tie that, like breathing, was recognized only too late, when it broke.

No, there was nothing to do, except stand by the chair and see the fountain of life spill out; and finally, when the silence was ruptured by the long insistent double buzzing, and the door had to be opened to the inspector, there was still nothing; only to help him clean his face, wipe off the blood that trickled from his lip where he'd struck it on the back of the chair, and casually, as if without seeing, take away also the final humiliation of the tears he hadn't been able to control, tears for the lost love. The little brother jumps in the road. Clout, clout! Now have a sweet, under my arm, walk together, I didn't mean it. I love you.

Ah, Christ! Who'll explain that lot? And who, nowadays, will believe it? Better to leave it in its simplicity, though nothing is simple; his cousin was kissing his girl, so he killed him. The facts, as usual; but not the whole truth.

—

Luke sat at his desk. I stood. It was the finish, at least of the part that required me to stay; for the rest of them the ends straggled away, untied, in an indefinite future. However, I felt the twittering inside that always goes with ends and finishes, the foolish staring at rooms simply because you know you won't see them again, trying to impress them on your mind's eye. Why should I have wanted to take the memory of Luke's office with me to the grave? The celadon walls, the white mouldings, the pieces of nineteenth-century fake porcelain; they were only too clearly the background to what I'd rather have forgotten.

'You haven't presented an account,' he said.

I looked at him. 'You know I couldn't.'

He sighed. 'Don't make things more difficult than they are. You must be paid.'

'Not for that. It isn't being difficult, it's just observing a minimum of decency. You think so yourself, but you don't care to say so.'

I put the neat quarto typescript on his desk.

'What's that?' he asked.

'Draft outline of the history of the firm and the illustrated booklet. If it proves to be what you want, send it down to me and I'll do it out in full. You can pay me for that.'

'When did you do this?'

'The typing I had done in Hanley.'

'No. The writing itself.'

'I found time. I don't sleep much after five. It was something to do.'

'Well, if you won't be paid, that's all, isn't it?' He paused. 'I shall see you again.'

Probably he would. At Stafford Assizes. We looked at each other, not attempting to conceal the gloom of our thoughts.

'There's no doubt it will be manslaughter,' he said abruptly. 'There'll be no difficulty, absolutely none.'

Only four years, if he's lucky, with remission. The springing muscular Freddy, with his black hair and fanatically polished shoes and his white shirts, the smiles, the stretch, the generosity. Four years in a mill of squalor and misery and monotony such as he could never have conceived.

What would it do to him, the fountain sealed? And Judith, the garden enclosed? His mother, his sisters—

'That's all, then,' I said. 'Now I'll let Brassick in. He's outside with his headache.'

'What headache?'

'To be blunt, you're short of two key staff and an assistant.'

He sighed. 'Yes, but we go on. Well—I have your address.'

'Why should you want it?'

He looked at me strangely. 'The book.'

'Of course, I wasn't thinking. I'm sorry.'

'For what?'

I shrugged, looking at him. A real staring match we were having.

He held out his hand, after all. After all? I shouldn't have been surprised, not at Luke. He'd asked me to work for him, I had, that was enough; he took the responsibility. And I wondered, as I went out of the room, why I'd ever smiled at him, called him paterfamilias.

I stopped on the landing between the two flights of stairs. I knew it all now, there were no more gaps, no more things that puzzled me. I knew even the inspector's weapons—the place of the fracture, the bruise on the jaw, the contusions on the back and the broken rib where it had hit the paddles, the usual amazing minute trace of hair that survived on the frame of the press, the alcohol on the clothes but not in the blood. Inquest stuff. But the inquest was over.

I walked along to the art room and opened the door. She was there, sitting at her table, working. The ash-blonde head, the familiar blouse and skirt. The others were there too, all of them, Anthem, Johns, Mitchell, Olive. Well, I couldn't send them outside. It had been worse for Judith and Freddy.

I went across and stood beside her. 'I'm going now,

Corinna,' I said quietly, so that the others shouldn't hear. I didn't want them to know, there was no need.

She didn't speak, didn't turn her head.

What could I say?

If you find yourself going over seven bottles a month, if you can't do without, if you're lonely, if you need a bolt-hole, if you're afraid, want protection, release from the husband, on any terms, please Corinna, even as an insurance policy—I ought to die before you—

But one can't offer such insults, such blackmail.

I put a card on the table, my name and address. Would she know, would she understand what I wanted to say, what I was offering?

It was all one if she did. She picked up the card and dropped it in her waste-paper basket, without a glance at me.

Accept, I thought, walk out. That's how it ends, with the stony lips and averted head, not even one more look from the tragic eyes. Don't stand there pleading that you did it for her, to help her, to get her out of the floor of the pit, to show that she could trust you. It wouldn't be fair to say so. Besides, would it be true? I knew what she thought, what she'd say. *You made sure of Freddy, black-haired Freddy, you wanted him out of the way.* And how could I swear that I didn't?

It was hopeless. Yet I had to tell her. I couldn't go without speaking at last, the truth, the only truth that mattered to me.

There was a plate beside her, a white glazed dinner plate, lying ready for her scribble, her trial and error. I picked up her china-graph, the fat black pencil. Not in English. In the language where it sounds less raw, more suited to our age. I wrote it. *Je t'aime.*

She looked. I saw the pause. Then she put her finger across the plate and wiped it out. There was nothing left, not even a grey smear. That was that.

'Goodbye, Corinna,' I said.

I went down to the yard, the long way round, behind the canteen, so that I didn't have to go through the hall. The car was at the end of the line, the cases were in the boot. I sat down behind the wheel. That was that. It didn't seem as bad as what I remembered of the teens. I hadn't said *I can't live without you, I'll throw myself in the river*. I knew I could, and wouldn't. I pushed the starter. No, it was worse than the teens. There was not even the delusion of a quick end in sight; only the long wait for forgetfulness.

I drove through the yard; leaving Shentall's, the milky cobbles, the floury windows, behind which piles of pipe-clay cups; leaving its shraff heap of broken lives. Rush Street, Canaan Street, past the others, past Copeland's, past Minton's, turning my back on Doulton's in cool remote Burslem, heading towards Wedgwood's in the fields. Leaving Stoke, *la belle laide,* the kilns, the chimneys, the grey hills, the slag, the quiet industry of six settled towns. Leaving it, when all I wanted was to stay, leaving the only truth I cared about, leaving Corinna.

I put my foot down and switched on the radio. I love my car, she is to me as mistress, child, and wife. One hundred and forty miles. Stone, Stafford, London.